Michael

Being traded after fighting with your coach on air isn't exactly a good look.
With one mistake under my belt, I knew I needed to focus on the game and nothing else.
But everything changed when I went to pick up my niece and came face-to-face with my very pregnant one-night stand from six months ago.

Jillian

Two pink lines changed all my plans.
So did the guy I had a one-night stand with, a man who made me laugh and smile, a guy who I called to share my unexpected news with, only to find out his number was no longer in service.
Once more letdown by the opposite sex, I figured I was doing this on my own.
Then one day, I was staring into the eyes of the man I hated, the father of my baby.

All it took was only one mistake to change everything

BOOKS BY NATASHA MADISON

The Only One Series
Only One Kiss
Only One Chance
Only One Night
Only One Touch
Only One Regret
Only One Mistake
Only One Love
Only One Forever

Southern Series
Southern Chance
Southern Comfort
Southern Storm
Southern Sunrise
Southern Heart
Southern Heat
Southern Secrets
Southern Sunshine

This Is
This is Crazy
This Is Wild
This Is Love
This Is Forever

Hollywood Royalty
Hollywood Playboy
Hollywood Princess
Hollywood Prince

Something So Series
Something Series
Something So Right
Something So Perfect
Something So Irresistible
Something So Unscripted
Something So BOX SET

Tempt Series
Tempt The Boss
Tempt The Playboy
Tempt The Ex
Tempt The Hookup
Heaven & Hell Series
Hell And Back
Pieces Of Heaven

Love Series
Perfect Love Story
Unexpected Love Story
Broken Love Story

Faux Pas
Mixed Up Love
Until Brandon

SOMETHING SO, THIS IS, AND ONLY ONE FAMILY TREE!

SOMETHING SO SERIES

Something So Right
Parker & Cooper Stone
Matthew Grant (Something So Perfect)
Allison Grant (Something So Irresistible)
Zara Stone (This Is Crazy)
Zoe Stone (This Is Wild)
Justin Stone (This Is Forever)
Something So Perfect
Matthew Grant & Karrie Cooley
Cooper Grant (Only One Regret)
Frances Grant (Only One Love)
Vivienne Grant
Chase Grant
Something So Irresistible
Allison Grant & Max Horton
Michael Horton (Only One Mistake)
Alexandria Horton
Something So Unscripted
Denise Horton & Zack Morrow
Jack Morrow
Joshua Morrow
Elizabeth Morrow

THIS IS SERIES

This Is Crazy
Zara Stone & Evan Richards
Zoey Richards
This Is Wild
Zoe Stone & Viktor Petrov
Matthew Petrov
Zara Petrov
This Is Love
Vivienne Paradis & Mark Dimitris
Karrie Dimitris
Stefano Dimitris
Angelica Dimitris

This Is Forever
Caroline Woods & Justin Stone
Dylan Stone (Formally Woods)
Christopher Stone
Gabriella Stone
Abigail Stone

ONLY ONE SERIES

Only One Kiss
Candace Richards & Ralph Weber
Ariella Weber
Brookes Weber
Only One Chance
Layla Paterson & Miller Adams
Clarke Adams
Onlye One Night
Evelyn & Manning Stevenson
Jaxon Stevenson
Victoria Stevenson
Only One Touch
Becca & Nico Harrison
Phoenix Harrison
Dallas Harrison
Only One Regret
Erika Markinson & Cooper Grant
Emma Grant
Mia Grant
Parker Grant
Matthew Grant
Only One Mistake
Jillian & Michael Horton
Jamieson Horton

Cover Design: Jay Aheer

Editing done by Jenny Sims Editing4Indies

Proofing Julie Deaton by Deaton Author Services

Proofing by Judy's proofreading

Interior Design by Christina Smith

ONLY ONE
Mistake

THE ONLY ONE SERIES

ONE

MICHAEL

"WE'LL BE LANDING in twenty minutes," the flight attendant announces. I just nod at her and look out the window at the clouds in the sky. My phone pings, and I look down and see it's from *The Hockey News* desk.

Breaking News: Michael Horton has been traded to the Dallas Oilers.

I close my eyes without clicking to open the article. They aren't going to tell me something I don't already know. When I woke up this morning, I was a member of the Columbus team.

I didn't have to read the news to know what was going around. I was getting text messages from my family asking me if I was okay.

I had been benched for the fourth night in a row. As the top sports news story, the spotlight was on me, and I hated every fucking second of it. It's not like it was because I wasn't producing on the ice.

No, it was all because my coach called me off the ice during the first period of a game against Montreal last week, and we got into a fight on camera. I knew I should have shut my mouth and just sat on the bench, but I couldn't hold it in anymore.

It had been six months of his shit on and off the ice. It all started last year during the playoffs. I made a couple of plays he didn't like. I fucked up on the ice by not producing, and then I gave up the puck in the neutral zone, and they ended up winning the game. He didn't like it, and he would call me out during the press conferences. I knew he was right, so I didn't say anything. I also knew I fucking hated being called out, but there was no way I would talk shit about my coach. So I waited for the summer to pass, and then at the beginning of the season, we had a meeting and said we would start fresh. I walked out of that meeting, hopeful it would stick.

He didn't last one game before he was riding my ass, and last night's game was the last straw for me. After benching me for four fucking games, he pulled me after one shift and sat me the rest of the game. I wasn't going to play for him again.

My phone rings in my hand, and I look down and see it's my father, Max. "Hey," I say, letting out a huge sigh.

"If it isn't the rebel of the family." He laughs, and I shake my head and close my eyes. "How are you?" His voice goes low, and I can hear the worry in his tone. I knew he was trying to joke about it, but these past couple of weeks have been just as stressful for him.

"You okay?" His voice goes low. "You need

anything?"

"I'm good. A little numb but it'll be good." It all happened so fucking fast. This morning, I called Erika, my agent, and then ten minutes later, I was being traded.

"Just say the word, and I'll be there in three hours. Either way, I'll be there this weekend."

"No, I'm good." But I'm not good. I'm the opposite of good. I hate that my name is being dragged through the mud.

"Uncle Matthew is there," he says softly. "If you need him, you pick up the phone and call him."

"I'm good, Dad." I close my eyes. "I'm landing and going straight to meet with Nico."

"Call me after," he says, and then I just wait. "Proud of you, son. Love you."

"Love you, too, Dad." I hang up the phone as the wheels touch down.

The plane lands without any fanfare, and when the doors open, the humid air hits me right away. "Welcome to Dallas," the flight attendant says. Slipping on my aviator glasses, I grab my backpack and sling it over my shoulder. I walk off the plane, looking for the black Lincoln waiting for me, and see my father leaning against the side of the truck.

"You didn't think I would let you do this by yourself." He grabs me around my neck and pulls me to him. "No fucking way." Closing my eyes, I let out a sigh as I hug him. "Let's get this over with." He lets me go, and the driver opens the back door for me, and I get in. Only when I'm sitting down do I let out a sigh of relief because he's here. I didn't even know how much I needed him until I saw him. My father gets in beside me, and I look over at him.

"I'm sorry."

"For what?" He looks at me, and it's like looking in the mirror. We have the same black hair and blue eyes. He helped push me this summer, making me bigger than I've ever been before.

"All this shit." My hands fly up. "All this fucking shit." I shake my head. "All the eyes on the family because of me."

He chuckles. "One, I couldn't be prouder that you are my son and help carry on my name." He raises his finger, and I see the tears in his eyes. "And two, fuck what everyone else says. You know the truth. The family knows the truth."

I watch the city go by me on the way to the arena, and my phone rings. Looking down, I see it's Nico. "Hey, we are just getting to the arena."

"Yeah," he says, and I hear him walking. "Press is here."

"Okay." I look out the window and see the press trucks. "I'm not saying anything."

"Good, we have a plan. See you soon." He hangs up, and I look over at my father, who is going nuts texting.

"Everything okay?" I ask, and he shakes his head.

"Erika is in labor," he says, and I gasp. "Her water broke after she called you." My heart speeds up. She's my agent, but she is also married to my cousin. "Uncle Matthew is, well, not handling it well."

I laugh. "What does Uncle Matthew handle well?"

"This," he says, pointing at the arena and the press trucks. "This is his playpen, and he's pissed he's not here walking in with you to show a united front." The lincoln stops, and I look at him. "If he could, you know he would be here."

"I know. Let's do this," I say, ignoring the lump in my throat. My father gets out first and then walks around, and the door opens. I get out, and I can hear the cameras clicking.

The silver door opens and I look over and see Nico walking out. His head held high, he's wearing a suit and the biggest smile on his face. "There he is." He holds out his hand. "Relax," he says, and I take a deep breath. "This picture is going to be posted in five minutes everywhere, so pretend you're happy to be here."

"I am." I smile, shaking his hand.

"Welcome home," he says, looking over my shoulder at my father. "Why am I not surprised that you are here?" My father shrugs. "Where is your sidekick?"

"Another family matter." My father doesn't want the press to know Erika is in the hospital.

"Shall we?" He holds out his hand. I nod at him and follow him into the arena. The minute the door slams behind me, I stop walking and look up.

"That wasn't so bad." Nico laughs, looking at my father.

"I thought he was going to throw up." My father slaps my shoulder. "You did good."

I watch Nico and my father walk ahead of me, and

he shows me the dressing room. "It's an off day today," Nico says. "Good thing for Erika she chose today to give birth." He laughs. "I mean, not surprising she scheduled that." He looks at me. "Now that all this is done, Coach is waiting."

I nod at him and look over at my father. "I've got this," I say, and he shakes his head.

"Oh, I wasn't coming in with you," he says. "That's a you thing." He motions with his chin. "You got this."

When I walk into the room with Nico, I see the coach sitting at the table on his phone. He looks up. "The big bad Michael Horton." He puts his phone down and gets up. "Martin," he says, holding out his hand. "Welcome to Dallas."

I shake his hand and sit down in the empty chair in front of him. Nico walks over to the other side of the table and sits down next to Martin. I look at both of them, and it feels like a big elephant in the room, and I know I'm already going to have to deal with it with the press. "Before we start." I think of the words to say and then finally just say what comes to mind. "I just want to thank you both for taking a chance on me." I swallow. "I don't know what you heard or what you read, but just know that there are three sides to the story."

"I know that," Martin says. "I also know John, and I know it's not easy to be coached by him."

I shake my head. "I have no problem working hard. I have no problem showing you what I can do. I have a problem with not showing you that I can do what you just told me I couldn't." Martin looks at Nico and nods his head. "I just want a chance to show the world I'm not the spoiled little shit that everyone is probably calling me."

"Fuck 'em," Martin says. "Press is going to be all over your ass."

"And we are going to make sure that it's respectful," Nico states. "I have no problem telling the press to get out of my arena," he says, and I nod at him. "With that being said, I think by you not saying anything to the press, it will be like putting a target on your back."

"I agree." Martin nods his head.

"I'm not pressuring you to do anything you don't want to do," Nico says, folding his hands on the table. "But I think if you did an interview." He holds up his hand for me to let him finish. "We can set it up, choose the reporter we want to talk to, and—"

I hold up my hand. "I'm not shitting on my other team," I say. "I am not going to sit down and point fingers, saying it was his fault and all that bullshit. I won't do it." I shake my head and wonder if I'm not shooting myself in the foot, before I even get on the ice. I look over at Nico and then at Martin. "I won't do it to them. I won't do it to you guys. That isn't who I am; that isn't who I was raised to be." I put my shoulders back. "So if you think it will help, then set up the interview, but I'm just telling you that I'm not throwing shade at anyone." I smirk. "No matter how much they deserve it."

"That." Nico sits up and points at me. "Respect right there." He pushes back from the table. "I think we are going to get along just fine." He smirks at me. "Welcome to Dallas, Michael Horton."

TWO

JILLIAN

LOOKING INTO THE mirror, I hold the clothes hanger with the black-and-white dress on it in front of me and contemplate wearing this tonight. I close my eyes and wonder why the hell I ever agreed to go out on a blind date. A date with a man I know very little about or have even seen a picture of. All I know is that his name is Zander, and he is meeting me at seven o'clock at Sullivan's restaurant. I throw the dress on the bed and walk over to grab another one-piece t-shirt red dress and hold it against me. After going back and forth a couple of times, I toss the two choices back on the bed and walk back to the closet for two more hangers.

Tossing the choices back on the bed, I plop down on the edge. Everything I own is scattered around the bed. And I mean everything. My phone rings, and I can hear it coming from someplace under the mountains of clothes on my bed. "Where is it?" I move the clothes aside as it rings, finding it under a white pillow.

"Hello?" I answer, lying on my stomach and my hair falling in my face. I blow the hair out of my face and then turn over to my back. A hanger stabs me in the back, so I get up to move it, then lie back down. I look down to see that she started a FaceTime call with me. I press the green accept button and wait for her face to fill the screen.

"Are you getting ready?" my sister, Julia, asks, and I close my eyes. When I take more than a second to answer her, she says my full name through clenched teeth, making me laugh so hard. "Jillian Lee Williams."

"You know it's serious when you use my whole name." I shake my head. "You do know what I'm doing, right?" I look around the room and wonder how long it will take me to clean this shit up.

"If I were to guess," she says, "you're probably at your computer with a spreadsheet with a pros and cons list as to what you should do tonight." I roll my eyes.

"Wrong," I say, happy she is actually wrong for once. Turning the camera, I give her a view of the explosion of clothes everywhere. I hear her whistle and then turn her back to me. "Besides, I already did that this morning when I got up," I confirm, making her laugh. "I'm lying in the middle of my bed, on top of every single piece of clothing I own." I look around the room at the disaster. "I'm not kidding. I took everything out. Jeans, yoga pants, joggers, skirts, shorts, dresses." I pick up a gray shirt with Warrior Not Worrier in the middle of it and toss it aside to the for-sure-no pile.

"What did you decide on?" I hear her tapping something, and I know it's either her index finger or a pen as her face comes closer to the phone.

"Either my black jeans." I pick up the jeans in question to show her. "And a black silk tank top." I pick up the black silky tank top with a bit of lace at the top.

"Or?" The tapping stops, and she sits up, looking around, and I can see she is sitting outside somewhere.

"Champagne shorts with the black silk tank top." I look around, and she blows out.

"You know why this is so hard." I hear a bird squeaking in the background. "Because you dress like a nun." She points at the phone.

I chuckle. "I like to call it respectable teacher attire," I say, getting off the bed. Placing the phone down on the bed faceup, I start to fold the clothes I will definitely not be wearing tonight.

"Is that what you are calling it?" She teases me as I look around at all the non-sexy clothes I have.

"I teach kindergarten," I remind her. "I can't go to school wearing stilettos and sexy clothes. All of my outfits are made for comfort. And after wearing a very expensive sweater one day, a cashmere sweater I bought for over a hundred dollars, and getting splashed by paint, I learned that it wasn't worth dishing out the big bucks. The amount of clothing I've had to throw out from being stained or glued is crazy. So I go affordable."

"If you want, you can swing by my place and borrow a couple of things," she says, and I laugh out loud. She has the same wardrobe I have, only she might have sexier tops for when she goes out cruising, which seems to be every weekend.

"You think you have a better style than I do? You're a social worker. You wear jeans and button-down shirts?" I ask her, trying to think back to the last time I saw her wear anything but jeans around me.

"The younger sister always has better style," she teases, making me laugh, and I look down at her, my eyebrows pinching together and making her laugh.

"You are younger by two minutes and forty-eight seconds," I remind her. "I don't know if that counts." It's her turn to roll her eyes, the same blue eyes that I have, just a touch lighter because she's sitting in the sun.

"Which is why you are my older sister, and I'm the younger sister." She laughs, making me shake my head. "Stop shaking your head," she says, and I sit down on my bed. They always say when you are a twin, you have a connection, and the two of us are no different. There are times when I feel what she is feeling and vice versa. Or the times I have a headache and call my mother, and she tells me that Julia has a headache.

The two of us are almost identical. The only thing is the way we wear our hair. We both have long hair down to the waist, but I part mine in the middle, and she flips hers to the side. When we were younger, we would try to trick people, and it usually worked except with our mom, who could tell us apart. She always knew who was who. I stop folding the clothes on the bed, picking the phone up again and looking straight at her. "Remind me again why I should do this?"

"Well, for one, it's been seven months since you broke up with the douchecanoe." She mentions my ex-boyfriend, Riley. We went to the same high school together, and she hated him even then, but when Julia and I went our separate ways in college, I caved and went out on a date with him. When I finally confessed to her that we were dating, she gave him a chance but still hated him. I should have listened to her because, three years later, I went on Facebook and saw one of my fellow teachers congratulating her sister on her engagement to my man. Or at least who I thought was my man. Needless to say, after I commented on the picture wishing the happy couple nothing but the best, we were done.

"Okay, fine, I'll give you that," I say. "But is a blind date really something I should have said yes to?" I ignore the way my head is screaming *you need to get out there and socialize* instead of sitting on your couch and watching Netflix.

She looks around, lowering her voice. "At this point, you've tried it all."

"I tried Tinder and Bumble," I correct her, holding up my two fingers. "There is still Christian Mingle and another one."

"You're an atheist," she says, laughing. "At least mom will be happy." My parents were high school sweethearts and raised us like they were raised, in a Catholic house. My father had a heart attack ten years ago, and Mom has never moved on, no matter how many times we urged her to find love again. The three of us are very close and always see each other a couple of times a week, and our

Sunday dinner is always a favorite of mine.

"You went on JSwipe." I laugh, reminding her.

"I could convert," she huffs out. "But seriously, are you ready for tonight?"

"No," I answer her honestly. "Not even a little. What if I get there and we have nothing in common?"

"What if you go and you have everything in common?" she counters, and I roll my eyes. We are similar in so many ways. We like mostly the same foods and have the same work ethics. We have the same taste in music and movies. The only thing we differ in is that I'm a planner, and she is a *go by the seat of her pants*, which always gives me the hives when we start to plan something, and she does the whole "let's wing it" thing. I gave in one time for three hours. "Listen, I know it's scary getting back out there."

"Now, who sounds old?" I joke with her, and she laughs.

"But the big question is, have you pulled up the carpet and laid down the hardwood floors?"

"What does that even mean?" I get up, going over to the dresser and carrying the clothes over and placing them in.

"It means…" She grabs the phone and shoves her face even closer as she brings her voice down to almost a whisper. "Have you shaved that jungle you started growing in lady town and made it smooth?" She laughs, and I can hear her hitting the table from her side of the phone. "Get it? Carpet means hair, hardwood floors no hair."

"Yeah, yeah, I got it," I say, shaking my head. "This conversation was enlightening." I walk out of my bedroom and toward the bathroom. "But with that being said, I have to go and get ready." I turn the water on. "Wish me luck."

"I wish you a big dick," she says. "And if it's the nicest you've seen, pictures or it didn't happen."

"That is never going to happen," I say. "Now I'm going to go and lay my floors, just in case he shows up looking like Chris Hemsworth and I have no choice but to have sex with him."

"This is what I'm talking about," she says with a huge smile on her face. "Call me when you leave the date."

I disconnect as I turn on the shower. "Here goes nothing."

THREE

MICHAEL

"HERE ARE THE keys to the condo," Nico says, handing me a square silver key. "Cooper said that the fridge is going to be stocked tomorrow." I look down at the key.

The last couple of hours have been a whirlwind, to say the very least. I just finished the interview with one of the reporters, and I know the guy was waiting for me to dish all the dirt. I could tell he was trying to slip in questions or would try to reword them. Nico and my father were in the room, and they would have had no problem yanking me out of there. After I walked out of there, my father took off for the hospital to sit with Matthew. He was not handling Erika in labor well.

"I'll be fine," I say. "I just need the address. I know the building, but I'm not sure of the address." He nods and takes out his phone and then texts me.

"That's my number," he confirms when my phone

buzzes in my pocket. "You need anything, you call me."

I nod at him. "Thank you, Nico," I say, turning the key in my hand. It's all a little surreal, and he turns and walks over to his desk, picking up more keys.

"I'm assuming you don't have a car just yet," he says, smirking. "You can have my BMW for tonight."

"I can take an Uber," I respond, not wanting to put him out more than I should.

"I don't need it." He hands me the keys. "Now, get out of here and get some rest. Tomorrow is an off day, but I expect your ass on the ice the day after that. It's time to put your money where your mouth is." He smirks, and I nod at him. My head's spinning in circles.

Walking out of his office, I make my way back to the garage and press the key fob to find the truck. I put the address in the GPS and make my way over to the condo. It's a four-minute drive to the condo, and I park at the same spot I did the last time. Grabbing my bag out of the back seat, I make my way to the silver door and the elevator. I slip the key into the door, and only when the door closes behind me does my head hang.

"I need a fucking shower," I announce, walking to the guest bedroom, dumping my bag on the bed, and heading straight into the bathroom. Undressing takes me five seconds, and then my hands are against the tile in the shower, and I let the hot water run down my neck as I close my eyes.

Getting out, I grab a towel at the same time my stomach rumbles. Walking over to my bag, I grab a pair of boxers and another pair of blue jeans. After I slide those on, I slip a gray short-sleeved shirt over my head. I walk over to the kitchen and pull open the fridge, finding just bottles of water and beer.

"He was not kidding about leaving this place empty," I say, closing the fridge door and opening the freezer to find just ice cream. "Not even pizza." Looking around the condo, I see how luxurious it is. Erika bought this condo when she first got here, and then apparently, she hated it, so she moved to the suburbs. When Cooper divorced his first wife, he moved in here with his two daughters, and as I look around, I wonder how he did it. The whole back wall is floor-to-ceiling windows. The kitchen is white with white and gray marble. The stainless-steel appliances look like they have never been used. I have stayed here a few times over the summer, but it's always been for a couple of days, so I never noticed how it never felt homey.

I walk back to the bedroom, slipping on socks and my running shoes. I grab my phone, keys, and a baseball hat and walk out the door. *Where am I even going?* I think, but I just get in the SUV and drive.

It clears my head, and when I finally look around, I notice all the turns have led me back to the same fucking place. I laugh as my phone rings, and I look down to see that it's Dylan. "Yo," I answer. Dylan and I are best friends and have been since we were eight, and my uncle Justin adopted him when he fell in love with Dylan's mom.

"Well, well, well, if it isn't the black sheep of the family," he teases, and I laugh, shaking my head.

"You know me," I say, joking. "Always the rebel." He laughs, knowing that between us, he's more of a rebel than I am. To be honest, before this shit, I was just another hockey player. My stats were good. I mean, not as good as Dylan's, but they were decent.

We were drafted the same year. He went first; I went third. I was drafted by Columbus and signed a three-year entry-level contract. I was invited to camp but didn't start out on the team right away. I waited for my turn, and in December, someone got hurt, and I got my shot to play with the big boys. On my second shift on the ice, I scored my first-ever goal, and it made it sweeter that it was against Dylan, who just glared at me when I chirped him. It took me two months to score my first-ever hat trick, and man, what a fucking night that turned out to be. It was hands down one of the best nights of my life. Four years later, we made it to the playoffs, and I scored another hat trick, pushing us to game seven, where we lost. It's during that time shit went down the tubes.

"You know why I'm so happy," he says. I can hear that he's walking, and I wonder if he's walking somewhere or just training. "Because no matter what I do this year, I'm always going to have this to throw on the table." He laughs a big belly laugh. "If I get suspended, all I have to say is, but did I get benched and then traded?"

"Like you would get suspended," I puff out. "Not the clean-cut Dylan Stone. Heaven forbid the hockey gods make you a bad boy." I laugh. Out of the two of us, he is the better player. He is hands down one of the best hockey players on the ice past and present.

"Fuck you," he says, laughing. "Where are you?"

"I'm sitting in Nico's BMW, wondering where I'm going to eat." I look around, spotting a restaurant that looks a bit busy, so I turn and look across the street and spot Sullivan's.

"Shit," he hisses. "Are you already in Dallas?"

"Got here a couple of hours ago." I lean my head back on the headrest.

"Wow, that fast?" he asks in disbelief.

"That fast. I couldn't wait to get the hell out of there, and Nico didn't want me getting on the ice." My finger taps the steering wheel. "So I got on a plane as soon as I could."

"I don't blame you," he says. "If that happened to me, I would have gotten in my car and drove home." He got drafted to Montreal, and home is New York for him, so it would have taken him six hours to be home. "I haven't even checked the press."

"It was a mess," I say honestly. "I sat down with a reporter this afternoon, and he was waiting for me to shit on my coach."

He laughs. "Idiot, like you are going to go on record saying he's an asshole." I laugh with him. "So what happens?"

"Now," I say, looking around, "I'm going to get something to eat, and then I'm off tomorrow, so I hope to sleep the whole fucking day and hope they are talking about something else when I wake up." To be in the press constantly was fucking with my head. The past five months have been mentally draining for me. "Actually, can you do me a favor?"

"Anything," he says without skipping a beat.

"Can you fuck up someone tonight? Maybe do an illegal hit," I say, and he just bursts out laughing.

"I'll see what I can do." He chuckles. "We are playing against Toronto, so who knows." His voice goes low. "Seriously, let me know if I can do anything."

"Yeah," I reply, tapping the steering wheel. "It's safe to say the worst is over."

He groans. "Don't fucking say that. Remember what happened when you said that two summers ago?" I roll my lips. "The worst is over. And then bang, I get stung by a jellyfish, and my foot swelled up five times its size. Alex kept taking pictures in case it exploded."

I laugh. "I think she made it her Christmas card that year." I shake my head.

"The headline was: If You Think You Are on Santa's Bad List, Check Out This Chump," he says between clenched teeth. "I didn't talk to her."

"For ten minutes," I remind him, and he huffs out.

"It was for two days," he counters. "And the only reason I caved is she bought me my favorite snacks and said sorry."

"I don't remember ever hearing an I'm sorry." I laugh. "I think it was more like don't be a pussy-ass bitch."

"I have to go," he huffs. "And I take back the *if you need anything*."

"No, you don't." He doesn't even say bye. He just hangs up, leaving me laughing. Driving over to Sullivan's, I park and get out.

I pull the baseball hat lower on my face and look down as I walk into the restaurant. The cold air hits me right away, and I look around. A brown hostess stand is to the left. A blonde stands there and then looks up at me, smiling. "Welcome to Sullivan's. Are we dining in or out?" she asks. I contemplate just taking the food back with me but then think of sitting on that white leather couch.

"I'll be dining in," I say. "For one. And can I have a table in the back corner?" I see that the bar spans the back wall of the restaurant, and they have sections on both the right and left side. All the tables are high-tops, and depending on the size of the table, they seat from two to eight.

She grabs a brown menu and smiles at me. "Please follow me," she says, turning and walking to the right and going all the way to the corner of the restaurant. My eyes are never roaming and making eye contact because if someone recognizes me, I'll spend the whole meal wondering if they are taking pictures of me. She stops in front of a table with four chairs. "Is this okay?"

There are two tables next to it, but none are taken. "This works," I say, going to the corner stool that puts my back against the wall but lets me have a view of the restaurant.

"Your server will be with you shortly," she says to me, and I just nod, grabbing the menu. The sound of people chattering fills the air, as well as the sound of plates clinking when I feel someone beside my table, and I look up.

My eyes meet the bluest eyes I have ever seen in my life. She gives me a little smile, and I can tell that she is nervous since she is wringing her hands in front of her. The girl stands there looking at me. "Sorry, are you Zander?"

FOUR

JILLIAN

My heart is about to come out of my chest or my throat at this point. "Sorry, are you Zander?"

I ask him, and he just looks at me. His blue eyes are a bit guarded as he scans my face. The longer he doesn't say anything, the faster my heart beats in my chest and the more nervous I get. His face gives away nothing as I stand here. I try not to let my eyes linger down to his muscled arms that fill out the gray shirt he's wearing.

The minute the Uber dropped me off outside, I got this feeling inside me that made me even more nervous. During the whole ride over, I kept asking myself why I didn't ask him for a picture. I kept asking myself why I didn't confirm the date with him today. I kept asking myself why the hell I put myself in this situation. With every step I took, my heart just beat faster and faster.

When I walked in, the chattering filled the area, and the hostess made eye contact with me before I could turn and run away. I had no choice but to pretend that I was okay, even though I felt like I was going to yack all over the place. I asked the hostess if there was someone here alone, and she pointed at this guy in the corner. I walked over to him, my hands shaky and my palms so sweaty I had to hold them together to calm myself down. The sound of my heels clicking on the floor echoed in my ears.

His head was down while I made my way to him, but that was good because it gave me a chance to check him out. He was wearing jeans and a T-shirt and a baseball cap. My head was yelling to turn away before he looked up. The guy came to a date in a baseball cap? Talk about not making an effort. "I'm supposed to be meeting a Zander here," I say as he just stares at me, and even if he wore the cap, I would forgive him because holy fucking shit, he is the hottest man I've ever seen. If he is desirable in a baseball hat, can you imagine how hot he is when he really makes an effort? "We were supposed to meet here at seven." I start to word vomit and can literally hear Julia tell me to shut the fuck up.

He shakes his head. "I'm not Zander." His voice comes out smooth, and my face suddenly gets hot, and I wait for the ground to open up and swallow me whole.

My eyes go big as I think of what to say. Sorry, I'm looking for a date and I don't know what he looks like because I'm an idiot and thought a blind date would be fun. "I am so sorry," I apologize, trying not to feel like an idiot. "I won't keep you any longer. Have a great evening," I say and turn around, walking away from him and waiting to trip over something and be roadkill in the middle of the restaurant. My eyes focus on my feet as I try not to make a spectacle of myself.

I walk back over to the hostess stand and see the same girl who smiled at me when I walked in here. "That's not him." She tilts her head to the side, not sure what to tell me.

"He is the only one who came in alone," she says, pointing over at the guy, and I look and see the waitress taking his order. "Other than him, there are no other single guys." She looks down at the paper in front of her. "Did you make a reservation?"

"It would be for Zander or Jillian," I say, not sure if maybe Zander made the reservation. She looks down at her paper as the door opens again, and I turn my head, hoping to see a single man come in, but I see a couple instead. They stand behind me, waiting for the hostess.

"There is no one under that name," she says, and if I didn't feel like a loser before, I feel like one now. Especially considering the weird face she just gave me.

"Is it okay if I wait at the bar?" I ask, looking around the restaurant and seeing that it's starting to get a touch busier than when I walked in. The door opens again, and five girls walk in.

"That's okay, but if we need the seat," she says, and I just nod at her and walk toward the back of the restaurant to the bar. I glance over my shoulder to look back at the stranger I interrupted and see that he's on his phone. He laughs and picks up his hand, bending it to scratch the back of his head, and I see the muscles in his arms flex.

"Jesus, Mary, and Joseph," I mumble. *How can he get hotter? Why couldn't he be my blind date?* I think to myself and turn, getting on a stool, ignoring the need to look back over and see if he's still laughing.

The bartender comes over. "What can I get for you?" he says, and I want to say a bottle of wine with a straw, but instead, I smile.

"I'll have soda water with lime, please." I look down at my phone to see if I have a missed call. The screen saver of Julia and me greets me and nothing else. The bartender comes back and puts down a white napkin in front of me and then puts down the short glass of bubbly water with a wedge of lime in it. "Thank you," I say, and he slides the paper bill to me. I grab the small clutch purse in my hand and take out my credit card. I look down the dark burgundy bar top seeing most of the chairs taken as people talk to each other. I look back over to the door and see a line of people, but no one is looking around for anyone.

My phone buzzes, and I pick it up so fast I'm surprised I don't drop it. I turn it over and see that Julia texted me.

Julia: *You look amazing.*

I smile, opening the chat and seeing the picture I sent her right before I left home. It was me in the hallway of my condo wearing the black jeans that fit a touch tighter than I remember and the black silky tank top that went a touch lower in the front, showing off a bit more cleavage than what I usually wear.

Julia: *How is it going?*

I shake my head while I answer her and quickly look

over at the hot guy who is not Zander.

Me: *I just met the hottest guy I've ever laid eyes on. IN. MY. WHOLE. LIFE.*

I press send and take another sip of water. The citrus from the lime hits my tongue right away, and then the bubbles explode on my tongue. It doesn't take long for my phone to buzz, and I pick it back up to check, smiling when I see her name.

Julia: *So, the blind date turned out to be hot. What are the chances? You should play the lottery!!!*

I laugh. "Oh, the chances are slim to none," I say to myself as I type out my response to her.

Me: *He's not my blind date. I thought he was and went over to introduce myself, and it turns out he's not Zander.*

Julia: *SHUT UP!*

Me: *I thought I was going to die. I was so embarrassed, and then my whole body was shaking, and I was afraid that I was going to trip with these stupid heels that I decided would be a good idea to wear tonight.*

I look down at the black shoes I bought for my cousin's wedding last year and decided to dress it up tonight. The minute I put them on, I felt the pinch in my baby toe, but I figured why not.

Julia: *What if he is and is lying to you???*

I gasp and turn to look back at the table and see that he's eating a burger as he scrolls on his phone. His eyes never look up.

Me: *Very doubtful. He is definitely not dressed for a date. He is wearing a baseball hat, for heaven's sake.*

Even if he was Zander, would he show up on a date looking like he didn't care?

Julia: hmmm…

I look back over and take another look at him.

Me: He looks like he just got out of the gym. There is no way he would show up for a date in sneakers. Don't you want to make a good impression?

Julia: He could be sizing you up. Maybe see you, say damn she's hot, and then I don't know, make an excuse and then meet you again when he's all dressed up.

Me: How would any of that make sense since I saw his face? I would remember his face.

Julia: I don't know. I've never done the whole blind date because people are crazy out there.

Me: Thanks for all of your uplifting comments.

I press send and take another sip of my drink.

Me: Seriously, how long do I give him to show up?

Julia: How late is Mr. Blind Date?

I look at the clock.

Me: Eighteen minutes.

Julia: One second, let me check and see if there are any accidents with casualties.

"Oh, good God," I say and then look over to see the hot guy on his phone again.

"Excuse me." I hear the hostess and turn my head, picking it up, wondering if I spot someone waiting at the door, but there is only a couple. The whole place is jam-packed. Not one table seems to be free. "I'm going to need to seat," she says.

"Of course," I say, the heat running up my neck as I

try not to make eye contact with her. I grab my purse off my lap and push away from the bar, taking my phone in my hand. Walking back to the front door, I keep my head down, afraid to look up and see the stranger watching me do another walk of shame. I push the hair back from my face once I get to the front door and go to the corner.

My hands tremble as I look back at my phone, trying not to focus on the sting of tears working their way up to my eyes. I blink away faster and faster to push it back.

My hands are clammy from sweat and nervousness as I pull up the text thread between Julia and me, taking a huge deep breath in.

Me: *I'm giving him fifteen more minutes, and then I'm out.*

FIVE

MICHAEL

MY EYES KEEP flying back to the bar every ten seconds, and I have to tell myself to knock that shit off. When she walked away from the table, I took a long look at her ass. And I mean long, her blond hair swaying left to right as she walked.

When she stood in front of me, I could tell she was nervous, and then when I said I wasn't Zander, I could feel that she was mortified. She put on a brave face and then turned around. I spotted her a couple of minutes later, walking back to the bar and sitting down. She looked around a couple of times, but she was mostly on her phone, her fingers going crazy. The restaurant is packed to the brim, and I'm happy I came when I did. I'm also happier that no one knows who I am.

Spotting the hostess, I follow her with my eyes as she zigzags her way over to the bar. She stops next to the blue-eyed girl, and then I see her smile and push away from the bar, walking to the front door.

Maybe Zander finally arrived, I think to myself, looking at my phone and seeing that it's seven forty-five. The asshole is forty-five minutes late, and he didn't think to call her. I shake my head as the waitress comes over and hands me the small black folder with the bill inside. I take out my credit card and place it inside. My eyes focus on the entrance to see if the hostess comes back with the blonde.

I push away from the table before I even know what I'm doing and stop at the hostess stand. My eyes roam, and I see the blonde standing in the corner, facing out, with her arms crossed over her chest. *Mind your own business*, my head screams while something else screams, *go get 'em, cowboy.*

The hostess spots me and smiles at me as I walk past her. "Are you still waiting?" My voice comes out higher than I wanted it to come out. She turns, and I can see the tears in her eyes.

"I'm sorry," she says, trying to blink away the tears, and I know that is what she's doing because I've seen Alex do it enough times in my life.

"You're still waiting for Zander?" I ask, putting my hands in my pockets before I do something stupid like pull her in for a hug.

"I was," she answers, putting her phone in her purse, "but I'm officially done waiting." She tries to shrug it off, and I have a chance to look at her up close. His lips are full and plump and are dying to be kissed.

"Why don't you come and let me buy you a drink?"

I say the words before my brain even registers what's coming out of my mouth.

The blonde stares at me with her mouth open, and I notice how slender her neck is. "No, no, no, no, no, no," she says, shaking her head and trying to laugh it off. I can tell she's nervous. "Now that would be even sadder."

"Please," I say. "Let me do this."

"I'm not taking a pity drink." She shakes her head.

"It's not a pity drink." I smirk when her eyebrows shoot up. "I have a sister, and if she was stood up, I would want someone to make her feel better."

She folds her arms over her chest, pushing her tits higher, and I can see the swell of her breasts, my mouth waters. "If your sister got stood up, you would want a stranger to buy her a drink?"

I listen to the words and grimace, making her laugh, the sound making my cock perk up. "Okay, fine." Taking my hands out of my pockets, I hold them up. "I would probably hunt down the guy."

"Probably?" she says, shaking her head and looking down. When she looks up again at me, it's like time stands still.

"Okay, fine." I laugh. "I would probably hunt him down, and it would not end well." I'm about to say something else when commotion from the side makes me turn my head, and I see my waitress there with my credit card in her hand.

"Oh, thank God," she says. "I thought you forgot your card." She walks over to me and holds the black folder with the bill in it.

"Actually," I say, looking at her and then turning to look at the blonde who has her back to the window. "I was just getting my friend," I say, pointing at her, and I can see the look of confusion on the hostess's face. "What do you say, friend?" I say. "Let me buy you a drink."

"Jillian." She says her name, and her whole face lights up, making her blue eyes crystal blue, but if you look deep enough in them, they have a light green on the bottom. "My name is Jillian." She holds out her slender hand for me.

My hand reaches out to take hers. "Michael," I say, smiling at her. "Or Zander, whatever." She laughs, but her hand still stays in mine. "So what do you say, Jillian?" I tilt my head to the side and smirk at her, hoping she says yes. "Have a drink with me or a meal. You can order food also."

She smiles shyly and looks down. Her hair falls in front of her face, and she lets go of my hand to tuck it behind her ears. "Sure," she agrees, looking at me. "Why not? I don't think my ego can get more bruised than being stood up."

I let go of the breath that I was holding as I hold out my hand for her to walk in front of me. I put my hand on the base of her back and then immediately drop my hand, and I can still feel the silkiness of her shirt.

The waitress follows me, and when we get to the table, Jillian takes out the seat in front of me that was empty not five minutes ago. "I'll be back with a menu," she says, smiling at me, and I sit back down in the chair

I was just in.

I'm about to say something when the waitress comes back. "Would you like to start with something to drink?"

"Um," Jillian says, looking at me, and then the waitress, and I can see her hesitating.

"I can afford whatever you want to drink," I say, and she laughs even louder. It's the only thing I can hear, and I love it.

"I'll have a whiskey sour and a shot of nineteen forty-two," she orders and then looks at me. "I'm not driving." I look at the waitress who waits for my order.

"I'll have water," I say and look back at Jillian. "Do you want something to eat?"

"No," she says. "I'm planning on drowning my sorrows." It's my turn to laugh out loud, and I swear in the ten minutes I've been with her, I've laughed more than in the past five months. "Oh," she says, "actually." She puts her fingers up. "I'll have a plate of french fries." The waitress looks at her. "Like a whole plate." She uses her hands to make a circle.

I look at her, and I'm suddenly so fucking nervous my heart starts to speed up, and my mouth gets dry. "So do you come here often?" I ask and then groan, putting my head back. Taking the cap off my head, I dig my nails into my scalp and put it back on my head when she just laughs. I hold up my hands. "As you can tell, I have no game." I shake my head.

With a chuckle, she puts her purse on the table next to my phone. "Are you saying you don't go on many dates?"

I look at her for a second and see if she's playing with me. Does she really not know who I am? "Not really," I say, and she tilts her head to the side.

"I find that hard to believe." Her eyes go big when she realizes what she said, and I'm about to ask her what she means when the waitress comes over with our drinks.

"Here is the whiskey sour and a shot of nineteen forty-two," she says. "I brought another one on me," she says, looking at Jillian with a smile and walking away.

"Well, I get stood up and get drinks," she jokes. "It's not as bad as I thought it would be." She smiles sadly. She grabs the one shot of yellow liquid. "To Zander. For making me cross off blind dating from my list." I shake my head as she takes the shot and then hisses. "Smooth," she says through clenched teeth.

"I have to ask…" She looks at me, her thumb wiping away something from the corner of her mouth. "What made you decide to go on a blind date?"

She laughs. "Well, I figured why not." She shrugs. "I tried the whole Tinder thing and then Bumble, and it was all…" She holds up her thumbs and points down. "So I figured why not."

"Did you know him?" I ask, so curious, and she nods.

"He is my hairdresser's son," she says. "Guess who is never going back to that hairdresser?" I can't help the laugh that escapes me as she picks up the second shot. "I knew that it was a bad idea." She shakes her head. "Besides rescuing women," she asks, "what does Michael do?"

I think about how to answer this, and for the first time,

I lie, saying the first thing that comes to mind. "I'm a fitness trainer."

She picks up her whiskey sour and looks at me. "It definitely shows." She winks at me, and I shake my head as the waitress comes back with a plate full of french fries.

"You checked me out?" I ask. She shrugs and takes another sip of her whiskey, and I am the one watching her. Her arms look thin, and I'm obsessed with looking at her lips as she takes a fry and bites the tip. Leaning over to grab the ketchup bottle, she pours a mountain next to her fries.

"When I got here, I was like, wow, he is really comfortable with himself if he's going to show up wearing a baseball cap to a date." I love that she just says what's on her mind, and I just look at her, my mouth hanging open. "I mean, I was like, wow, he's good looking." She just continues to talk, taking another sip of her whiskey, and I wonder if it's liquid courage or if she is just this open. "Then, well." She dips a fry in ketchup. "You looked up, and I was like, I just won the lottery." I shake my head, the laughter escaping even if I didn't want it to. "Then I thought I was going to die." She grabs a fry and then chases it with another sip. "I was mortified."

"It happens." I try to make her feel better, and she chuckles.

"When was the last time you got stood up?" she asks, and I just look at her. "That's exactly what I thought," she says. "Someone who looks like you will never get stood up."

"Well, Jillian," I say, leaning forward. "If it's any consolation prize." I make sure she is looking at me when I say the next words. "There is no fucking way he would have stood you up if he knew how you looked."

SIX

JILLIAN

"WELL, JILLIAN," HE says, leaning forward and my hand stops on its way to my mouth with the French fry in it. "If it's any consolation." His eyes stare into mine, and my whole body falls into a puddle-like form. "There is no fucking way he would have stood you up if he knew how you looked." My mouth suddenly goes drier than a desert, and I pick up the whiskey sour and finish the whole drink. The sound of the loud restaurant becomes silent, and all I can hear are the words he just said to me. All I can hear is his smooth voice.

"Um," I say, holding up my hand with the french fry in it, aiming at the waitress who looks at me. "More drinks?" I say, pointing at the three empty glasses in the middle of the table. I look back over at Michael and try to swallow, but it feels like a huge lump is in my throat. "You said you had no game," I'm finally able to say when I swallow a couple of times. When I met him, I thought he was hot, but talking to him, he just went into another category altogether. The category of the once-in-a-lifetime kind of thing.

With a chuckle, he leans back in his chair, pulling his shirt across his chest. If I had more saliva available, I would be drooling on the table. Heat rises up the back of my neck, and I have to wonder if it's the alcohol or the man sitting in front of me. "That wasn't a pickup line or game," he says.

"I say otherwise." I finally eat the fry in my hand. I point at him, getting another fry and dipping it in ketchup. "That was game." I wink at him. "Definitely keep that in the bank to use at a later date." If anyone who knew me was sitting at this table, they would not believe I just said that or did the whole eye-wink thing. When he found me at the door, I was five seconds away from having a crying session about being stood up. I was getting ready to call myself an Uber and looking forward to going home and sitting on the couch while I had a pity party with ice cream and pizza. But then he asked me to have a drink with him, and everything in my head said to just leave, but a little part inside me jumped at the chance. When I sat down at the table and ordered a shot of tequila, I made up my mind that this night would never happen again. A once-in-a-lifetime sort of thing. I mean, who gets stood up and then has a hot guy ask her to have a drink with him? True, it was a sympathy drink, but nonetheless, I was sitting at the table with said hot guy, and I was going to make every second count.

"Here you go," the waitress says, putting down

another two shots of tequila and a whiskey sour.

"Thank you," I say and turn back to look at Michael. "Are you from Dallas?"

"No, I was born and raised in New York," he says.

"That's my second favorite city," I say. "I mean, technically first if it had a beach."

"There is a beach in Long Island," he informs me, and my eyebrows pinch together.

"Okay, then I'll rephrase it, a beach with blue water," I say, making him laugh.

"It's a dark green." He tilts his head to the side as he looks at me, and I give him a look that says, *come on*. "Fine, it's not as good as the South."

"Thank you," I say, nodding at him. "So when did you move to Dallas?" I want to know more about him.

"I moved here today," he says, and my mouth drops open.

"Like today, today?" I point at the table, maybe misunderstanding him.

"Like today, today." He looks at his watch. "Like ten hours ago, I was getting on a plane to move here."

"Oh my God." I shake my head and take a shot. "This is not your day," I say, grabbing another fry.

"Why do you say that?" He leans forward, and his arms just bulge. "I had an okay burger, and I'm sitting with a hot girl." He winks at me, and I can't help but snort. "Was that not good game?"

"It was," I say. "It's just." I take a big inhale. "It's weird being told I'm the hot girl," I admit to him. "Pretty eyes, yes, but hot girl, no." I look around and spot a table with six gorgeous girls all dressed to the nines, posing with their phones. I point at their table. "Now those are hot girls."

He looks over and shakes his head. "That is Instagram versus reality." I can't help but laugh out loud. "If I take you home tonight…" He looks at me and takes off his hat, scratching his black hair. "I know I'm waking up with you tomorrow." He points with his thumb. "I take any one of those girls home, and I'm probably waking up with Cruella."

"Oh, that," I say, smirking. "That means there is a story behind that."

He shakes his head. "No story," he says, avoiding my eyes.

"Lies." I slap the table, smiling, and I think I'm flirting with him. I mean, I want to flirt with him, but I haven't flirted with a guy in well, forever, so I don't even know if I'm doing this right or not. "There is a story behind that," I prod, the alcohol in my body giving me added confidence. "Spill the tea."

He runs his hands through his hair, and I wonder if it feels as silky as it looks. "There was one time," he finally says, closing his eyes. "It was summer, and I was with my cousin and…" He trails off and just shakes his head.

"And and," I say, clapping my hands together, waiting for the juicy part of the story. The smile on my face hurts my cheeks, but I haven't smiled this much in a long, long time, if ever, for that matter.

"Let's just say I woke up with her eyelashes stuck to my cheek," he says, putting his hands to his face. "Stuck

stuck."

I can't help the laughter that roars through me at this point, throwing my head back and smacking the table with my hand. "Stop it," I plead, holding my stomach.

"Imagine my surprise when I looked over at her and saw that." He puts his palm on his forehead. "It was not something you need after spending the night drinking. You think you are taking home the hot girl, and it's all an illusion." I grab my drink and take another sip. "So trust me when I say that you, Jillian, are the hottest girl in here."

"Well, after that." I shrug. "I guess I'll take it."

The waitress comes over. "Can I get you guys anything else?" she says, and my heart sinks just a little, knowing this date is over. I mean, it's not really a date, more like a drink with a friend.

"I'm good," I say, grabbing my purse to pay for the drinks.

"Don't you even think about it," he says, grabbing the black folder that the waitress came running to him with when I was at the door. "You can use this card."

She grabs the black folder from him and smiles. "I'll be right back." Turning, she walks away.

"You really don't have to do this," I say. "This is…" I try to think of the words to thank him for saving me tonight, but no words would do it justice.

"This was a really great night," he says, and I just smile at him as the waitress brings the black folder to him. He signs the paper in scribbles and puts away his card. I push away from the table, my heart thumping, and

I don't know if it's because I'm nervous again or the fact that I'm going to say goodbye to him.

I get off my stool, grabbing my purse, and he waits for me. "After you," he says, holding out one hand as he puts his hat back on his head. He puts his hand on the lower part of my back, and I can feel the heat from his hand coming through the silky fabric.

"Thank you," the hostess says to us with a huge smile. "Come again."

"Thank you," I say to her as I walk out of the restaurant and move to the side of the door, not to stand in the way. The wind has picked up, and my hair is flying all over the place. I stop and look at Michael, who is a head taller than me, and now that he's standing, I can take in his whole body. You can tell from the way he wears his gray T-shirt that his chest is defined. His legs look thick in his jeans. "Well," I say, pushing the hair away from my face. "I have to admit." He waits for me to talk. "I'm going to go out on a limb right now and say that I had a better time than if my blind date had shown up." I tuck my hair behind my ear. "Thank you for that, Michael."

He nods at me. "It was my pleasure." He starts to lean in, and I hold my breath, thinking he's going to kiss me. My eyes stay open the whole time, just in case my head plays games with me later on and says it didn't happen. His lips come to my cheek, and my whole body lights up. "A great welcome to Dallas," he says, smirking.

"Drive safe," I say, and my heart sinks when he turns and walks away. I want to watch him, but my eyes fly back down. "No use in drawing out the inevitable," I say, taking my phone out of my purse and seeing twenty missed text messages.

I pull up the Uber app and order a car. I wait for the black dot to stop spinning, and it says that my driver will be here in ten minutes. Switching over to the text app, I scroll to the missed texts from Julia.

Julia: Where did you go?

Julia: Did he show up?

Julia: Um, hello?

Julia: You are freaking me out.

Julia: You are really worrying me. Can you tell me that you are okay?

The rest of the messages are the same, and I think about what to text her back. What can I possibly say? I had the best time ever with a guy who was not Zander, and I let him leave without even asking him for his number? I close my eyes, and all I can see are Michael's blue eyes.

Me: I'm fine. On my way home. I'll call you tomorrow.

I press send and see the three dots come up at the same time as a car pulls up. I look up to see the SUV, and the passenger window rolls down. He leans over, and I can see that he took off his hat as he looks at me. "You are not Riccardo," I joke with him.

 SEVEN

MICHAEL

JUST DRIVE AWAY, my head told me. *You did your good deed for the night, let her be.* I sat in the SUV, looking in the rearview mirror. "Just drive away." I closed my eyes. "But she drank, and what if." I knew she was beautiful when I saw her, but she became even more beautiful when we started talking. She made me feel things I didn't know how to explain or put my finger on. I also never wanted her to stop laughing. I could have spent the whole night just listening to her laugh. Even when she asked me about the girls and wanted to hear about one of the dates I've been on. I omitted telling her that I didn't even score with said girl. Instead, we both passed out mid-make-out session, and when she rolled over the next morning and kicked me in the balls, that is when I woke up. The woman thought I had game, if only she knew how many times I've gone home alone instead of with someone.

When we walked out of the restaurant and she turned to me, the wind blowing her hair, her cheeks a slight pink, and her lips were so plump they were dying to be kissed. Or at least I was dying to kiss her. My head moved before my brain realized what it was doing, and at the last minute, I went for the cheek. I ran out of there so fast I didn't even get to ask for her number. I got in the car, and if she wasn't close by, I would have screamed out my frustration.

Starting the car, I pull out of the parking spot. I look over at her, and her head is down as she types on her phone. Driving slowly in front of the restaurant, I stop beside her. Her head is down as I press the button for the window to roll down. "You are not Riccardo." She laughs back at her phone. "Definitely not Riccardo. He's driving a Honda Civic, and this is not a Honda Civic."

She bends, and her blond hair falls to the side of her face. "I am not Riccardo," I say. "Get in the car."

She gasps. "Absolutely not." She shakes her head furiously. "You've done enough for the night." She puts her hands on her legs. "I can say you have done it for the month. No more good deeds."

I just look at her as she stays leaned over, and I can see the black lace bra under that flimsy satin top. The whole night I kept looking at the thin straps and wondered how it would feel with me pulling them down. "So you can either get in the car." I look at her and then ahead and then back to her. "Or I wait for your Uber and follow him to make sure that you get home okay."

"Or you can pretend I'm not here," she says, and I

want to tell her there is no way I could do that, nor do I want to do it.

I lean more into the seat so she can see my eyes. "You don't know my father or my uncle," I say, shaking my head. "But if you did, you would know that if I left you out here by yourself, they would kick my ass." I close my eyes. "Tag team and then both of them together." My voice goes soft. "Get in the car, Jillian."

She steps off the sidewalk and puts her arm on the window. Just being near her and her scent has my cock waking up. I don't think I've ever been drawn to a woman like this before. "You really aren't going to leave?" I shake my head. "You really are that perfect," she says, and I pfft out.

"Trust me, I'm far from perfect." If only she knew what the fuck hell I just went through, she would know I'm not perfect.

The door opens, and she gets in. "I have to cancel Riccardo," she says, taking her phone and canceling her ride. She turns and looks at me. "My mother would not be happy with me. The whole stranger-danger thing."

"I think she would be less happy about you getting into a stranger's car," I say, and she looks at me.

"I met you an hour ago," she points out.

"You don't even know Riccardo." That's all I can say as I put the SUV in drive and take off. Turning right, I look over at her as she laughs. "Now, where do you live?"

"Oh, no, I'm not giving you my address," she says, and it's my turn to laugh.

"I don't even know what area I'm in," I respond, and she gasps.

"How did you pick Sullivan's?" She turns in her seat with her back against the door, bending one leg and tucking it under her butt.

"I was driving around, and well, the car led me to that place, and it looked good, so I stopped," I say and turn right. "Guess it was my lucky night." She laughs.

"You lied to me." She hits my arm, and I just look at her, not saying anything. "You have no game, my ass." I immediately think back to the way her ass swayed when she walked away from me. I also think about how it would look in my palm. My cock becomes so hard I'm afraid she is going to see, so I toss my hat on my lap and scratch my head. "You have this whole big bag of game."

I laugh. "The last time I went on a date was two years ago."

She rolls her eyes. "Just because you don't date doesn't mean you don't have game." She looks around. "At the next light, turn left." I nod at her as I follow her directions. I don't notice any street names, and at this point, I could be an hour away from my house, and I wouldn't even know.

"I blame my sister, who lets me watch all those sappy love stories." I smirk over at her, and she claps her hands.

"Which one is your favorite?" Her voice is radiant as she waits for me to answer.

"I don't remember the names," I say. "She just had me watch the historical piece on Netflix."

"*Bridgerton*?" she says, her eyes lighting up. "If you

like it, you should read the books."

"I think I'll pass." I chuckle. "I don't even know everyone's name. All I know is the duke and then the girl he married. The brother who bangs against a tree."

She throws her head back and laughs. "Okay, fine, what is another movie?" she asks, and I look ahead and stop at a red light. "Turn left here." I put the blinker on.

"She went through this stint of *The Notebook*," I say, and I swear to God, I think she sighs. "That fucking movie. She could probably recite it word for word."

"If you're a bird, I'm a bird." Jillian puts her hands over her chest, and I groan.

"Are we going to forget the fact that she was going to marry another man?" I point out the same thing I told Alex when we watched it.

"But she always loved Noah," Jillian says with a shriek. "He built her the house."

"Yeah, and she came, banged him, and left." I turn left at the red light, and I hear Jillian shriek.

"She went back." She makes the same case that Alex made. "She went back."

"Yeah, whatever." I roll my eyes, and she just shakes her head, making me laugh. "What about you?" I ask. "Which one is your favorite?"

"It's a toss-up," she says, looking in front of her. "At the next light, you are going to turn right."

I switch lanes, looking around, and all the lights in the businesses are closed. "Toss-up between?"

"It's between *Titanic*," she says, and I groan so loud, "and *Pride and Prejudice*."

"One," I say, holding up my finger. "Rose was a hog. She could have shared the door with him, but no, she had to take the whole door." I roll my eyes. "I'll never let go, my ass." I turn on the street. "She let go in a heartbeat as he sank."

"She survived and lived with his memories for her whole life," she says, and I just look over at her.

"I would have haunted her," I admit. "I would have haunted the fuck out of her."

She throws her head back and laughs, putting her hand to her stomach. "You would not."

"Oh, I would," I confirm. "I would not give up. But which *Pride and Prejudice*?"

"Keira Knightley," she says, and I nod.

"Right answer," I say with a chuckle, focusing on the road.

"See that white building?" She points at the only white building on the street. "That's me." I pull up to the curb in the only empty parking spot, a couple of feet away from her door. I put the SUV in park and look over at her. "This was fun." She smirks as she reaches for the handle. I can see she is thinking because she looks over at me, and I can tell she's nervous.

"If you are going to drive me home, the least you can do is walk me to my front door and make sure I get in okay," she jokes, opening the door and putting one foot out. "I could fall right before I put my key in my door, and then what?" She gets out and then leans down again, looking into the SUV. "Which is going to make everything you did tonight moot."

"Moot," I repeat the word. "Did you just use the word moot?"

"I did." With a laugh, she closes the door. I take the keys and put the hat back on my head. I open the door and see her waiting for me on the sidewalk. Her face goes into a huge smile. "You really are all that."

"I blame Alex," I say to her. "For not only making me watch love movies but also *Unsolved Mysteries*."

She laughs as we walk quietly toward her place. "There hasn't been any crime in this area," she says, looking around, "in at least a month."

I stop and take a look around, and I can hear her snickering. "I'm just kidding," she says, putting her hand on mine. "It's a safe area." She turns toward the white building. "Before I moved in here," she adds, pulling open the glass door and stepping in, "we checked out all the newspapers."

"Is there no locked door?" I look around as we head to the stairs on the side, and she laughs. "That is not safe."

She walks up the flight of stairs and then turns right down the carpeted hallway, stopping in front of the door with a four on it. "I'll bring it up at the next condo meeting." She takes her keys out of her purse and puts it in the door to unlock it. "Thank you for walking me to my door," she says, biting her lower lip. "I will never forget this."

I look at her and figure that I'll regret it for the rest of my life if I don't do anything. "Jillian," I say her name, and before I do anything else, we lunge for each other.

EIGHT

JILLIAN

"JILLIAN," HE SAYS my name, and everything in me stops and lights up all at the same time. This guy who saved me the embarrassment of being stood up and then went out of his way to make sure I got home safe. This guy who literally fell from the sky is standing in front of me, and the only thing going through my mind is to kiss him. So I just went for it. For the first time in my life, I took what I wanted. I lunged for him the exact time he lunged for me. His hat flies off his head, landing right by my foot, but I'm too engrossed in his eyes to even look down.

His arm circles my waist, pulling me to him, and I've never felt so safe before. My hands wrap around his shoulders. His other hand goes straight to the nape of my neck, where he grips a handful of hair and pulls back so he can claim my lips. My mouth opens for his as his tongue slips in to meet mine. My eyes close as I take in the feeling of being in his arms; his tongue slides against mine and going around in a circle. He turns his head to the side to deepen the kiss and pushes my back to the door. One of my hands goes to the nape of his neck and slides up to touch the hair I've been itching to touch all night long. I moan when I feel him on my stomach through his jeans.

"Inside," I say, panting, letting go of his lips for just a minute to say what I needed to say before going to kiss him again. If the night were to end right now, I would be okay with that because I've just had the best kiss of my life. The kiss that starts giving you flutters in your stomach, the kiss you hold your breath for. The kiss that makes your toes curl and you go to bed at night wondering if it really happened. The kiss that will forever be in my memory.

Moving my hands from his shoulder but never letting go of his lips, I reach for the handle, gripping it, and then stopping when he nips my lip and then sucks my tongue back into his mouth. He lets go of my hair, his hand coming out to hold my face as he kisses me with so much need. My hand turns the handle as I push the door open, and the hand still holding my waist picks me up as he walks us into my house. He turns and slams the door with his foot, pushing my back up against the door. He lets go of my lips as the both of us try to catch our breaths, my chest rising and falling as I look at him in the dark. The only light on is the little one on top of my fan over my stove that I never turn off. I place my hands on his chest, and I can feel his heart pounding underneath his shirt. "Jillian," he says my name again, this time in a whisper. "I don't know what I'm doing right now."

I smirk at him as his hand comes up to push my hair away from my face and his thumb runs along the side of my face going toward my lips. "This is called making out," I inform him, smiling and leaning in to nip at his lip. I'm so afraid he's going to walk away from this and from me, and my heart's not ready for the letdown yet. "And I don't want to fluff your ego and all that, but that was one hell of a first kiss." I lean in again and kiss him softly.

His hands come up as his fingertips touch my cheek, and my whole body explodes with goose bumps. "You are so fucking beautiful," he murmurs. "The minute you want to stop this." He kisses me back, his tongue sliding and dancing with mine, my eyes closing and then fluttering open when he stops kissing me, his eyes on mine as he says the next words. "You just say the word."

"Michael…" I move my hand up and down his chest. "Can we do less talking?" I look up at him shyly. "And more kissing and other stuff." It's a good thing we are in the dark because I can feel my cheeks turning bright pink.

"Other stuff." He laughs softly, bending his head and kissing under my chin. "What other things were you thinking about?" He trails his tongue toward my ear. "Tell me what other things you were thinking about." I close my eyes when I feel him nip my ear, and my back arches against the door. He trails kisses down my neck and stops, making me groan. "You need to tell me what other things you were thinking about, or I'll stop kissing you," he says, and my stomach fills with flutters, shooting down to my core with need.

"I was hoping." My head spinning from his touches, he continues to kiss me while I talk, and all I can do is think of all the things I want to do with him. "That we could maybe," I say, stopping when he nips my clavicle. "Maybe," I repeat, and his head comes up, and he kisses me again. This time the kiss is hungry. It's needy, and it's even better than the soft kisses he's been giving me.

He pulls away from my lips to continue kissing my neck. "All night, I wondered how you might taste," he says, his hands going to my hips, and I push out my back, hoping he takes the hint that I want his hands to grab my tits.

My hands go to his hips as I peel the shirt up a bit. "All night, I kept wondering what you looked like," I say, my head falling back as my fingers make their way slowly up his chest under his shirt.

"Well," he says, using one hand to reach behind him and pulling his shirt over his head in one smooth movement. "I don't want to keep you guessing." He smirks, and I push him away from me for a second, and he just looks at me.

"I need the light for this," I say, pushing him down the short hallway that feels like it's never ending. He laughs as he steps back to the small kitchen attached to the living room right off the bedroom.

"Is this good enough?" he says, dropping his shirt on the floor by his feet. His chest is huge, and his abs are chiseled and on point. He even has the side abs you hear about and see in pictures but have never actually experienced in real life.

"Holy shit!" I exclaim when my hand comes up and touches said two parts of his body. "These actually exist," I say in shock, and I drop to my knees in front of him, and if I was thinking like my regular self, I would never even imagine being so bold. But this is one night, and I'm going to make it fucking count. My hands come out as my finger traces them. "Like for real," I say, and he laughs, looking down at me.

"Also, while I'm down here." I look up at him, and I can see he is clenching his teeth. My hands go to his legs as I rub up his jeans. "I was also wondering what you looked like," I say, my hand moving up his jean-covered cock, and then my eyes go big as I realize how big he is. "Oh, my," I gasp as I slip his button out of its hole. "If you want me to stop," I say, giving him a second to change his mind as my thumb and forefinger draw down the zipper. "Now would be a good time." I open the flaps of his jeans and come face-to-face with his white Calvin Klein boxers and his cock trying to escape. "Last chance," I warn him before pulling down the top of his boxers and coming face-to-face with…

"This is the most beautiful penis I've seen in my whole life," I say the words out loud instead of in my head, pushing his pants down over his hips and thanking all the gods in the world for giving him to me. "Okay, fine, I've only seen one other penis, but this one is so much better." Only when I hear him laughing do I realize

I'm actually saying these words out loud. "I'll shut up," I say, leaning forward and taking his cock in my mouth. I close my eyes as I twirl my tongue around the tip. I push his pants all the way down to his knees to get his cock out so I can hold it in my hand. My fingers don't even close around the shaft as I try to take as much of him in me as I can.

"Fuck," I hear him hiss out, and my eyes open to look up at him, his eyes looking straight into mine. One of his hands grips the countertop, and the other goes into my hair. "Jillian," he says my name, and his hips move to keep up with the way my mouth is sucking him off. My hand is moving up and down, getting wet from my mouth, letting his cock go as I lick down the whole shaft. "I'm not going to last long," he groans out as I suck one of his balls into my mouth and then do the same with the other, then lick back up to the head of his cock. I take his cock in my mouth and move up and down. "So fucking good," he says, and I look up at him as he fucks my mouth. "I'm going to come," he warns and tries to pull away from me, but there is no fucking way I'm not going to swallow everything he has to give me.

"Come in my mouth." I let go of his cock long enough to tell him as I pick up speed, and I feel his hand grip my hair. The fact that I've made him lose control turns me on so much. I've never wanted a man so much in my life.

"Jillian!" He roars out my name at the exact time his cum hits my tongue. I swallow everything he has to give me. I take it all, and when his hand falls out of my hair, I look up at him, and I can't help but smile when his cock slips out of my mouth. "I knew that mouth was trouble," he says, panting. "But I didn't expect it to be so much trouble." He pulls me to him. "Fuck, I'm going to have so much fun," he states with a glimmer in his eyes as his hands go to my silky tank top, and it's off me before I know it, and his mouth is already attacking one of my perky nipples. "All night, this lace has been taunting me." He bites down on the nipple as I feel the tip of his tongue flick it. "All fucking night, my cock was hard, wondering what you looked like naked." He moves his head to the other breast. "And I'm going to fucking find out," he says, ripping the lace with his teeth, and I swear I almost come right here in the middle of my kitchen.

NINE

MICHAEL

I LOOK AT her as my pants are down to my knees, my cock throbbing for her. "All night, this lace has been taunting me." I bite down on the nipple that's been taunting me, then flick it with my tongue through the lace. "All fucking night, my cock was hard, wondering what you looked like naked." I move to the other breast, repeating the motion. "And I'm going to fucking find out." I bite down on the side of her breast and rip the lace away from her. She moans, and her head falls forward. My hands come up, taking the flimsy bra in my hand and pulling it off her. Her tits are hanging and waiting for me. "Jillian." Her eyes open as she looks at me, and I can see that lust has taken over. I roll her nipples, and her eyes close just a touch. "Focus on me," I say to her, and her head lolls like a rag doll.

"Michael," she says my name, and it's like an angel calling me. "This is going to sound really bad." I watch her, and my hand stops as my heart pounds in my chest.

"You want to stop?" I ask her, and my cock about screams out. My hands drop from her tits, and move up to her face. "We can stop."

Her eyes go big as she just stares at me. "God, no," she says, shaking her head. "I wanted to let you know that I think I'm going to come from you playing with my nipples," she admits, arching her back. "I've never," she says, and I bend and kiss her, my hand roaming over her shoulders, down to her tits where I play with her nipples, pinching and tugging them. She lets go of my mouth to pant out, and I thought she was kidding, and I know she was not. She puts her knees together, and I can see it's for friction. "Please," she huffs out.

I let go of her tits and move my hands down to the middle of her legs. Cupping her pussy through her jeans, I can feel the heat. "Tell me," I whisper in her ear, and I rub her through her jeans. "Do you want to come on my hand?"

She nods her head. "Yes," she pants out without hesitation, and I love that she is so open with me. When she got on her knees before, I thought I was going to have a heart attack, and then when she took my cock in her mouth, I thought my legs would give out, and I had to hold the counter. "I want your hands."

I smirk as her hips move with my hand. "What about my mouth?" I say, dying to taste her. She stills, and I look at her.

"I've never…" she starts. "I tried it once, and it was…" I look at her as she looks down at my hand shy, and that shit is not going to fly with me.

I put my finger under her chin and tilt her head back. "You've had me down your throat," I say, smiling. "Don't get shy with me."

"It's just that…" She hesitates. "I can never really orgasm with oral."

"Really?" I say, my hand is going to the button of her jeans. "Are you sure?" I ask her, and she laughs.

"I mean," she says. "I faked it." I laugh as I slip down the zipper.

"You know what this is?" I ask, and I spot the same lace as her bra sticking out of her jeans. "This is a challenge."

"No challenge," she says. Her tits call to me, so I bend and take one of the nipples in my mouth. She's more than a handful, and I plan on doing lots of things with them tonight. "I just want to."

I look up at her. "Oh, I know what you want," I say, peeling her pants down over her hips and taking one leg off, leaving her one shoe dropping to the floor. I pick her up from her hips and place her ass on the cold counter. "You want to come."

"Yes," she says, and I step between her legs that she opens for me. I place her foot with no shoe on the counter, and I can see her wetness all over the lace panties.

"Do you trust me?" I ask, taking my index finger and rubbing it up and down her open slit through her panties. My finger is getting wet from her.

"Yes. Of course."

"Good," I say to her as the other shoe falls to the floor,

and I peel the pants down. "Put your other leg up." She obeys what I say. "I'm going to eat that pussy," I say, and she just looks at me. "And you are going to watch me make you come."

"Michael," she says my name, and I don't know if it's a plea or if she's scared I'm not going to make her come.

"Trust me." Squatting down in front of her, I can smell her, and my mouth waters. "You're wet," I say, licking up her slit through her lace panties. "How much do you love this thong?" I ask her as I rub up where my tongue just was, and I finger her clit. I can tell from her chest that she's having trouble paying attention.

"Well, you destroyed the bra," she says, taking one hand and placing it behind her to lean back.

"Good." The sound of ripping fills the air. "Fuck," I say when I look down and see that she has a little landing strip and everything else is bare. "I can't," I say. My tongue comes out, and I lick her up and down two times, the taste of her making my cock harder than it's ever been before in my life. I've never been so turned on. I've never had my cock sucked like she did. Everything with her is in a whole different atmosphere, and I don't want it to ever end. I hold her lips open while my tongue finds her clit. She moans out my name, and I look up as her eyes close. "Eyes open," I demand, and she opens her eyes. "Watch me eat you." Licking her again, and fuck, I haven't even finished, and I am already looking forward to eating her again. My tongue slides into her pussy, she moves her hand to my hair, and she holds on to it. "You like that?" I ask, licking her up and down.

"Yes," she says, her nails scratching my head. "Oh, God."

I move my hand down, and when I slip my tongue back into her, I add two fingers, and her ass jumps up off the counter. "Michael!" she shrieks, and the only thing I can do is look up at her. "Oh my God." My finger and my tongue fuck her while my thumb rolls around on her clit in soft circles. "Oh my God," she pants again. This time, I know she is close because she's literally pulling the hair on my head to stop me from moving.

"Yes." My fingers are getting squeezed as they move faster and faster in her. "I don't know what is happening," she says, and I want to roar and pound on my chest. But instead, I flick her clit harder and harder as my fingers get wetter and wetter. "It's happening," she says as I look up at her. "Oh my God." Her foot falls off the counter as she tries to focus on me, but her eyes are glazed over. "I'm…" I don't stop my fingers, and I know she's about to come, so my mouth sucks in her clit at the same time as I feel her come all over my hand. I watch how she tries to keep her eyes on me, but her head falls back, and her hips rise up to meet my fingers. I finger-fuck her until she stops moving and lets go of my hair. My fingers slip out of her, and when she opens her eyes finally, I lick my fingers clean.

I turn my head and kiss the inside of her thigh and stand. "What were you saying about not….?" I don't say anything because she sits up, and her mouth finds mine. She slips her tongue into my mouth, and my cock is so hard, and it's at the perfect place to slide into her. I step away from her before I do something stupid.

"That was a first," she says, looking at me and biting her lip when she sees my cock. She gets off the counter, coming to me. Her body is fucking smoking hot. She has perfect tits, her curvy hips, and I can't wait to squeeze that ass of hers. She stands in front of me. Her hand goes to my cock, and she jerks it. "You know what else I've never done," she says, and my tongue feels heavy in my mouth as she moves her hand up and down. "I've never been fucked so hard before that I can't walk the next day." She steps close to me and gets on her tippy-toes. "Think you're up to that challenge?" she dares, letting my cock go and then walking around me. I look over my shoulder as she makes her way to what I'm assuming is the bedroom. "Actually, come to think of it, I've never been thoroughly fucked." She smirks. "Any help with that will be greatly appreciated."

I have to count to ten before I rush into the room and pound the shit out of her. "She's going to be the death of me," I say, looking around her small condo at the clothes strewn everywhere. Pulling up my pants, I walk to the bedroom to find her kneeling in the middle of the bed. "Jillian." She looks at me, her open shades letting the light from the moon come in.

"Yes," she says and then falls back on the heels of her feet.

"I'm hanging on by a thread," I say, kicking off my shoes and then pulling my pants down. I grab my wallet out of my back pocket and look inside, grabbing the three condoms I have in there. I toss the condoms on the bed, and I see her face with disappointment on it.

"Three?" She shakes her head. "You better make them count, Michael," she says, laughing when I get on the bed. I'm kneeling on the bed, and I grab the condoms from her, and she bends over to take my cock in her mouth. "I'll keep him busy while you get ready." She winks at me.

"Jillian." I call her name. "Challenge accepted."

TEN

JILLIAN

I LOOK AT the three condoms, and I swear if I could pout like one of my kindergarten students, I would. "Is three even enough?" I ask him as I take his cock back into my mouth.

"Move," he growls between clenched teeth, and I move out of the way, getting onto my back as he takes his cock into his hand and rolls the condom on it. When he set me on the counter before, I was so shy to tell him that I've never had any luck with oral. But with him, I feel like I can tell him everything, and I did, and fuck, did he blow my fucking mind in more ways than one. I've never come so hard in my life. "Lie back," he says, and I lie on the pillow as I watch him jerk his cock as he comes to me. My legs open for him as he settles between them. His cock is the biggest I've ever had, and I'm almost afraid he's going to split me in half. But I'm also more afraid of him not having sex with me. "Now you want it hard?" he asks as he rubs his cock up and down my slit, then moves away. "Fuck, your pussy screams fuck me."

"Good," I say to him. "You should listen to it and fuck me," I tell him, and he smirks.

"I'm going to make sure that you feel me inside you for days after," he says, and I swear I almost come again. "And I'm going to make sure your ass stings when you sit down."

I close my eyes, my hand going to play with my clit. "Put your cock where your mouth was," I say, and it's like my words pushed him over the edge. He slams into me so hard I swear my eyes roll behind my head.

"Fuck," he hisses out, not moving. "You're so fucking tight." I look down to see his cock all the way in me.

"I should have warned you," I say as I get used to his size. "It's been a while."

He bends his head down and sucks my nipple into his mouth. "Jillian, you're going to be the death of me."

I want to say something snarky, but he pulls out and slams into me again, this time my pussy getting used to him. I lift my legs to wrap around his waist, and he shakes his head. "Oh, no," he says. "We are going to watch me fuck you." He pushes my legs back, and his hands hold down my legs to the bed. "I want you to remember every single time I pound into you."

"Harder," I say, trying to move my hips up. "More."

He pulls out and slams into me over and over again, never letting go of my legs. I scream when I come thirty seconds after he starts fucking me. My pussy begging for more. "So fucking tight," he says in the middle of the second time I come, and this time, I can feel how wet he's making me as it leaks down my ass.

"More," I say, taunting him, and he just drills me. "Harder," I bait him, and I feel a big one coming. "Michael." I grunt out his name, my hand going back to my clit to play with it. My toes literally curl as I come so hard I see fucking stars. I come and come and come, and only when I'm close to the end does he pull himself out of me and turns me over.

"Not yet," he says, and I groan when he pushes my head down so my ass is in the air. He slams into me again, holding my hips. "This ass." He smacks it hard and then rubs it, and my pussy squeezes him again. "Is." He smacks it again. "Going." He smacks the other side, and my hand slides between my legs as I play with my clit. "To be red." He smacks it again, and I come. This time, my body shakes as he doesn't let up. He pounds into me like a fucking jackhammer, and I'm here for all of it. Whatever he wants to give me, I'll take. "I'm going to come," he says, and I fuck him back. His fingertips grip my hips so hard I know I'm going to be bruised, and I don't fucking care. "Come with me," he says, and he doesn't have to ask twice before I'm coming all over his cock again at the same time as he plants his cock balls deep into me and roars out my name.

I collapse on the bed, and he follows me, and I can feel his sweat all over me. I don't even know who I am right now, but I want to turn over and ask him to fuck me again and again. "That was a good start," I say, and he chuckles as he turns to the side, taking me with him, his cock still in me, and my pussy pulsing around him.

"I need a minute," he says.

"One of those condoms has to be saved for me riding you," I say, thinking about all the positions I want to try.

"Duly noted," he says and slips out of me and gets off the bed. I get up on my elbow as I watch him. "Why do I feel like a piece of meat?" He looks over at me and laughs.

"Just bring the meat back over here," I tease, and he looks around.

"Bathroom is through that door," I say of the side door that opens. He walks into the bathroom and turns on the light. I put my head down just to rest for a second, and when he comes back out, he finds me fighting sleep. "I might need a little."

"Oh, no, no, no," he says, getting on the bed and tossing my legs apart. "Round two starts," he says, burying his face between my legs, and he is not fucking wrong.

I HEAR THE alarm coming from somewhere in the house, but I can't fucking move my body. "What is that?" I ask, and I feel the covers fling away from my body, and I groan. I'm in the middle of the bed like a starfish, literally. I open one eye and look over at the side table and see that it's seven in the morning.

"It's my alarm." I hear him from beside the bed and look over at him.

"If I had the energy, I would look up," I say, and I can

hear him laugh. "Why are you waking up at seven o'clock on a Sunday morning?" I ask him over my shoulder.

"I have to get to work," he says, grabbing his jeans, and something in me sinks. I turn, and my whole body screams at me. The pain of my muscles from being bent into positions I didn't think were human to the number of times I begged him to do it harder.

I look at him right when he's putting on his jeans. "You got a couple of battle wounds," I say, laughing as he buttons his pants and looks down at his chest. I bit him sometime during the night. Don't ask me which round because I lost track. "I need water." I get up and grab my robe from the chair in the corner.

"You got a couple of battle wounds yourself," he says, and I look over and see that his teeth marks are on my shoulder.

"It doesn't beat this one," I say of his bite mark on my hip. "And then the fingertips."

He puts his hands on his hips. "You can't issue a challenge and think that there won't be battle scars." I laugh at him as I put on my robe. "Um, Michael," I say, and this shyness comes over me, which is stupid since he spent most of the night buried in me, eating me, pleasing me. "Before you go, I want to say something." I look up at him, and my heart stops in my chest. His blue eyes are so light blue that you can almost see through them, his black hair is pulled every which way, and he has a mark on his face from the pillow. "I don't do this," I say, pointing at the bed. "The whole bring a guy home and have sex with him." I hold my hands in front of me.

"I don't do this," he says, "ever." I laugh.

"There is no way that the things we did yesterday were a one-time thing," I joke with him, and he shakes his head.

"I meant, I don't go to bars and pick up women and have one-night stands with them." I tilt my head to the side. "After that whole eyelash thing," he counters, and I want to go to him and kiss him, but I don't because his phone rings again.

"That's the second alarm." He takes his phone out of his pocket. "I have to go." I nod as he walks out of my room, and I wince when I take a couple of steps forward. He was not joking with the *I'll feel him the next day*. I walk out of the room, finding him picking up his shirt off the floor by the front door.

I walk to him and stand in front of him, neither of us sure what to do. "Thank you," he says. "For a memorable night."

I laugh. "Thank you for all those challenges."

He looks down and then looks back up. "Can I get your number?"

"Yeah," I say, smiling, and he takes out his phone.

"What is it?" I give him the number, and he presses send, putting it to his ear. My phone rings from the counter, and I walk over to it. Grabbing my purse, I slide to answer. "Hello."

"Hey," he says, and I can hear the echo in the room. "It's me."

"Hi," I say, smiling at him.

"Now the ball is in your court." He hangs up. "Call

me." I nod as he opens the door. I wait for him to walk out, and he's halfway out of the door when he turns back and comes in. He doesn't say anything to me. He just stops in front of me and brings his hands up to cup my cheeks.

"Call me," he says softly before bending and kissing me. Though the kiss is like so many we've had over the night, it always feels like the first one. "Call me," he reminds me again. I just nod and watch him walk out. The door closes softly behind him, and I raise one of my hands to my lips.

I walk over to the coffee machine and start the coffee when there is a knock on my door. For some reason, my stomach flutters, thinking it's him. A smile fills my face when I open the door and see my sister there bending over and picking up a hat from the side of the wall. "Hi."

"I swear to God," she huffs, coming over with the hat in her hand. "You are so lucky that you share your location with me, and I saw you were home because I was about to send out a search party," she says, and I laugh, turning to walk back to the kitchen. "What happened to you?"

I look over at her. "I'm fine."

"You are walking like you have a baseball bat stuck up your ass." She points at me and then looks down at the hat in her hand. Her eyes go wide. "You brought him home."

I shake my head, grabbing a cup of coffee. "I did not," I deny, and I'm not lying, but she can see the glitter in my eyes.

"You brought someone home," she accuses, gasping

and looking around. "Is he still here?"

I shake my head. "He is not," I say, and she shrieks and puts the hat on the counter.

"You little hussy," she teases, shaking her head. "I want all the details."

I know that I share everything with her, but something stops me from sharing Michael. "The only thing I'm going to say is you know those pictures you see on Instagram?" I look at her, and her eyebrows pinch together. "The one where the guy has the set of abs and then the side abs?"

"Those are airbrushed on." She shakes her head. I shrug.

"I can confirm that they do exist." I laugh, taking a sip of my coffee and wondering when will be a good time to call Michael.

ELEVEN

MICHAEL

Five Months Later . . .

I SLIP ON my cashmere jacket and grab my backpack as I open the hotel door and head out. "I need a coffee," I say when I see the captain, Manning, standing at the elevator with his own cup of coffee. "Did you go out already?" I ask, and he smirks at me. He is wearing pretty much the same thing I am wearing but with a black hat covering his head.

"My wife sent it to me," he says, and I swear he gets googly eyes talking about her. From the talk in the locker room, they met one night, and it was all it took.

"How did you get coffee?" my cousin and linemate, Cooper, says from beside me. I look at him and see that we have the same jacket, but I'm not surprised since our aunt Zara, who is a professional shopper, probably bought it for both of us. "There was nothing in the room." We've been on the road for the last fourteen days, two whole fucking weeks, and I, for one, can't wait to not see these guys for a few days. Everyone is fed up with each other, and it doesn't help that we lost the last four games.

"His wife sent it to him," I say when the elevator doors open. I walk into the elevator and look at Cooper, who looks at Manning, who lifts his coffee to his lips as he walks in beside me, leaving Cooper to look up. "Why didn't your wife send you one?" I roll my lips when he glares at me, walking into the elevator next to me. "I'm just asking. I thought maybe it was a wife thing." I shrug my shoulder as Manning tries not to laugh at him.

"It's not," he says, reaching out and pressing the L button.

"My wife loves me," Manning leans into me and whispers loudly, and I can't help but laugh. Cooper and his wife, Erika, were best friends for years before they got together.

"I can tell you without a doubt," I say, looking at Manning, "that Erika loves this buffoon more than she should." I point at him with my thumb. "Sickleningly so. To the point she fawns all over him." I make fake vomit noises. "At Christmas, we found them making out in the laundry room."

"Don't be jealous that you don't have anyone to kiss." Cooper pushes my shoulder, and I don't have time to answer him when the door opens, and we step out into the lobby. The bus is there waiting for us, and I look around to see if I spot anywhere to have coffee.

"How is there no coffee stand?" I ask, looking around,

and Nico comes out of the elevator holding a coffee in his hand.

"If you tell me your wife sent you that…" I point at the coffee, and he just laughs.

"No, it's called Uber Eats," he says, standing next to me. "You should try it."

Shaking my head, I walk out of the lobby, and the bone-chilling cold hits me right away. So cold the snow crunches under your boots, and breathing in makes your nostrils freeze. "How the fuck does Dylan live like this?" I say, getting on the bus and sitting down.

"You get used to it," Cooper says, sitting down next to me. "Or like he says, your blood gets thicker."

"His head is getting thicker if he thinks anyone can get used to that fucking cold out there," I grumble, putting my hands together and blowing heat on them. The bus fills with cold air as everyone loads on. "It's minus thirty-three outside. How do you even leave the house?" I ask Cooper, who just shrugs.

Once the bus is loaded, we take off and can't even see outside with the amount of ice on the window. "I can't wait to get home," Cooper says from beside me, and I look over at him. "I also hope not to see your ugly mug for a couple of days."

I burst out laughing. "You were the one coming to my room," I point out. "What are you doing? You sounded like a lost puppy."

He shakes his head. "I was looking out for you." The phone pings in his hand, and he smiles. "Look at him," he says, turning the phone for me to see his son with a gummy smile. "I can't believe he's five months already."

"Good thing he looks like Erika," I say, joking with him, and he pushes my shoulder.

"He looks just like us," he says, and the bus comes to a stop.

"I think he looks just like himself," I reply.

Cooper shrugs his shoulders. "You'll see when you have yours how different it will be." He walks out to the plane, and I follow him, not saying anything.

I walk up the silver stairs to the plane. "I swear I think my eyeballs are frozen," Ralph, my teammate, says from the other side of the plane when he throws his backpack in the empty seat by the window.

"My balls crawled back up into my scrotum," Miller, my other teammate, gripes as he walks by me. "Where do I send my complaints?" He holds up his hand as Nico walks onto the plane and looks at him. His cashmere jacket is buttoned up with his Burberry scarf as he puts his leather backpack on the seat and then takes off his gloves. "I would like to file a complaint."

Nico laughs at him. "I can't wait to hear it," he says, taking off his jacket and putting it over his chair.

"Coffee," he says, holding up his finger. "We have to have coffee."

We all laugh at him. "I'll make a mental note and tell my people." He shakes his head and sits down in his chair. "Now, get your ass in your chair, so I can go home to my wife and kids."

Miller shakes his head and sits down as I put my head back as the plane takes off. The flight takes thirty minutes, and everyone is excited to be home.

When the plane lands, there are a few of them who clap, I get up, throwing my jacket over my arm as I walk out of the plane and the sun hits me right away. I take my phone out and snap a picture. "Who is that for?" Cooper asks me as we walk to our cars.

"Dylan, to show him what it's like not to have white shit all around me," I say, looking down at my phone and sending Dylan the picture with the following text.

Me: Someone's balls just melted.

I put the phone away when I get to my BMW SUV that I bought the week after I got here. It worked out that I sold the one I had in Columbus to another player. The drive home takes me no longer than six minutes, and when I put the key in the door and open it, I yell, "Honey, I'm home," to the four empty walls.

I haven't moved from Erika's condo, only because it makes more sense to just stay put until the end of the season and then get a place. I sold the house I had in Columbus as is, so I have no furniture.

I carry my bag straight to my bedroom and dump it in the closet, walk to the bathroom, and turn on the shower. "Fuck, it's good to be home," I say when I step into the big shower and turn the jets on.

Once I step out, I don't bother getting dressed. Instead, I slide into the bed and fall asleep as soon as my head hits the pillow. My eyes flicker open when my phone rings. My hand snatches it off the side table, and I see that it's Cooper. "What happened to you don't want to talk to me for a few days?"

"Very funny," he says, and he's huffing out. "I need a favor."

I close my eyes. "Depends," I say, throwing the covers off me and rubbing my face.

"Erika had an accident." His voice is frantic. My heart picks up, and I'm already in the closet getting dressed.

"Is she okay?" I ask worriedly. "Where is she?"

"She's fine. She got rear-ended on the highway," he says, and I can hear crying in the background. "I have the baby, but I have to get to the hospital to be with her."

"What do you need from me?" I ask, slipping on jeans and a shirt.

"Can you get Mia and Emma from school?" he asks, and I snatch my leather jacket and a baseball hat. "I already called the school, and Mia's teacher is going to wait with them."

"I'm walking out the door right now." I grab my keys and slam the door behind me. "Text me the address."

"Thank you," he huffs out. "I owe you."

I press the button to open the BMW door when I get in the garage. "Text me the garage code also."

"I gave it to you fifteen times already," he says, and I can hear him running around.

"Well, make it lucky sixteen and stop giving me a hard time. Hug Erika for me," I say, disconnecting the phone and then waiting for his text. The address comes through within two seconds, and I put it in the GPS.

Parking in front of the school, I get out and walk up the long concrete pathway to the two brown doors. I pull one of them open and then come face-to-face with two more blue doors. I look over to see the secretary of the school waving at me as she buzzes me in. I walk in and turn to the right. "You must be here to get Mia and Emma," she says to me, and I smile, showing her my ID.

"I am." I smile at her, looking around.

"They are in the last classroom to the left. It's a red door," she says, holding out her hand toward the hallway.

Walking down the hallway, I see children's artwork hanging outside of the classroom and a couple hanging down from the ceiling. I stop outside the red door and look inside and smile when I see Mia and Emma sitting at two desks. My eyes go to the teacher sitting with them, and I swear the earth shifts underneath my feet.

I stop mid-step, and she looks up at me. The woman who has been haunting my dreams for the past five months. The woman who is more beautiful than I even remember, the smile fills my face as I see her look up at me. Her eyes meet mine, and I whisper her name. "Jillian."

She looks at me, the smile on her face freezing and then going away. In its place is a glare. "Uncle Michael!" Emma says, and I look at her as she runs to me and then hug her.

Lifting my eyes again, I see that Jillian is standing up, and she looks a lot different than she did the day I left her, and she said she was going to call me. She stands there with her hair in a ponytail wearing a tight white dress with black stripes across it and a belt under her boobs but on top of her pregnant belly. "What the hell?" comes out of my mouth.

TWELVE

JILLIAN

IT ALL HAPPENS in slow motion. It's like one of those slow-motion car accidents that you see happening right in front of you, except you are the one driving the car. "Uncle Michael!" Emma shouts, and the smile on my face freezes. This can't be happening. There is no way this would happen like this. When I look up, my eyes meet his.

Yes, the universe is really doing this to me right now. He stands there in pretty much what he wore the first time I met him. Except I know what he looks like naked, and my body reacts to it like the traitor it is. The only different thing is the leather jacket, which just makes him even hotter, if that is possible. He looks at me up and down, and when his eyes land on my stomach, the only thing he can say is, "What the hell?"

What the hell, indeed, I think to myself, along with other things that I can't say in the presence of my students. The last thing I need is to get fired right before I have a baby.

"Miss Jillian," Mia says, looking at me. "That Uncle Michael." She points over at him, getting off her chair and running to him. His face goes into a full smile when he sees her running to him. He bends and picks her up and kisses her neck.

"Hi, you," he says softly, and she hugs his neck and lays her head on his shoulder for a second. His arms bulge from holding her, and I wonder if he got bigger. The memories from that night come crashing back, making me angrier with him. I want to yell at him and kick him in the balls, but instead, I put on a brave face. The same brave face I've worn since I found out I was pregnant and most likely going to be a single mom.

"Did you bring me candy?" she asks, and the smile fills my face even though I don't want it to. When I look at him, my heart speeds up just like it did the first time, but then my hand goes to my stomach, and the sorrow and anger come in.

"I did not," he says, looking at Mia and then at me. His eyes travel down to the hand on my stomach.

"Can we get McDonald's?" Emma asks, and he looks down at her.

"Why don't we call Dad when we get in the car, and we can see," he suggests. "Go get your things, and I'm going to talk to Miss Jillian."

"Oh, no." I shake my head. "There will be no talking to Miss Jillian." I put on a fake smile. "Because Miss Jillian has been waiting, and she needs to leave." I walk over to my desk.

"I'm sure Miss Jillian can spare a minute," he says, putting Mia down, and Emma comes over and grabs her bag.

"I assure you she probably can, but she doesn't want to," I say, and I feel like one of my students when they fight with each other. I need to stomp my foot, fold my arms over my chest, and pout.

I watch her walk over to me. "Thank you for the snacks." Emma hugs my waist, and I bend a bit to hug her back.

Looking down at her, I smile. "It was my pleasure," I say and look over to see that he's stepped more into the classroom. I can smell him, and my nipples perk up. I look down and am thankful that my padding doesn't show it.

"Miss Jillian," Mia says to me. "Can I bring home this book?" She holds up the book I was helping her read.

"Only if you promise to bring it back," I agree, and she smiles so big and nods. "Then you can borrow it from me." I squat down in front of her. "If you practice, maybe tomorrow you can lead storytime." She gives me a hug, then turns to tuck it in her bag.

"Jillian." I hear him say my name, and even though I'm angry, the tears come, but I blink them away. All I can remember is the way he said my name all night long. The night that I held on to for the past five months. Racking my brain for clues as to why he did what he did.

"If you don't mind, I need to head out," I say, getting up and walking over to my desk. He's about to say something else when there is a knock on my door, and I look up to see Sharon, my co-worker, standing there.

"Sorry to interrupt," she says and then looks at Michael and walks in, swaying her hips. I almost roll my eyes.

"You are not interrupting anything. See you girls tomorrow," I say, giving him the hint to get the hell out of here.

He looks at me, and I avoid looking into his eyes because there is no need to go down that road. The last thing I want is for him to see how much he hurt me. "Let's go, girls," he says, holding his hand out to them. They slip their hands in his, and he looks back at me one last time, and I make the mistake of looking into his eyes. I can tell that he's trying to tell me something, but I hope he sees in mine that I don't ever want to see him again.

"Have a nice night, girls," I say, waving my hand and then turning to my desk as I pack up my things. I see Sharon following them out with her eyes, and when they walk out of the classroom, she tiptoes to the doorway and watches them through the door crack.

"Holy shit, who was that?" she turns over to ask me.

"That's their uncle, I assume," I reply, avoiding her eyes as I pick up my papers to grade at home.

"Did you see the ass on him?"she asks, and I want to say yes, I have. I even want to say that I've smacked it and went so far as to bite it, but instead, I shake my head.

"Did you need something from me?" I ask, picking up the bag and putting it over my shoulder.

"It was just about the plans next week. It can wait until next week. You should go and rest. You look exhausted," she says and turns to walk out of my class, and the only thing I have energy for is to stick up my middle finger at the space she was just in.

"You look exhausted," I mimic her words as I walk out of the classroom and close my door behind me. "You try carrying a human child," I say when I pass her class and find her sitting at the desk with her feet up as she talks on the phone to someone.

I shake my head and walk out the employee entrance to my car. I look around, and for some reason, I expected Michael to be there waiting for me, and then my heart is let down once again when he isn't there. "What did you expect?" I ask, getting into the car and putting my bag on the passenger seat. I let out a breath because these past two weeks I've gone from having just a tiny bump to looking like I have a soccer ball. "Well, that was your dad," I say to my stomach, and I feel flutters. My hand rubs my stomach as a tear escapes and falls onto my hand.

Only when I'm alone do I let the tears fall. "We are going to be fine," I reassure. "Just peachy." I start the car and make my way over to my house.

Parking my car in the back of my building, I grab my bag and head inside. As soon as I get into my apartment, I kick off my shoes and head to the kitchen.

Opening the fridge, I look for a snack. I gave the one I brought to eat after school to the girls. Grabbing a cheese stick, I turn to head over to the fruit bowl and grab an apple.

My phone rings from my bag, and I walk over to it and see that it's my sister. "Oh, boy, do I have a story for you," I say without saying hello.

"I can't wait," she responds, and I hear the sounds of beeping in the background. "I just left court, and let me tell you. Taking a ten-year-old child away from his parents sucks monkey balls. Especially when the child is being abused and still loves his parents."

"Jesus." I put the phone to my ear and walk back into the kitchen. I grab the cutting board and a knife. "You will never guess who I ran into today," I say, slicing the apple and taking a piece.

Turning, I open the cupboard to grab the peanut butter and fetch a spoon. "Chris Evans," she guesses, and I roll my eyes as I take a scoop of peanut butter and place it beside the apple on the plate.

"Where the hell would I meet Chris Evans?" I ask, laughing.

"I have no idea, but ever since he leaked his dick pic on Twitter, I've been waiting for him to answer my private message," she says, and I gasp.

"You did not," I say, shocked but I'm not sure why I'm shocked when it comes to her.

"It was a simple question," she says. "I wanted to know if he was a shower and a grower or just a shower. It's a question I'm sure everyone was asking."

"You are insane, and he probably blocked you," I declare, sitting on the couch, and as soon as I sit down, I want water.

"He did not. I checked." She chuckles. "Also rude for not answering me."

I shake my head as I take a glass out and fill it with water. "Now, who did you run into today if it wasn't Chris Evans?"

"Oh, no one special," I say. "Just my baby daddy." I wait for her reaction, and she doesn't make me wait long.

"Shut the fuck up right now," she says, her tone totally serious, and I can hear the car door shut.

"You did not."

"Oh, but I did," I confirm, taking a drink of water. "He came to get his nieces."

"I don't believe you," she rebuts, and I can just picture her face.

"Why the fuck would I lie about this?" I shriek out louder than I want to and hear a knock on my door.

"How did he look?" she asks, and I don't have a chance to answer her before she asks another question. "Did he see your stomach?"

I'm about to answer her when I pull open the door, and my mouth hangs open. "I'm going to have to call you back," I say, hanging up when I hear her yelling. "What the hell do you want?"

THIRTEEN

Michael

I PARK MY BMW exactly where I did that night we spent together. Getting out, I jog to her door, my head spinning, my heart pumping exactly like it did that first night. The sun is setting, and more people are on the street. I walk over to her apartment and see a couple of people sitting outside on their patio.

Pulling open the door, I'm irritated all over again because I can just walk up to her door. As I walk up the steps, the sound of my heartbeat pounds louder and louder in my ears. Turning down the hallway, I feel my palms get sweaty. I stand outside her door for a while, the whole time trying to get the courage to knock on the door. The memories of our first kiss play over and over in my head. A first kiss that, to this day, I think about every single day.

"Just do it." I try to pep-talk myself. "What's the worst that can happen?" I hold up my hand and knock on the door. My stomach sinks, and I swear I'm going to be sick, so I hold the doorjamb. It feels like every second is a minute, and every minute is an eternity. I don't even know if she's home, but I know I'm not leaving until we talk.

Walking out of the school holding the girls' hands, I felt like I was in a daze. My feet were making the motions, but my head was still in that classroom staring at her. Taking her in, I was so into the memory of her that I didn't hear Cooper yelling my name. It took Mia pulling on my hand for me to look over and see him. He rushed over to me, his hair wild from all the times he ran his hands through it. The fear and worry that was in his voice over the phone showed in his eyes. The girls were happy to see him since he'd been gone for two weeks and it's that reason that Erika forced him to come and get the girls and then go get her. I took in his frazzled look, and for once in my life, I knew exactly how he felt. Sitting in the car, I pulled up the address that I took down when I left her house that morning.

The sound of her voice comes through the door and makes my nerves speed up. Shit, what if she's with someone? I put my hand to my stomach when it sinks and then rises again. What if I'm doing all this, and it has nothing to do with me? The what-ifs all stop when the locks click and the door opens. All the what-ifs are out the window when I take one look at her.

She stands there looking even more beautiful than she was when I saw her at the school. She's even more beautiful than she was that first night, and even that is hard to believe. She has the phone to her ear, and she tells the person she's talking to that she will call them back. Her face goes from shock to anger in a blink of an eye. "What the hell do you want?" she hisses with her hand still on the door handle.

All the words get jumbled in my brain, and the only thing that comes out is, "I think we should talk," looking at her and then down at her belly, which looks bigger. Her eyes go into slits as she looks at me.

"The balls on him," she mumbles. I want to laugh, but I don't have time because her voice goes higher when she says, "We have nothing to talk about." Her hand attempts to slam the door in my face. My foot comes out before the door can close, making her even angrier.

"You have got to be kidding me," she says, shaking her head when the door opens back up. "What do you want?"

I look at her and think about how to word this question. She stands there with her hand on her hip. "Are you..." I point at her stomach, my heart racing, and I think I'm going to be sick. "You're pregnant?" I ask, and her mouth hangs open.

"No," she retorts, shaking her head as her eyes go big. "I'm retaining water." She folds her arms, and I notice how perfect her tits look, and my mouth waters. Fuck, everything about her turns me on. And I mean everything. Her eyes when she looks at me even with a glare. Her hands when I think of them on me. Her lips when I think about just kissing the shit out of her until they are swollen and then starting all over again.

"Can you be serious right now?" I look her in her eyes, and she just shakes her head. Voices come from the side, and I see one of her neighbors is coming in. She stands there just looking at us, not moving. Jillian sees this and then steps out of the way for me to step into her apartment, and I have to figure that is a good sign. Unless she wants to bring me inside to stab me.

"I am being serious right now, Michael," she says, and all I can do is look at her. She takes my breath away.

"How far along are you?" I ask, and I wait with bated breath for her to answer me. The thought goes through my head that this baby might not be mine. The thought also makes me feel something I can't explain, but I do know it's not a good feeling. Nothing about that thought is good. Not. One. Thing.

"Why don't you just come out and ask me if it's yours?" She looks at me, shaking her head when I raise my eyebrow. "Unbelievable," she says to me. "Such an asshole."

"Hey," I reply, holding up my hand. "I don't know why you are the one who is so pissed off." I take off my hat and scratch my head as the pounding comes on full force. I point at her. "You were the one who didn't call." I put my hands on my hips. I wait for her to say something, but she shocks me when she whips her phone at me. Her aim is on point, and I have just enough time to block it from hitting my head. My hand comes out to catch it when it deflects and crashes against my chest.

"I didn't call you?" she shrieks. "Oh, I called you all right," she says to me, and my eyes go big. "Two days after you left here. Ball's in your court," she mimics me. "My ass, your girlfriend answered your phone." I look at her, confused. "Like an idiot, I actually asked for you and she informed me that you were busy, and if you wanted to talk to me, you would call me back." Her voice goes low. "You never called me."

"I can explain," I finally tell her when I see the tears well in her eyes. All I want to do is go to her and hold her in my arms.

"Well, I don't want to hear it," she says strongly, putting her shoulders back and shaking her head. "I don't care. It doesn't matter."

"It matters to me," I say. "I went away on a road trip the day after we…" I point at her and then to me. "I thought I lost my phone, but it turns out that I forgot it on the plane. I thought, easy, I'll get it back, but it turns out, the flight attendants who had it weren't going to give it back so easy." She just listens, and I wonder if I'm explaining for nothing. I wonder if she already made up her mind about me.

"We set up a time for me to get it when I got back to town, and when I went to get it, she said she wouldn't give it back to me unless I went on a date with her." I close my eyes, thinking about how the conversation went, and I'm giving her the CliffsNotes. It got so fucking bad.

"When I told her to dream on, I went to my boss. He was not happy when I told him that she basically tried to blackmail me into going on a date. He called her and reported her to her boss, and well…" I explain. Nico was not playing games. He had her fired and blacklisted from any other airline. It was just another cloud that followed me. "She leaked my number on Twitter." I close my eyes. I would get calls at all hours of the day from fans, from people who thought I was a traitor to Columbus. "I had to change my number."

She looks at me, not sure if she should believe me or not. "You expect me to believe that?"

"I can show you the pictures," I say, taking out my phone, ready to show her if I have to. "We have to keep them for the court case."

"A court case for someone who stole your phone?" she asks, shocked. "A little extreme."

"She gave away private and personal information," I say. "And she tried to extort me."

"She used your phone as leverage," she points out, and I glare at her.

"And when I said no, she refused to give me my phone back." I shake my head. "Whatever it is, I didn't get your call." I close my eyes. "I didn't want to, but I had to change my number, and all of my stuff from my other phone couldn't be retrieved because of the fucking cloud that I still have no idea what it means." I take a deep breath. "Which is why I couldn't call you."

She looks at me, not sure. "You would have called me?" she asks, putting her hands together in front of her.

"Of course I would have called you," I say. "What we shared, it was…"

She holds up her hand, and when she utters the words, I'm still in shock. Even though I knew she would say those words, when she finally does, all I can do is stand here and stare at her with my mouth hanging open.

"It's yours."

FOURTEEN

JILLIAN

HERE IN THE middle of the room where we started our one-night stand, I tell him what I was planning on telling him when I called him and got the stupid pre-recording.

The number you are calling is not in service. Please check the number and try your call again.

I called every day since then, hoping it would change. Hoping—always fucking hoping—I would hear his voice, but it was always the same thing.

I wring my hands together. "It's yours," I say, and his mouth hangs open, and he puts his hand in front of it, gasping.

"What?" he asks, shocked, and I just look at him.

"The baby is yours," I confirm again, and all he can do is blink. He looks like he's going into shock, and at this point, I'm worried he'll pass out.

"How?" he whispers, taking off his hat and tossing it on the counter. His hands run through his hair. "Like how?"

"I mean, if I have to explain that, I don't think we were doing it right," I say, trying not to freak him out, yet getting a little freaked out myself.

"I don't mean how, how," he says, walking past me to the living room, where he starts to pace. "We used protection."

"We did," I say. "All three times but…" I shrug. "But the condom is only ninety-eight percent effective."

He just shakes his head. "It didn't break," he points out. "They were all intact. Trust me, I remember." I'm about to say something when he just looks at me. "Two out of every hundred people get pregnant, and we are the one."

I don't know how they do research, and I don't know why this conversation bothers me. I don't know what I was expecting. Maybe I was expecting him to be a little happy. Maybe the irrational side of me was hoping he would be even a little bit excited, but standing here in front of him, having to go over all this, is making me angry. I'm about to say something to him when my stomach suddenly sinks and then rises. "Oh, no," I gasp, running to the bathroom and closing the door behind me. I rush to the white toilet and make it just in time to throw up whatever is inside my stomach. I put my head down on my arm as my body decides that none of the food I ate today is good enough. I'm dry heaving as tears stream down my face. I give myself a couple of minutes before I ease myself away from the toilet enough to sit, but I don't have the energy to move.

Sitting on the floor with my back to the wall, I close my eyes and wait for the nausea to pass. The knock on the door has me opening my eyes. "Are you okay in there?"

I roll my eyes. "Yes, I'm having a tea party. I'll be right out," I sass.

I get up to grab a glass of water and rinse out my mouth, then wet a washcloth and put it behind my neck. Looking at myself in the mirror, I cringe, knowing I have to go back out there. Walking to the door, I pull it open and see him leaning against the opposite wall. "It might look like I'm crying," I say, "but don't flatter yourself." He stands up in front of me. "Why are you still here?" I ask, and he just looks at me and down at my stomach.

"Why would I not be here?" he questions, and I walk away from him because my body might tempt me to lean in closer to him and hope that he hugs me. I walk over to the counter and grab my water and take a drink. "Do you always get sick?"

I look at the plate of apples and take a piece. "In the beginning, it was bad," I confirm. "I lost about nine pounds and couldn't keep anything down. I ended up in the ER twice for dehydration."

"What?" he asks in a whisper.

"It's fine, I'm fine, the baby is fine. Everything is hunky-dory," I say, dipping the apple in the peanut butter. "The first trimester is over, so the doctor said I should be fine."

"But you just threw up." He points at the bathroom. "Is that normal?" He puts his hands on his hips and takes out his phone. "Should I call 911?" The panic in his eyes makes me forgive him just a touch.

"No." I shake my head. "I'm fine. I just have to eat something. If I don't eat snacks between meals, it makes me sick, which doesn't really make any sense, but it is what it is," I explain, taking another piece of apple.

The door opens, and I look over as Michael whips his head toward the door. "What in the hell is going on?" my sister, Julia, says, standing there with the door open and still in her hand. She looks at me and then at Michael and then back at me, her eyes big. "Am I interrupting something?" she asks, closing the door and coming in. "I'm Julia," she says to Michael. He does a double take from Julia to me and then back again.

"Michael." He nods, and I close my eyes when she gasps.

"Michael, as in…" I hear in her tone that she is just as angry as I am. "The sperm donor?"

"Wait, what?" I open my eyes and look at Michael, who looks at me, then back at my sister.

Julia ignores the look I'm giving her, and instead, she continues on her tirade. "The one who changed his number after a girl answered his phone?" She folds her arms.

"It's complicated," he defends, and I get up to stand in front of him, knowing Julia is going to go off on him.

"I got this," I tell my sister and then turn to Michael. "Why don't you go home, and I'll call you later."

He looks down at me, and I know he wants to refuse. "You have a lot to think about," I say. "We can talk more in the morning when you've had time to let it sink in,"

I reason, and he doesn't move. "You know where I live. I'm not moving." I throw my hands up in the air.

"Do you have a pen and paper?" he asks, looking at me. When I walk past him, I can see that Julia is standing there with her arms crossed as she glares at him.

I walk over to the bag that I dumped at the door when I walked in, grabbing a piece of paper and a pen. "Behave," I mumble to my sister as I walk back to Michael. "Here you go." I hand him the pen and paper, and he walks over to the island.

"Can I have your number?" he says, and my sister snorts, then laughs.

"Classic." She shakes her head, and I mouth at to her to stop it.

"It's four, six, nine," I say, and he writes it down. "Two, one, eight, forty-seven, fifty-eight."

"Mine is fifty-nine," Julia adds from the side. "In case you forget hers." She dumps her bag on the floor and walks over to the cupboard to take out the bag of chips. She takes one chip out and chews it. She holds the bag for me, asking me if I want any, and I just shake my head.

I look at Michael, who takes his phone out and dials the number. My phone rings from where it sits on the counter. "Did you not believe her?" Julia asks him, leaning against the stove and glaring at him.

Any other guy would ignore her, but not Michael. He gets in the ring with her. "I was storing it in my phone," he says, his fingers going crazy.

"What do you have her under? Jillian or baby momma?" She tilts her head, and he just looks at her.

"And are you going to add her to your favorites?"

"I'll call you later," he says to me softly and leans down to kiss my cheek, and my heart speeds up. He looks at Julia. "It's nice to meet you, and I look forward to getting to know you."

"Smooth," she says as he walks out of the apartment. The door closes behind him with a click, and all I want to do is ask him to come back because I'm scared I won't see him again. Julia pushes away from the counter, her eyes going big as she moves to the door and opens it. She sticks her head out, then comes back into the room. "Oh my God," she says, shaking her head. "Oh my God." I get on the stool and take a sip of water, my hand shaking as I take a sip. "I swear I thought you hired a stripper," she admits, coming over to the counter and looking at me. "That…" She points at the door. "That was your baby daddy?"

"That would be him," I confirm, looking at her. "In the flesh."

"Jesus Christ, Abbi." She uses my nickname. "How did you let that get away?" She shakes her head, holding up her hand. "How can you let that get away?"

"What the hell was I supposed to do?" I ask her, laughing.

"I don't know, go door-to-door," she says, laughing. "Did you google his name?"

"Do you know how many Michaels there are?" I ask, and she rolls her eyes.

"It's the fourth most common name for men," I say. "Trust me, I checked."

"You should have put up pictures of him. Like have you seen my dog, but instead have you seen the man who finally made me orgasm during oral," she jokes, and I glare at her. "What did he say about the baby?" she asks, and I just shake my head.

"He was in shock and started asking how it happened," I say, and she laughs. "You couldn't walk properly for two days." She holds up her hand with two fingers.

"Can we talk about something else, please?" I say, putting my head in my hands. She comes over to me and puts her arm around my shoulder.

"You freaking out?" she asks softly, and I nod my head.

"I had finally gotten used to the fact I was doing this by myself," I disclose. "And this happens."

"You know what they say, right?" I look at her. "When you think everything is going good…"

"Duck for cover," I fill in and lean my head to hers. My phone rings, and I look down at my phone, and I see that it's the same number Michael called me from. "Hello?"

I can hear that he's in the car. "Hey, it's me." I smile as I hear his voice. "Just wanted you to know that I'm with you in this," he says. I get up from the stool, not sure I want Julia to hear this conversation.

"What do you mean?" I ask softly as I walk into the bedroom and sit down on the bed.

"I mean that you won't ever have to do anything alone," he clarifies, and the lone tear falls out of my eye. "We're a team."

"You don't have to do that," I say, giving him an out.

"There is nothing else I would rather do than stand with you," he says, and my heart speeds up in my chest. "Will you call me when your sister leaves?"

"Yeah," I agree, looking into the kitchen and seeing her open the fridge. "It may be a while."

"I'm sorry, Jillian," he says, and I can feel the pain in his voice.

"Michael," I say his name to stop him from talking. "There is time to talk about all of this."

I expect him to just hang up or say goodbye. Instead, he shocks me with, "You bet your ass there is."

FIFTEEN

MICHAEL

"YOU BET YOUR ass there is." I want to say more, but I also don't want her having this conversation with her sister looming. Goddamn, when she walked in the room, I did a double take for one second, and it took two seconds more for me to spot the differences. Jillian's hair was a touch lighter than Julia's. Her eyes were almost brighter than Julia's, and she was more beautiful than Julia. "Call me later."

"Okay," she agrees, and I look down. It took everything for me to leave, but I knew Julia wasn't going to let up on me. I also know from my aunts that if one is pissed at you, it's a matter of time before the other one is pissed at you. The bond with twins is something no one can explain, and having grown up around it and seen it, I know that I have to tread carefully, especially with Julia. So I bowed out, but I will be having a conversation with Julia as well.

"Today, right?" I joke with her, and she huffs out. I wonder if she changed her outfit or if she's still in the black and white dress she wore earlier.

"Goodbye, Michael." She hangs up the phone. I take a deep breath when I make the next phone call.

My palms sweat as I hold the steering wheel. A part of me hopes he doesn't answer, yet the other part of me wants nothing more than to hear his voice. It takes five rings before he answers, and I don't even realize it because I'm going over a speech in my head. A speech that is forgotten the minute I hear his voice. "Hey," he answers. "Sorry, I left my phone downstairs."

The minute I hear his voice, the tears well in my eyes. He's been the best father you could ever wish for. He's sat back and watched me fuck up and never once told me what to do. Never once did he try to steer me his way. He waited until I asked him what I should do. He waited for me to find my own way, and I'm the man I am because of him. "It's okay," I say softly. "Um…" I hesitate. "I need you to come down here." I come right out and say it.

"Okay," he replies softly, and I can picture him sitting down as he waits for me to say more.

"I'm not asking you either," I say. "I'm telling you that you need to come down here." I stop the car as my heart beats so fast in my chest.

"We can get on a plane within the hour." His voice stays calm, and it's like he knows I need to hear the calmness in it. "Do I need it before?"

"No," I say softly. "It can wait until tomorrow. I just need you and Mom to come down here."

"Son," he says in a whisper. "Are you okay?" His voice cracks, and I know he's probably freaking out right about now.

"I'll explain everything tomorrow," I reassure him. "But I'm okay."

"Do you need anything tonight?" he asks, and I smile.

"No, I just need you and Mom to come and see me."

"We'll be on the plane at eight o'clock," he says, and I hit the steering wheel with my finger. "If you change your mind and want me to come tonight," he offers, "all you have to do is say the word."

"I'll be okay. Text me when you take off."

"I will. I love you, son," he reminds me, and I put my head back on the seat. "Proud of you." The tear runs down my cheek as he says the words, and I can hear the tears in his voice also. "Best thing besides your mother was you and your sister."

I smile. "Didn't you call Mom the b-word the first day you met her?" I ask, and he gasps.

"Who told you that?" he hisses.

"Mom. Last year when she got mad at you," I say. "On the beach." My parents never fight. Like I can count on my hands the number of times I've heard them arguing, but last summer, my father took my uncle Matthew's side for I don't even know what. I'm sure if you ask her, she won't even remember, but she was pretty heated, so she probably would know. She was livid.

"I didn't mean it like that," he deflects. "I didn't even know who she was."

I hiss out, "That doesn't make it any better."

"I have to go and tell your mother to pack," he says. "We will both see you tomorrow."

"Thanks, Dad," I say, leaving out "for taking me out of my freak-out moment." Just hearing his voice settled me.

"Anything for you," he assures me, and I hang up.

I put my head back on the headrest and think about how the hell I'm going to tell them. This is so not how I wanted this to happen, this is so not how I thought it would happen. I thought I would meet the girl, fall in love, and then get married. Then the kids would come. I mean, that is how I was told it happens.

I pull off from the curb and call Dylan. I have to tell someone, and he's the closest thing to a brother I have. "Well, well, well, if it isn't the palm tree boy."

I laugh at him. "You got my picture," I say, and he just laughs.

"I did," he breathes out. "I have to say I love it here. I love the city. Love the team. Love the fans." He has been with Montreal from the first day they drafted him. After his rookie contract, he just stayed there. They paid him more than enough to stay there also. "What I don't love." He huffs out, "The fucking cold."

"It's insane," I say. "When you would send me pictures, I would think you were joking."

"Why the fuck would I joke about the weather?" he asks, and I can hear his dog barking in the background.

"Did you hear about Erika?" I ask.

"Yeah, your sister texted me," he says. "Even though she said she was blocking me. She okay?"

"Yeah. Last I heard, she was okay. You'll never guess who I saw when I went to get the girls at school," I say. I keep him hanging for a moment before saying, "Jillian is Mia's teacher."

"Jillian?" he shrieks. "Jillian, the one-night stand Jillian?" His voice goes higher. "The one where you stalked her."

I shake my head, turning onto my street and pressing the button to open the garage door. "I didn't stalk her. I went to her house once." I park my car in the assigned parking spot and turn off the BMW. "It was one time, and I didn't go back because Alex said that she was going to call the police on me."

"She would," Dylan agrees. "She's cutthroat like that. She sent me a text after the game," he says, laughing. "It was just the knife emoji." I laugh, getting out of the BMW. "So how is the mystery girl?"

"She's good," I reply, and then I stop walking. "She is even better looking than I remember."

"Sweet," he says, and I can picture him smiling. "Did you give her your new number?"

"Oh, yeah," I say. "And I wrote hers down on paper and put it in my wallet."

"You going to call her?" he asks, and I close my eyes.

"Definitely going to call her," I confirm, and then it's like he knows I have more to say. "She's pregnant."

"IIIsssshhh," he says. "Bad luck, dude."

"It's mine," I say, and the call goes silent. Like you-can-hear-a-pin-drop silent.

"Excuse me, what?" he says, and then his dog barks.

"Thunder!" he yells at his dog. "Quiet. Did you just tell me she's pregnant with your child?"

"I did," I admit, pressing the button of the elevator. The doors open right away, and I step in, pressing the button for my floor.

"Oh my God," he says, gasping. "You aren't kidding."

"I'm not kidding," I say, and the elevator door opens on my floor.

"Didn't you wear a condom?" he shrieks. "It's like Planned Parenthood 101."

"We used protection," I say. "But it's only ninety-eight percent."

"Did you go play the lottery?" he asks. "I would play the Powerball with that luck."

"My parents are flying in tomorrow, and I'm going to tell them," I inform him, taking a deep inhale and letting it out.

He laughs. Like full-on belly laughs. "You going to tape this conversation? Because I will pay you money to see Uncle Max's face when you tell him."

"Fuck off," I say. "You can't tell anyone."

"What???" he shrieks. "You didn't tell me it was a secret. You can't just come at me, tell me this massive news, and expect me not to say anything."

"You can't tell anyone, not even Alex," I say, and he groans.

"What fun is that?" he moans. "Fine, I won't tell anyone, but you owe me." I let myself into the condo, and I kick off my shoes. "You're going to be a dad," he says. "Holy shit." His voice is still shocked. "That's a big fucking deal."

"You really have a knack for this pep talk shit," I jest, rubbing my hands over my face. "Anyway, I had to tell someone, and you are that lucky person."

"Wow, lucky me," he says. "Are you okay, though?"

"I'm in shock a bit. I woke up this morning thinking my biggest problem was not bringing gloves with me. I'm going to be a father."

"Crazy," he responds. "Someone is at the door. I'll call you back." He hangs up, and I look around the living room.

The white leather couch I'm sitting on has to be the most uncomfortable couch of my life. The condo is so quiet it's eerie. I pick the phone back up and call Cooper.

"Hey," I greet when he answers. "How is Erika?"

"All good," he says, and I can tell he's relieved. "Thank you again for getting the girls."

"Yeah, yeah," I say, rubbing my hands down my jeans. "It was my pleasure." I tap my finger on my thigh. "Listen, I wanted to ask you something."

"This sounds serious," he says, and I can hear him walking around on his end.

"How well do you know Miss Jillian?" I ask, thinking that it's coming out casually.

"Are you insane?" His voice goes loud. "You can't date her. Absolutely not. Plus, she's pregnant. What kind of sick bastard are you to go after someone else's woman? Did we teach you nothing?" I laugh. "I'm going to hang up the phone and pretend this conversation didn't happen. You sick, sick freak. I should kick your ass myself for even thinking about doing what you are thinking about doing." He doesn't wait to answer. He just hangs up, and when I hear the two beeps, I look down at the phone and see he really hung up.

I'm about to call him back when a text comes through from him.

Cooper: Stay in your own lane.

I laugh, putting the phone down on the coffee table. Jillian's face pops into my head. "Oh, I'm definitely in my lane."

SIXTEEN

JILLIAN

I HEAR THE sound of ringing, and my eyes open slowly as I look around the room. The sun is trying to come in from the blinds, but my eyes are just so heavy, so I close them again and hope the ringing stops. I'm about to drift back to sleep when the ringing starts again. I reach out of the covers and grab the phone. "Hello." I put it to my ear and close my eyes.

"Were you sleeping?" I hear his voice in a whisper.

"Yeah," I say, snuggling deeper into my bed. "What time is it?"

"It's nine," he says. "Go back to bed and call me later."

"No," I mumble out. "I'm up."

"Did I wake you?" he asks softly.

"No." Rolling onto my back, I open my eyes and look at the ceiling. "The phone ringing one after another did." My bladder lets me know it's time to get out of bed. I throw the quilt off me and make my way to the bathroom.

He laughs. "If I told you that I was sitting outside of your condo, and I had food, would that make it better?" I stop mid-step and run to look out the window, but I don't see his SUV there.

"I'm looking outside, and you are not there." I see movement in a black SUV, and the driver's side door opens, and he steps out. He's wearing another fucking hat, and he has scruff on his face.

He holds up a hand. "Can you see me?"

"You changed SUVs?" I ask, and he leans back into the SUV. I move my head to see what the hell he's doing. He comes back with two brown bags of food and two drink trays.

"The last one was a loaner," he explains as he walks toward my building. He stops as he sees me standing in the window. "Why don't you have a patio?" I just look at him standing there in gym shorts and a shirt. His arms are bulging, and my hormones kick in. *He's so fucking hot* is the only thing I can think of. Everything else is pushed aside.

"Why are you carrying so many drinks?" I ask, and he looks down at the trays. "I'm going to the bathroom. I'll leave the door open," I say, pushing away from the window and walking to the front door. I unlock it and then step into the bathroom and look at myself.

I shriek when I see my reflection. My hair looks like a rat's nest, the white tank top getting to be a touch too small around my belly, but the booty shorts fit me perfectly. I turn on the water in the sink and wash my face after I go to the bathroom, then grab the white robe hanging on the door. Even though he's seen me naked, I cover myself up. I brush out my hair and braid it on the side. "Here goes nothing," I whisper as I pull open the door to the bathroom and step out.

He's sitting on the stool at the counter with the curtains in the living room open to let in some light. "Morning," he says, smiling when he looks up from his phone. "How are you feeling?"

"Good," I reply, walking over and sitting down on the stool next to him and wincing.

"What's wrong?" he asks frantically.

"Nothing. My back just hurts," I share, leaning back. "What did you get me to eat?"

"I didn't know what you like," he says, grabbing the two bags of food. "So I got you a mix of everything." He looks over at me and smirks. "I got you the regular pancakes, French toast, waffles." He takes out the first black container with the clear lid, handing it to me. My hand reaches out to take it from him, and our fingers graze each other. My pulse picks up speed as his eyes find mine.

"Thank you," I say, averting my eyes in case he can see how much his touch affects me.

"Then I got you eggs." He pulls out the second black container. "Scrambled, over easy, and sunny-side up." My mouth opens as he places it down on the counter. "I got all the meats, sausage, ham, bacon, and some hash browns." He puts another container on the counter, and at this point, we are running out of space. "Then I also got you bread, wheat, grain, and white," he continues, taking out three brown bags. "I didn't know if you wanted baked goods," he says, taking the second brown bag and pulling it to him. "I got you a fruit platter." He takes a bowl out of the bag and puts it down, and I see that it has all the fruits in it. My mouth waters as I open the top and take a strawberry out. "Then I got you croissants and muffins." He takes out two more containers.

"There is enough food here for a family of eight." I look around, and he just shrugs.

"You can snack during the day," he says. I smile and put my head down, some of my loose hair that escaped the braid, falls to the front, and I tuck it behind my ear. "So you don't get sick." He remembered.

"Thank you," I say softly, putting my hand on his. "That is very thoughtful."

"For you, Jillian," he says my name softly. "Anything."

I blink away the tears and get up to go get two plates and some forks. "Did you eat?" I ask, and he nods.

"I couldn't really sleep," he says. "I got you something to drink." I want to ask him why he couldn't sleep. I want to ask him if he tossed and turned. I want to ask him all the questions, and I want to know everything about him. "From all the things I read online," he says, "I got you one of everything. Orange juice, tea, milk, and decaffeinated coffee," he says, but all I can hear is that he read things online.

"You read things?" I ask, and he nods his head, opening the containers.

"Yeah, I didn't know how far along you were, so I

had to like google and stuff, but I got to see what the baby looks like," he says, and my heart just grows in my chest. "I took the day we were together, and then it told me to add two weeks because that is when you were ovulating."

I push away from the counter and walk into the bedroom to the frame by my bed. I pick it up and then open the drawer, taking out three more pictures. I walk back over to him. "This was taken about four weeks ago," I say and hand him the frame. Inside is the black-and-white ultrasound of our baby. He takes it in his hand, and I can see his hand shaking as he looks down at it.

He looks over at me with tears in his eyes, and I smile as my own tears come to my eyes. "Do you know if it's a boy or girl?" he asks, and I shake my head.

"I wanted it to be a surprise," I say. "I mean, it's already a surprise that I got pregnant, so I might as well just hold out for all the surprises." He laughs.

"My parents are coming in today." I just look at him with my eyes big. "We should talk," he says. "About a couple of things."

"Yes," I say to him, not moving.

"We can talk while you eat." He points at the empty stool beside him. "I don't want you to get sick."

I sit back down on the stool. My head's spinning, and my heart's thumping faster and faster. "I don't know if I can eat," I claim. "What do you want to talk about?" I ask, my hands getting just a touch shaky. I look down at them, and he sees it also. He reaches out and takes my hand in his. "I'm fine."

He grabs the orange juice with his other hand and hands it to me. "The sugar will stop the shaking." I let go of his hand, taking the glass to sip. "Now, is Julia your only sibling?"

I nod my head as my stomach rumbles. "I guess I'm hungry," I say, opening the lid with the pancakes in it. "Do you have syrup?" He nods, reaching in the bag and pulling out two little containers of syrup. "Is this the good kind?"

"What is the good kind?" he asks, laughing as he pops a raspberry in his mouth.

"The extra sugary one that you should never eat?" I get up and walk over to the cupboard, taking it out. "I only tasted this after I got pregnant, and I'm not going to admit this to anyone, but I eat Eggo waffles every night before bed," I share. "With butter and syrup."

"Noted," he says, nodding his head.

"Why are your parents coming down?" I ask nervously.

"I asked them to come because I want to tell them about the baby," he explains. "I can just imagine what your father must think of me."

"Well," I say, looking at him. "He passed away, so you're off the hook with that one." I take a waffle out of the container with a pancake and cover them with syrup, watching it seep into the pancake. "But my mom, on the other hand," I say, and his face goes white. "She was not pleased with me." I see his shoulders slump. "It's one thing your daughter getting pregnant but then you have to be like 'oh and I don't know the dad's last name or how to reach him.'" He puts his hand to his stomach as I take a bite of pancake. "She prayed for this," I say, pointing the fork at both of us. "So she is going to be really happy her prayer worked and brought you back to me." I laugh, and he just looks ahead.

"I think I'm going to be sick," he says. "She must think I'm a…"

"Nah." I shake my head. "I mean, it was a rough couple of days, and she and I had heated words, but she's come to terms with it," I say. "When I told her, she went from shock to laughing, thinking it was a joke." I laugh. "Julia and I thought she was having a stroke. Then she went into a rage and said some not nice things." I shrug, thinking about the words she took back the minute she said them, and then I was the one consoling her after she had a nervous breakdown.

"I'm so, so sorry," he says softly, "for not being there. For letting you do this all on your own." He puts his hand on my cheek. "I don't know how I will ever make it up to you," he confesses, and my eyes go to his lips, then back to his eyes. "But I'm going to die trying."

I swallow down the lump in my throat as I look at him. "If you bring me food," I say in a whisper, "that will always help."

SEVENTEEN

MICHAEL

"IF YOU BRING me food." Her voice drops to a whisper, and my whole body tingles. "That will always help." She winks, and I can't help the smile that fills my face.

"Duly noted," I say, and my thumb rubs her cheek. When she came out of the bathroom this morning, she looked gorgeous. I wanted to hug her and kiss her lips, but I knew that I had to tread carefully.

My phone pings, and I look down and see that it's from my father.

Dad: Landing in thirty. We will come right over.
Me: I'll be waiting.

"There are so many questions I want to ask, but my parents are landing in thirty minutes."

"Are you going to pick them up at the airport?" she asks, and I just shake my head. I have yet to tell her who I am, so I'm not ready to tell her about my family.

"No, I have a car getting them," I reply. "I'm nervous," I admit to her. "I called my dad yesterday to tell him, and I swear I almost cried."

"I know how you feel," she says. "When I found out." She swallows. "It took twenty-five tests to convince me. Then it took a week of shock, and I thought they were all wrong until my stomach lurched and I almost threw up while singing 'Row Row Row Your Boat' in the middle of class." She shakes her head and chuckles. "When the doctor confirmed it, I cried for four days straight from Thursday to Sunday." My hand flies to hold hers. "Closed all the curtains and did nothing for four days but lie on the couch and then the bed. It was a yo-yo. I snapped out of it when Julia came over and threatened to call the health inspector."

My heart sinks when I think about her going through that without me. She must have been petrified. "Well, I'm here." I bring her hand to my lips and kiss it instead of reaching over and kissing her lips. What if she doesn't want to have a relationship with me? My heart speeds up when I think about this.

"You should go," she says. "The last thing I want you to be is late." She points down at her stomach. "This is changing everything."

"Not changing. Making us better."

"Good one." She points the fork at me. "Now go."

"I'll call you after," I say.

"Does your father own a gun?" she asks. "He might shoot you in the ass."

"More like my mother," I answer her. "My father, I

think will be okay, but my mother…" I shake my head. "Time will tell."

"Godspeed, Michael." She laughs, and I walk out without kissing her face. I jog out of her condo and make one phone call.

It takes me four minutes to order it, and then I call her. She answers after one ring. "You literally just left," she says, laughing.

"You are going to get a delivery in the next two hours," I inform her.

"Of what?" she asks, shocked.

"It's a surprise," I say. Hanging up the phone, I'm smiling to myself. She is either going to hate it or love it. I mean, it's a fifty-fifty chance. I just hope she doesn't think I'm overstepping. But in time, she will learn I need to take care of her and the baby.

I park my car just as my dad sends me a text

Dad: Landed early, be there in ten.

I get into the elevator, and my leg starts to shake with nervousness. I walk into the house and try to sit on the couch, and when that fails, I pace the white floor, going over my speech in my head.

I put my hands on my hips and tilt my head back and sigh. I'm about to pace again when I hear a knock on the door, and I suddenly feel like I'm sixteen years old again and I just smashed my mother's new truck that was a week old. Another knock comes, this time harder, and my heart speeds up so much it echoes in my ears. This time, the knock is more like pounding, and my feet move on their own. "Here goes nothing," I say. Pulling open the door, I see my parents standing there with my uncle Matthew behind them.

My eyes go back to my mother whose eyes are red as she puts on a fake smile, and I can tell she's been crying. "Hey." She comes in and gives me a hug, and it's tighter than any hug she's ever given me. I can feel her tears through my T-shirt. I put my hands around her shoulders and look at my dad, who just shrugs at me. His eyes look red also, and I want to kick myself for worrying them so much. Maybe I should have just FaceTimed them.

My mother pushes away from my chest, and she holds up one hand to my cheek. "There is my boy." Her voice cracks, and she tries to fight away the tears, but one escapes. "I need to use the bathroom." She ignores my eyes as she walks down the hallway toward the bathroom.

"Is she going to be okay?" I point with my thumb over my shoulder toward the bathroom my mother just went into.

"She will." My father comes in and grabs me around my neck and squeezes, pulling me to him. I can feel his body tight with worry.

I look back at my uncle Matthew, who just looks at me. "You didn't think you would call an urgent meeting and me not be here," he says, shaking his head, coming in when my father steps aside. He slaps my shoulder, walking into the condo at the same time my mother comes out of the bathroom. My father waits for my mother before they walk to the living room. I can hear my father whisper to her, and she just holds her head down as they walk toward the living room.

Closing the door, I give myself a couple of minutes before going into the living room. My father is sitting next to my mother with his arm around her, as she tries to pretend nothing is wrong. Matthew sits on the other side of her, giving her his strength.

"I guess you're wondering why I asked you to come," I start, and I have to sit down because my knees are knocking together. I sit on one of the single chairs that face the couch. My mouth is so dry that it's hard to swallow, and I really wish I would have gotten a bottle of water. "There is no easy way to say this, so here it goes." I look down at my feet and slump forward, putting my hands in the middle of my legs. Looking them all in the eyes, I take a deep breath and say the words that will change my life forever. "I'm going to be a father." My eyes fly over all three of them to see their reaction.

My parents just look at me dumbfounded, both of them blinking their eyes. "I'm sorry." My uncle Matthew is the first to say something. "Did you just say you are going to be a father?" His eyebrows pull together, and he leans in to make sure he can hear what I'm saying.

"I didn't even know you were dating anyone," my father says, and the knot in my stomach rises to my throat when I have to tell them the next part.

"I'm not dating her," I admit, and my uncle Matthew throws his arms in the air and huffs out.

"Oh my God, she's married?" my uncle Matthew says, shaking his head back and forth. "What is it with the Hortons that they have to steal all these women away from their families?"

"One." My father puts up his hand, looking at my uncle Matthew. "Who are all these women? It's two women." My parents dated in secret many, many years ago and eloped without anyone knowing. Matthew and my dad weren't exactly best friends, and to this day, he never lets my father live it down. My father also gives zero fucks about it since he's married to the love of his life. I look at my mother, who has tears just streaming down her face, and she doesn't even try to wipe them away. Her hand goes to her mouth as she starts to sob quietly.

"I'm not married," I tell them, and Matthew and my dad both whip their heads back to stare at me. "We are not married," I repeat again, holding up my hand.

"When are you getting married?" my uncle asks me.

"I don't think I am," I tell them. "I mean, as of right now, we are not getting married."

"But she's having your baby?" my father questions, leaning back on the couch.

"She is," I confirm and swallow. "But," I say, trying to come up with the words.

My uncle holds up his hand, and I can see it's shaking. "Let's all calm down here for a minute," he says, and I look at my mother, who looks over at him. He isn't the one who calms down for anything.

"Michael," my mother says my name softly. "Why isn't she here?" She reaches over and grabs a tissue from the middle of the glass table.

"Well, because she doesn't live here," I answer honestly.

"But you two will be moving in together, right?" my uncle Matthew asks or maybe tells. I'm not sure.

"What aren't you saying, Michael?" my mother finally says, and I look at her.

I look down at the floor, and I know I have to just rip it off like a Band-Aid. When I look back up, all three sets of eyes are on me. "The first day I got here, I went to this restaurant," I start, and my father puts his head back and looks at the ceiling. "We spent the night together."

"And...?" my mother says, the tears gone as she glares at me.

"And well, we exchanged numbers, and then you know I had this whole thing where my phone got stolen. I didn't have her number, and well, I changed mine," I explain. My uncle Matthew puts his fist against his mouth to either stop the smile or maybe he's going to punch me in the face.

"Michael Horton," my father says with clenched teeth.

I close my eyes. "I didn't know until I picked up Emma and Mia at school and came face-to-face with her."

My mother springs off the couch. "What the hell is wrong with you?" She looks at me, then looks at my dad. "What the hell is wrong with him? Didn't you teach him the whole condom thing?"

My father just looks at her shocked. "First off, we had this talk with him together." He points at my mother. "And second, I think he's smart enough to know what to do with his penis." He looks at me. "You did know what to do?"

I get up. "Of course we used protection, but it's like…" I run my hands through my hair. "It's not a hundred percent."

"You know what is a hundred percent?" Matthew says, leaning forward. "A baby."

"Your wisdom sometimes is just groundbreaking," my father says to him sarcastically. "Why are you even here?"

"Enough!" my mother shouts and then looks at me. "Where is she?"

"She's at her house," I tell them.

"You need to go and get her, and we need to meet her," my mother insists, her voice tight.

"Mom, really," I say and look at my father and my uncle, who both shake their heads.

"Yes, really," she hisses. "You dumbass. You left a woman pregnant with your child for four months." She holds up her hand with four fingers.

"Actually," my uncle says, "I think it's more like five months."

"I'm going," I say, getting up and walking toward the door. "What if she doesn't want to?"

"You convinced her to have sex with you," my mother says, folding her arms. "You better convince her to come and meet us."

EIGHTEEN

JILLIAN

"I DON'T KNOW, Julia," I say to my sister on the phone. "All he said is to expect something in the next two hours." When he left, I ate a bite and then got up to go get dressed. I was slipping on a pair of black capris and a gray T-shirt that used to be loose and is getting tight on my belly. I pin my hair on top of my head to keep it out of my face.

"What the hell could it be?" she asks, and I shake my head, picking up a strawberry and popping it into my mouth. "Do you think he would come to you with his dick in a box?" I roll my eyes and groan out. "What? Justin Timberlake did it."

"Well, I don't think it's his dick in a box," I tell her, omitting that I would not say no to his dick in a box. I put the lids on the containers, leaving some on the stove and putting some away in the fridge for later. "His parents are flying in today." I clean up the kitchen, trying to keep my head from thinking about the fact that Michael is probably sitting down with his parents right now, telling them about the baby.

She gasps out. "What?"

"Yeah, apparently, he called them yesterday to tell them about the baby and asked them to come in." I shake my head, wiping down the counter and then walking to my bedroom. I grab the six pillows off the bed, starting to fix it, but the minute I put my head down, I get dizzy, so I sit on the bed.

"What's going on in that head of yours?" she asks, and I just look at the floor.

"I don't want them to think that I go home with every man I meet," I say, wiping away the tear that escapes. The fact that these people will be the grandparents to my child is huge, at least for me. I want my child to be loved, regardless of my relationship with the father. I put my hand on my stomach, vowing to make sure that this child is never a burden.

There is a knock on the door, and I get up. "Oh my God," my sister says as she hears the sound. "Is that your surprise?"

"I have no idea," I respond. Walking to the door, I open it and see two guys standing there.

"Jillian," one of them says, and I just nod. "We have a delivery for you."

"Um," I say while Julia yells at me to ask. "What is it?" I look at one man and then the other.

"It's a king-size mattress," the other man says. "We are going to pick up the old one at the same time."

"He bought you a new mattress." Julia laughs out loud.

"I'll call you back," I say, hanging up the phone.

"I'm sorry, a mattress?" I repeat. "Like to sleep on."

"Yes." The man nods his head. "Is the other mattress ready?"

"Can you hold just a second?" I say and take my phone and call Michael, not even caring that he's probably with his parents.

"Hey," he says, and I can hear that he's walking and then hear a car door slam. "I was just calling you."

"Did you buy me a new mattress?" I ask, turning to look at the men. One raises his eyebrows, avoiding looking at me while the other guy grimaces.

"Yeah," he says as if he just sent me a pizza. "You said your back hurt. So I called my guy."

I walk into the bedroom. "Who the hell has a mattress guy on speed dial?" I hiss out in a whisper.

He totally ignores my question. "Make sure they take your old mattress and don't touch anything. You shouldn't lift anything."

I look around my room. "I like my bed," I say even though it's old, and I got it when I was in college, and it should have been replaced. "How much is this mattress?"

"I'm on my way to you," he says, and I just look at the phone. "See you soon." He hangs up the phone.

I shake my head and walk back out where the two guys are just standing there. "I have to take the covers off the bed," I say, and they nod. I move as fast as I can and dump the bedding on the couch. "There you are."

The men come in and take out the mattress and then come back and take out the headboard. "Um, I thought you said that…"

"This frame is too small for the king one, so we have a new one also." I nod my head.

"Of course you do," I say, folding my arms over my chest. The men come back with the new headboard that's almost the same as the one they just took out but a beautiful cream color. I walk over to the couch and start folding my sheets.

It takes them ten minutes to put it all together and then another ten minutes to bring in the mattress. "This is the best mattress on the market," one of the men says. "You'll sleep like a queen."

"I'm sure I will," I mumble. When they walk back out of the bedroom, they look at me, and it seems they are scared to tell me the next part.

"We have two boxes of bedding," one of the guys says when they walk out. I get up and walk over to my bedroom and see the massive bed. I shake my head, walking over to the bed and sitting on it. It's hard at first, and then I sink in. My hand rubs the mattress as the guys come back in with two massive boxes. "We will leave these right here," the guys says, dumping the boxes. No doubt wanting to get the hell out of here before Michael gets here.

They walk out, and I get up, walking over, but another knock is at the door. I shake my head and pull the door open. Michael stands there, wearing the same thing he was wearing before, one of his hands squeezing his neck.

"You are out of your mind," I huff out, ignoring the way his eyes are clouded. "A king-size bed?"

He walks in, going straight to the bedroom. "It fits perfect," he says, looking at me. "And I also have like special pillows coming in."

"What special pillows?" I ask, closing the door and walking back into the house to stand in front of him.

"I don't know. I read about them. It's like this whole long pillow that twists and turns to wrap around your body." He tries to describe it. I just stand here with my mouth hanging open because I can't come up with any words. "Anyway," he says, turning to look at me. "Are you ready?"

"Ready?" I tilt my head to the side. "For?"

"To meet my parents," he says, and my eyebrows rise. "They kind of want to meet you."

My palms get sweaty, and my mouth gets dry. "What do you mean they kind of...?"

"Well, I told them about the baby," he says and scratches his head. "At first, my mother started crying," he shares, and I have to walk over to the stool and sit down. "By the end, she basically said if I don't come back with you, not to come back."

"But..." I say. "But I haven't showered."

"You look amazing," he says, and I shake my head. "You going to grab your purse?"

"One," I say, getting up, and my heart starts to speed up. "I'm not meeting them in loungewear," I say. "And two, we are not finished talking about the bed."

"How about we do one thing at a time?" he bargains. I

look at him, and he still makes me want to do all the things we shouldn't be doing. "One, let's meet my parents, then we can discuss whatever it is you want to discuss."

"This is crazy," I say, walking to my room. "Like out-of-the-norm crazy."

"Oh, baby." He shakes his head, and I ignore the way my body responds to the nickname. "You have not seen crazy yet."

"Good to know," I reply, walking to the bedroom and slamming the door on him.

My back leans against the door as I wait for my heartbeat to calm down. I'm kidding myself because nothing could calm me down.

I walk over to the closet and pull it open, taking an inventory of what I have. I haven't really bought much since I was still semi-normal until last week. My hand pushes one hanger after another.

A soft knock on the door has me looking over my shoulder. "Are you okay in there?" I'm about to answer him when I hear him laughing. "Or are you having another tea party?"

I roll my eyes. "Not this time." I shake my head. "Just shining my jewels."

He chuckles. "And I thought I was the one who had the family jewels."

"How are we feeling about those jewels right now?" I shout back. "Also, what was your mother wearing?" I look at the closed door.

"Jeans, I think," he says. "With a pink top. Maybe it was green."

"So, not formal," I say quietly. Looking back into the closet, I snatch the gray dress from the hanger. I bought it a couple of weeks ago, but putting it on, I look into the mirror and find it too sexy. So it's thrown aside, and then I just snatch a pair of black tights and a white shirt. It's crisp and clean, the sleeves go to the elbow and then flare off a bit. I look into the mirror, deciding that it is a good clean outfit.

When I open the door, I see him sitting on the stool, his head down, typing something on his phone. When he hears the door open, his head looks up, and he smiles at me. "How is this?"

His eyes go lighter as his face fills with an even bigger smile. "Looks good." Then his smile turns into a smirk. "I like the tiara." I shake my head at him and look down. "What's wrong?"

"I'm nervous," I admit to him. "It's not easy meeting the guy's parents to begin with the first time. Throw in the fact that I'm carrying your child, and we..." I wipe away the tear from the corner of my eye.

He gets off his stool and comes over to me. His hands come up and cup both my cheeks. "We got this," he assures me softly. "Whatever happens, I'll be right there."

NINETEEN

Michael

SHE STANDS IN front of me, looking like an angel as she wrings her hands together. I get off my stool and walk over to her. My hands move up to take her face in them, my thumbs rubbing her cheeks as I try to calm her down. "We got this," I say, looking deep into her eyes, wanting her to hear what I just said. "Whatever happens, I'll be right there." Knowing that no matter what they say, I'll be in her corner.

"I've never had to do this," she admits. "Usually, parents love me."

"My parents will love you," I say. "You'll see. I promise you." She swallows and nods her head. I want to lean in and kiss her lips, but I know that if I kiss her, I won't stop, and then we'll have a whole different story to tell my parents. "Are you ready?" I ask, and she nods.

She grabs her phone and her purse as she locks her door behind her. "Don't think I forgot about the bed," she huffs out as we walk down the hallway toward the door. I chuckle. "It's not even funny, Michael. How the hell did you even get it here in a couple of hours?" She looks at me as we walk down the steps to the glass door.

I push the door open and hold it for her to step out of. "I ordered my bed from him," I answer her. "He said if I ever needed anything, to call him." I stop by the BMW and open the passenger side door, waiting for her to get in.

"And just like that, he sends over the bed?" she asks, getting in and looking up at me. I think about how to answer this. I had to beg and offer him a signed jersey and a couple of tickets to the games.

"It was in stock," I placate. "I have the same one."

"How much was it?" she asks, and I just stare at her.

"Watch yourself while I close the door," I say, and she glares at me as I close the door and walk around to my side of the BMW. I get in and look over at her. "Ready?"

"Nope," she says, buckling her seat belt, and I can see her little bump even more. When she came out of her room before wearing black pants and a white top, I couldn't help but smile because she looked perfect. The white shirt is loose but shows her little baby bump, a bump that I have yet to see or touch. It still blows my mind that she is carrying my baby, that my baby is growing in her. She is giving me something that I will never ever be able to repay her for. It's a gift worth more than all the money in the world, than all the sponsorships, than all the Stanley Cups in the world. It's worth everything.

"It's going to be fine." I pull away from her condo,

and she puts her hands in her lap. "Are you hungry?"

"Even if I was." She looks over at me. "The nerves in my stomach would just reject it, and then I'd be barfing on someone's shoes." She shakes her head. "But I do need water."

I pull over at a gas station, and I'm getting out of the BMW when she looks over at me. "And can you get me an apple juice?" she asks, and I nod. I walk into the gas station and get her two bottles of water, an apple juice, and then also an apple grape juice. Walking back to the car, I see she's on the phone, and when she sees me, she hangs up quickly. Something in my stomach burns. What if she is with someone? The thought is just more than I care to bear.

I get into the BMW and hand her the water bottle first and then put the juice in the middle cupholder. She opens the water bottle and drinks it halfway. "Thank you," she says, as I put my seat belt on and start driving toward my house.

Neither of us says anything, but my head is going around and around, thinking about the big elephant in the room. "What's got your panties in a twist?" I hear her say and look over at her. "You've been tapping that finger on your steering wheel since we left the gas station."

"I know this question is going to sound out of the blue," I hedge. "And I know that I really don't have any say in how you live your life." She just stares at me. "Are you with anyone?"

"You are joking, right?" She turns in the seat and puts her back to the passenger door. "Like for real, are you joking?"

"I am not joking," I say, huffing out. "It's an honest question."

"It's a stupid fucking question," she says and shakes her head. "Who in their right mind would date a woman who is pregnant with another man's child?" she asks and doesn't even give me time to answer. "Between working, sleeping, and growing a human in me, I've been a bit busy to date." She shakes her head. "Are you with anyone?"

"What?" I ask, shocked. "Why would you think I was with anyone?"

"For the same dumb reason you thought I was with someone," she counters with her sass.

"I came out of the gas station and saw you on the phone, and then when you saw me, you hung up the phone," I say. "And for the record, I haven't been with anyone since you."

She blinks as she looks at me. "Okay, one, I was on the phone with Julia, who went by my house and saw I wasn't there. She heard the nerves in my voice, then she threatened to show up at your house, so I had to turn off my location. Because I think we should ease Julia in with your family, and two." She holds up her second finger. "Regardless of how easy it was for you to get me into bed, you were only the second person I ever slept with." My heart beats so fast in my chest when she says that, and I can't help but smile.

"Well, it's good to know," I respond, trying not to sound so happy about the fact that she hasn't been with anyone since me. Not that it would matter, but it's good to know.

"You live downtown?" she asks when I turn down the street as she looks at the high-rises.

"For now," I say honestly and turn into the underground parking garage. "I haven't had time to do the whole house-hunting thing." I park the BMW and look over at her.

"You've been here five months," she says, putting her hand on the door handle and looking around. "How do you have no time?"

"It wasn't an issue," I answer her honestly. "But I'll be looking for a house starting tomorrow." I put my hand on the door handle. "If I know my mother, she has already called my aunt Zoe and is getting some listings sent to her." She nods her head and opens her door and steps out. I open my own door and wait for her at the back of the car. I see her eyes looking around at all the luxury cars.

"Um?" she asks when she gets next to me. "Are we in the right spot?"

"The elevator is over there," I say, pointing at the two stainless-steel doors. I put my hand at her lower back as I guide her toward the elevator. When I press the button for up, my heart starts to beat erratically because she still doesn't know my full name. Or what I do, or who I am. The doors open a second later, and I hold out my hand for her to step into the elevator. I step in right next to her and hold my breath when I press the PH button.

She looks over at me. "Who exactly do you train?" she asks, and I look over at her and take a deep breath.

"I'm not really a trainer," I say, and she just looks at me, her eyes blinking, and the elevator ride is over so fast she doesn't get to ask another question.

She shakes her head and steps out of the elevator. "You aren't really a trainer?" she hisses, not raising her voice, and looks around to see that there is only one door on this floor. "Wow."

"I didn't know what to say." I hold up my hands.

"Here is a shocking piece of advice." She leans in. "Tell the truth. Good God, are you a trust fund baby?" she asks. "Are you in the mob?"

I chuckle at the last one. "One, I'm not in the mob. Two, I'm not a trust fund baby. I might have a trust fund, but I earn my own money."

"Great," she says. "So who exactly are you?"

"Fine." Ignoring the burning in my stomach, I look into her eyes. "My name is Michael Horton," I say and wait for it to click in her head. Wait to see it in her eyes that she's heard of me, wait for anything, but nothing changes.

She just looks at me, waiting for more answers. "Is that name supposed to mean anything to me?" she asks, her eyebrows pulled together.

I let out a huge breath. "I play hockey for the Dallas Oilers," I reply, and her mouth hangs open. "When we met, I had just gotten traded here." I wait for her to say something. "It was why I wore a cap out."

Her mouth opens and closes, and the only thing that comes out is, "You play hockey for the NHL?" She points at me.

"I do," I confirm. "I'm not the only family member who does. Obviously, Cooper is my cousin, and I have a couple of other cousins who play. My uncles used to play and my father also."

"Oh my God," she says, her voice in a whisper as tears start to fill her eyes, big tears that even if she blinks them away, they are still going to escape. "Oh my God." She gasps out in shock, "Is your father Max Horton?"

I get a little annoyed she's heard of my father but not me. "Yeah."

"He was," she says, the tears just streaming down her face. "He was my father's favorite player," she shares and then puts her hand over her mouth when a sob comes out of her. "He used to watch the New York games all the time. He tried to get me to watch it with him, but I wasn't into it. Julia," she continues, her voice quivering. "She used to watch with him. It was their thing, and when he passed away, she never watched hockey again." I walk to her, holding her face in my hands, my thumbs wiping away the new tears that spill onto her cheeks. She smiles through the tears. "He would shit himself if he ever got to meet him." I don't know what to say to her, my own tears coming to me with the thought of ever losing my father. She puts her hands on my chest. "I can't believe this," she says. She smiles up at me as she tries to blink away the tears. All I can do is look into her eyes, and my head is moving on its own, my lips dying to taste hers and see if it's like I remember. She licks her lips, seeing me bring my face closer to her, and she closes her eyes. Right before my lips touch hers, the front door swings open.

The two of us jump away from each other and look over to see my uncle Matthew standing there, looking both shocked and excited. "Um, they have arrived," he says over his shoulder.

TWENTY

JILLIAN

"THEY HAVE ARRIVED," the man says over his shoulder, and his shock and excitement quickly change when he sees my face. "Why is she crying?" He looks over at Michael. "What the hell did you do to her?" He doesn't wait for any of us to answer. Instead, he shouts again over his shoulder. "Max, your son is making his woman cry," he says, and I'm about to step forward when I feel Michael put his hand on mine.

My eyes go to his. "This is the crazy," he mumbles, and I shake my head, looking back at the guy who stands there with his hands on his hips.

"She's crying, and she looks scared," he accuses, and all Michael can do is chuckle from beside me.

"I don't look scared." I look at Michael. "I'm not scared," I mumble to him. The sound of feet rushing toward the door has my eyes going big. "I'm fine," I tell the man standing there.

A woman and a man join him, and I know right away these are his parents. His mother is so beautiful as she stands there with her hair loose and curled at the ends, wearing jeans and a cashmere ivory sweater. I take one look at her outfit and make a mental note to discuss clothing with her. She looks at us, first at me and then at Michael. "What do you mean she's crying?" the woman says, and I know that this is Michael's mom. They have the same shaped eyes. Her hand goes to her mouth in shock. She looks at me and then looks over at Michael. She glares at him as she hisses, "What did you do to her?" She comes out of the doorway to join us in the hallway. I see another man standing behind her, and I know for sure this is Michael's father. "You had one job. One." She holds up her finger at Michael, who stands exactly like the other guy with his hands on his hips.

His father comes out and puts his hands on his mother's shoulders. "Jesus Christ," he says, looking at me and then at his son. "What the hell did you do to her?"

"Are you okay?" His mother comes forward to me and puts her hand on my arm, and she squeezes. "Did he hurt you?"

"Oh my God," Michael says from beside me. "Seriously, you think I would hurt her?"

"Well, why is she crying, Michael?" the other man asks, shaking his head. "What did you teach your boy?" He looks over at Michael's father.

"That is all Grant in him." He crosses his arms over his chest.

"You two," his mother says to the two guys, "knock it off." Then she turns back and looks at me. Her eyes so warm and loving, and I'm about to say something when my stomach does a little flutter.

At least, I think it's a flutter, but then it comes back more like a smashing wave, and my stomach starts to rise, and I look over at Michael with my eyes wide. The panic takes over as the heat rises up my neck. "Bathroom," I say fast, and he just looks over at me. "Bathroom." He must see that I'm going to be sick because he swings into action.

"Move!" he shouts to all of them, moving them aside as he runs with me into his house. I don't have time to look around before I slam the white door behind me and make it to the toilet. The water from the car comes right back up. It's a good thing my hair is up in a braid. I sit on my knees and close my eyes, trying to get my breathing under control. "In through the nose, out through the mouth," I say right before I dry heave into the toilet. Closing my eyes, I put my arm on the toilet seat and lay my head down as I slip from my knees to my butt.

I look around, and it just makes it even worse. I'm sitting in what has to be the nicest bathroom I've ever been in. The floor is a white marble with gray lines in it, and it's so shiny I can see my reflection. The marble flows all up the walls to the ceiling. The big floor-to-ceiling window lets all the light in with a big tub right in front of it. It looks like it can fit at least three people.

I look over and see the long white counter on the other side of the room with two white marble sinks and gold faucets. A long gold-framed mirror hangs over it. A glass vase is in the middle of both sinks. The bottom of the vase is gold, and it holds white flowers. There is a small white tray on the side of each sink with soap and hand towels. I'm afraid to touch any of this, and I close my eyes as I hear his words again. "I play for the Dallas Oilers." The minute he said that, everything clicked. I really wish I could call my sister and tell her because I feel like it's a dream.

My hand comes out to rub my stomach, as I feel flutters. "Hey, you think you can do me a solid and not make me barf on your grandparents?" I whisper to him or her. "I'll let you vomit on them when you come out." I smile and wipe the tear from the corner of my eye.

I get up slowly, taking a step toward the sink, and then think twice. There is no way I'm touching any of this. Instead, I lean over and grab some toilet paper and wipe my mouth. Flushing the toilet and then getting up to go to the sinks. I turn one gold faucet, and the water flows out softly. I cup my hand under it, bringing some of it to my mouth, rinsing it out, and washing my hands.

Looking around, I decide to dry my hand on the back of my pants. I mistakenly look in the mirror and cringe when I hear voices coming from outside the door. I try to listen, but all I hear is shushing.

Walking over to the door, I turn the handle, and when I open it, I don't know why but I'm not surprised to see Michael there, but I am surprised to see his mother and father there. His mother is dabbing her eyes, his father has his arm around her as he rubs her back.

All eyes turn to me as I walk out of the bathroom. "I'm sorry."

"Are you all right?" Michael asks, coming to me. "I have water," he says, holding up the bottle.

I smile at him and grab the water, then look at his parents. "This is not how I wanted to meet you," I say softly, looking down and then looking back up to see that his mother is crying.

The doorbell rings, and then I look over to see who else is here, and I'm suddenly scared that my sister tracked me down. I wait to hear her voice, but nothing comes out. Instead, the other guy comes back in again. "Hey." He smiles at me. "I got you something." He holds up a brown bag in one hand. "I'm Uncle Matthew, by the way." He holds his hand out. "His favorite uncle." He looks over at Michael, who just rolls his eyes.

"I'm Jillian," I say to him and hold out my hand to shake his. "It's nice to meet you."

He hands me the bag, and I look at Michael, who is trying to look into the bag. "What is it?" It's a lot heavier than I thought it would be.

"I got you some things," his mother says softly, and my eyes go to hers. His father holds her around her shoulders and rubs her arm up and down. "To help with the nausea." I can tell she is nervous by this, but the only thing I can do is look down at the bag. "There is some ginger ale, ginger tea, some saltines." She looks at me with tears in her eyes. "We can get you something else if you need."

"You bought me stuff," I say, looking at the bag, and

the tears come even though I fight them. Michael puts his arm around my shoulder and pulls me to him. He kisses my head, and all I can do is look down at the bag.

"If you need anything else," his father says. "Whatever it is, we can go out and get it."

"You guys," I say and stop when my voice cracks. "You don't hate me?" I ask, and my stomach sinks, and it's not because I'm going to be sick.

"Why would you think we hate you?" his mother asks and comes to me. "Did you tell her this?" She looks over at Michael and glares at him. "Me and you." She points at him and then her. "We are going to have a nice talk when she leaves."

"Mom," Michael refutes. "I never said that."

"He didn't say anything," I finally say and look up at them. "He never ever said anything like that." I look over at him and smile as I wipe away tears. "It's just this whole situation. How it might look for me. Sleeping with him and then showing up pregnant," I explain, and I wish I could stick a cork in myself. I wish that I would stop talking right now, but this baby has shifted everything inside me. "I'm not a woman who sleeps around," I say, and my lips quiver. "Whatever you think of me, know that I don't sleep with just anyone."

His mother comes forward, and she puts her hands on my upper arms and rubs them up and down. I look up at her. "Hey," she says, smiling. "One, we would never ever hold anything against you or think anything of you." She blinks, and her own tears roll down her face, and she lifts one hand to cup my cheek, exactly like my mother did.

"Everything is going to be okay." She smiles, making me smile.

"Max was an asshole when we met him," Matthew says, pointing at Max. "And then he stole my sister, and we still love him." The five of us laugh.

"Let's go sit," his mother says to me. "And get to know each other." Her hand falls from my face, and she grabs my hand. I walk with her. "Everything is going to be okay," she whispers to me. "I promise." I look at her, and my heart settles. She looks at me without judgment and without accusation, and at that moment, I know my baby will be so loved.

TWENTY-ONE

MICHAEL

I WATCH MY mother hold Jillian's hand in support as she walks to the living room. "Idiot," I hear from beside me and look over to see my uncle Matthew shaking his head. "Why would you let her think that?" He puts his hands on his hips.

"Did you even talk to her?" my father whispers, looking down the hallway that they just went down. "All this is not good for the baby." He shakes his head. "Did we not teach you anything?"

"I told her you guys would love her," I finally say, my heart sinking in my chest thinking about how scared she was. "I know that it would never cross your mind."

"Hey, three stooges," my mother hisses out in a whisper. She glares at all of us. "Get your ass in here." She points toward the living room. "I can just imagine the stupid things you guys are planning."

"One, we aren't planning anything," Matthew says.

"And two"—he looks at my father—"why is she so angry? What did you do to her?"

My father shakes his head. "It's him." He points at me. "He did that." Turning his finger back to my mother.

"What did I do?" I hold up my hands and look at my mother, who is not happy with me.

"You need to go and make sure she is comfortable." She points at the living room. "And then we will come and join you."

I nod at my mother and walk into the living room and see Jillian looking around. She sees me walking into the room, and she smiles. "You live here?" she asks, her eyes moving all around, "I don't even want to touch anything."

"I'm staying here for now," I say as I walk toward her and sit beside her. "It's Erika's place." She nods as she continues to look around with her hands on her lap. "How are you feeling?"

"Okay," she answers quietly. "I mean, the big talk is coming, right?"

I hold out my hand to grab hers. "It's not that big of a talk. They just want to get to know you." Her fingers link to mine, and I'm not letting them go. I want to make sure that my parents and my uncle know we are united in whatever happens here today.

She nods, leaving her hand in mine as she leans to the side for her water bottle. "I didn't want to put it on the table," she answers the question in my eyes. "I was afraid of the ring marks."

It's my turn to glare at her. "Put the bottle on the

fucking table, Jillian."

She glares at me, and I think she is about to ream me a new asshole when my parents come into the room with Matthew. They walk over to the couch facing us and smile at her when they sit down. "I really wish I would have been able to warn you about them," I say, and the three of them look at me. "You guys can be a bit much."

"We haven't been formally introduced," my father says. "But my name is Max, and this is my wife, Allison."

"Why do you have to be all, 'this is my wife'?" my uncle says. "We get it, she's yours, we know."

I lean in to whisper to Jillian, who smiles at the exchange. "This is crazy. They actually are best friends, but neither of them admits it. They always troll each other. But," I say, watching them exchange words, "they have each other's back without question."

"It's nice to know," she says as she watches them.

"Anyway," I continue. "These are my parents, and that is my uncle." I look at Matthew, who smiles. "And this is Jillian."

"It's a pleasure to meet all of you," she says with a smile, and I can feel her hand shaking in mine. I squeeze it, and she looks over at me. "Forgive me for being nervous."

"There is no need for you to ever be nervous," my mother assures her. "Ever."

"Thank you," she says, looking down at our hands. My thumb rubs her finger. "I'm sure this is a shock to you."

"Why don't we start with the easy questions?" my

mother says with a small smile on her face. My father puts his arms around her. "Michael tells me that you are a teacher."

Jillian looks over at her, and her whole face lights up when she talks about her being a teacher. "I am. I teach kindergarten." She chuckles. "I tried teaching sixth grade, but I tend to like the young kids."

"How does your family feel?" my father asks, and my mother just looks at him. "About this whole situation." He finishes talking, and my mother gasps, and he opens his eyes when he rethinks his words. "Not situation like that. I mean situation like…"

"What he means to say is how does your family feel about you having a baby." Matthew corrects him, and for once, he is making more sense than my dad. "Was it a shock for them?"

Jillian smiles at my father. "I knew what you meant," she tries to comfort him. "My mother was not okay at the beginning," she says, and I can see she's trying to hold back tears as she thinks back to it. "But she has come around. I have a twin sister, her name is Julia, and she has been behind me the whole way."

"We have twin sisters also," my mother says. "Zara and Zoe, their bond is something we can't explain." She blinks her own tears. "I'm happy you had that support."

"I'm grateful also," I say to her, and she smiles at me. "Even though we started on a rocky ground."

"Zara would have skinned you alive," my uncle Matthew says.

"Zoe would have buried your body," my mother

continues.

Jillian laughs from beside me, and all of us smile when we hear it. "Will you let us be involved?" my mother asks softly. "Regardless of how you two end up." Her lower lip trembles. "All we want to do is support you and the baby."

"It's okay, angel," my father says to her in a soft voice. She looks up at him, and his hand comes out to wipe the tear away from her face.

"I want you all involved," Jillian confirms. "We don't have a big family," she says with her own tears in her eyes. "It's just the three of us," she shares, and my mother puts her hand to her mouth. "So I would love for you to all be there."

"Are you sure you mean all?" Matthew asks, and she laughs through her tears.

"Of course, the more people involved, the more love our child will have," she says, and the way she says our child, my stomach goes to my throat. "Regardless of how it happened." She side-looks me. "She or he is coming."

"I think it's a boy," Matthew says. "I can feel it."

"I really hope it's a girl," I counter. "Just so you can be wrong."

"I don't care what it is," my mother says. "As long as the baby is healthy, we will take it."

"When is your due date?" my father asks.

"I'm due the second of July," she replies, and Matthew looks over at me and smiles.

"Perfect timing," he says. "Off-season and right around family vacation time."

"We can do the family vacation here," my father offers. "Rent a couple of houses here." Matthew just nods his head.

"We can drive down to the beach," Matthew cuts in. "I'll throw it out to the family."

"What's going on?" Jillian whispers to me as she watches them make plans for July.

"We have a big family," my mother says. "As you can imagine with five siblings and then their kids. Plus extended family members."

"Our last family vacation." I use quotations around family. "We were one hundred and twenty-five."

"Oh my God," she says, her eyes going big. "And all of them will come here for the birth?"

"No," my mother says, shaking her head and looking at my uncle and my father. "It's not a circus. It's their first child. It will be who she wants there, and that is it."

"I'm not saying we all have to go in the room with her," Matthew retorts, then looks at her. "But we can show her our support by being here."

"Why don't we table this discussion for another time?" I suggest when Jillian squeezes my hand.

"How has your pregnancy been?" my mother asks, and I can see that she just wants to know everything.

"It's been okay," Jillian says, putting her hand on her belly and rubbing it. "I had severe morning sickness at the beginning and couldn't keep anything down." She shrugs. "I ended up in the ER a couple of times for dehydration. But I just get sick when I don't snack during the day."

My mother shoots up off the couch. "You've been here for over an hour and haven't eaten anything, and you have been sick," she says with worry all over her face, and all Jillian can do is put her hands on her face as she cries. I lean to her side and take her in my arms. Now I'm the one glaring at my mother for making her cry.

"Now you've done it," Matthew says, looking over at my mother, shaking his head. "You made her cry."

"No," Jillian denies from my chest. "It's not like that."

Jillian turns her face to look at my mother. "It's just so overwhelming that you care." Her voice is soft as she tries to talk without her voice quivering, and my mother comes around to sit beside her.

"Of course I care," my mother says. "We all care." She rubs Jillian's leg. "We all want the best for you. We all want the both of you to be okay. We will do whatever we need to do to make the rest of the pregnancy go as smooth as it can."

"Thank you," Jillian replies, and she sits up and looks at my mother. "And I promise you that I'm eating well and taking vitamins. I've gained some weight back."

"Oh, we have no doubt that the baby is in good hands," my father clarifies. "What Allison was trying to say, but her delivery was frantic and not calm, is that you've been here for a long time and haven't had anything to eat. Would you like a snack?"

I look over at my mother, who glares at my father. "You made her cry."

"The only one in this room who hasn't made her cry today is me," Matthew says, getting up and walking over to us, holding out his hand to Jillian. "Come on, let's get some food into you."

She reaches out and grabs his hand and gets up. "I wish I could offer you more choices, but he's a Neanderthal," he says, opening my fridge. "Has nothing but milk and protein powder."

"I was out of town for two weeks." I get up, going to the kitchen. "All the food would have gone bad."

"I can order whatever you want," my father suggests, coming into the kitchen with his phone out.

"Um," Jillian says and looks at me.

I smile at her, and the only thing I can say, "Welcome to Crazy."

TWENTY-TWO

JILLIAN

"WE SHOULD ORDER food," Matthew calls from the kitchen, looking at me. "What have you been craving?" He asks me, and I want to break out into tears again. It's all these hormones going through me, but it's also because of how I've been accepted without a second thought. They didn't judge me or blame me, and it means everything to me.

"I don't know if I've had any cravings," I say. "I have been eating more meat."

"That's because it's a boy," Matthew presses, puffing out his chest. "He needs the protein." I roll my lips to stop from laughing at him. "Burgers or steak?" he asks, looking at his phone. "I'll get both."

"I want both also," Michael says from beside me, and I look over at him. "I haven't eaten today."

I'm about to say something else when the front door opens, and everyone looks around. I look at Max, who pushes Allison behind him, and Michael does the same to me. "Oh, good, the gang is all here." I hear a woman's voice, and my heart starts to speed up. "Traitors!" she shouts and looks around the room. "You two." She points at Max and Allison. "I can't believe you." She stands there, her hair a chestnut color and her eyes so crystal blue, I swear I can see right through them. She wears black jeans and a shirt with a leather jacket. "Liars."

"Now wait a minute," Allison says, coming around. "We didn't lie."

"You said you were coming to visit Erika and the baby," she says, and I grab on to Michael's waist from behind. He looks over his shoulder at me and winks with a smile. I don't know why, but it calms me, and I know everything is going to be okay. "What you forgot to say is that you were coming, too." She looks over, and only then does she see me trying to peer over Michael's shoulder. "Oh my gosh," she says, getting tears in her eyes. "Is that her?"

"Oh, God," I sigh as Michael moves to the side. She comes over to me with tears in her eyes.

"Hi," she says softly. "I'm Alex." She doesn't put her hand out. Instead, she takes me in her arms in a hug. "It's so, so nice to meet you," she adds and then lets me go so she can wipe her eyes. "You are stunning," she compliments and then looks down at the baby bump. "Can I?" she asks with her hands out.

"Fuck no," Michael growls, getting in front of me. "I haven't even touched her yet." He pushes his sister away from me. "If anyone gets to touch her stomach, it's me," he says to her. "I put it there."

"Yeah, you did," Matthew comments and holds up his hand for a high-five, but no one gives him one.

Michael ignores Matthew and turns back to his sister. "Who told you?"

I look over at Alex, who shrugs and avoids looking at anyone. "I put two and two together."

"Bullshit," Michael says, and I pull his arm. "Dylan told you." He points at her. "That rat bastard. It was supposed to be a secret."

"When are you going to learn that Dylan will never keep anything from Alex?" Max says. "Also, young lady, how did you get here?"

"It's called an airplane, Dad," she sasses, rolling her eyes and walking over to the fridge. "Also they didn't have anything to go back, so I might have to hitch a ride."

"Hitch a ride?" I ask, confused, but no one pays attention to me.

"When are you guys flying back?" She looks at her parents.

"The plane is here on Monday," Matthew says to her, and she nods her head.

"The plane is here on Monday?" I repeat again, and then Michael looks at me.

"They fly private," he says, avoiding my eyes as I just shake my head.

"Of course they do," I say, and I can't wait to get home and call my mother and sister.

"Are you okay?" Allison asks me from her side of the counter.

"I'm tired," I answer honestly. "It's been a crazy couple of days."

"I'll get my keys and take you home. We can eat there," Michael says, walking toward the hallway.

"I want to say thank you, for today. All of you." I smile at them when Michael comes back into the room.

"Can I hug you?" Allison asks, and I just look over at her. "It's okay if you don't do hugs."

She blinks away tears, and I just walk to her and give her a hug, where she whispers in my ear. "Thank you for giving us a chance."

She lets go of me, and I walk over to Max. "Hugs for everyone," I say and hug him, and when he takes me in his arms, I swear it's like my dad is hugging me, and I sob out.

"I didn't hurt her," he defends, letting me go.

"It's a long story," I say, wiping my eyes with the back of my hands. "For another day." I walk over to Matthew.

"You take care, and you call me if you need anything," he says, and I don't even tell him that I don't have his number only because I have a feeling that by the time I leave here, they will have mine.

"Alex," I say to his sister. "Thank you for coming."

"I would have been here sooner," she retorts, and I let her go. "If they weren't liars."

I shake my head and walk to Michael, who slips his hand into mine. "I'll be back later," he says, and we walk out of his place.

"Oh my God," I say, getting into the elevator and looking over at him.

"They can be a lot to handle, but they mean well," he explains, and I laugh and nod my head. He opens the door for me, and I get in. My head is spinning around and around, and I literally just need to close my eyes. I hear him get into the car but give myself a second more before I talk to him.

"Hey." I hear his voice softly and open my eyes. "We're home," he says, and I look around.

"I can't believe I fell asleep," I reply, unbuckling my seat belt.

"The food is going to be here in ten minutes," he says to me, and I look over. "We got here about thirty minutes ago, but I let you sleep." My mouth opens. "If the food wasn't coming, I would have let you sleep longer."

"Thank you." I smile at him as I reach for the handle and get out of the BMW. "I guess I was really, really tired," I admit, walking up to my condo.

"It was an eventful day," Michael says from beside me, pulling open the door and waiting for me to walk in. When we get into my condo, I kick off my shoes and let go of a big sigh.

"I'm going to go and change, I need comfy clothes." He smiles and nods, and I walk into my room, going to the chair in the corner and seeing the big bed still sheetless. I pull off my shirt and look down at my stomach. Before I change my mind, I walk back out, and he is standing there on his phone as he looks up and sees me. "I never thought about letting you touch my stomach," I say as I walk to him. "I can only feel flutters as of right now," I say. "But by all means, you can touch the bump."

"Are you sure?" he asks, and his whole face lights up like a kid coming down the stairs at Christmas and getting the two-wheel bike that they asked for.

"You put it in there." I use his words, and he brings his hands to his mouth as he warms them up with his breath. Then he rubs them together. "You know it's just skin, right?" I tease as he brings his hand to my stomach and then stops, looking at me. "You aren't going to hurt the baby or me."

"Oh, I know. I just…" He hesitates. "I don't think I've ever loved anything as much as I do the baby," he finally says as he places his hands on my stomach. "Hey." He leans down to talk to my stomach. "It's me. Your dad," he says, and I can see the tears coming out of his eyes. "I love you, and I'm sorry for not being here before." He looks up at me and stands up. I'm expecting him to take a step back, but instead, his hands come up to my face. "I'm here," he assures me, and his lips lower to mine. He kisses me softly, and my whole body tingles from his touch. "You were beautiful before," he shares, putting his forehead to mine. "But there are no words that I can come up with to do you justice. You're exquisite," he whispers as he kisses me again, and I'm waiting for him to slip his tongue into my mouth but a knock on the door interrupts us.

"That's the food. Go get a top on," he says, and I nod, walking back into the bedroom. My hands go to my lips as they still tingle from his kisses. I close my eyes waiting for my body to calm down. I swear I almost climbed him like a monkey in heat. I put my hand to my chest and change.

"Where is she?" I hear Julia's voice, and I slip on my shorts when I walk out. "I've been calling you all day long."

"Sorry," I say softly, looking at her and then the bag of food on the counter. "I was meeting Michael's family."

"I'm going to head out," Michael says to me, and I want to tell him not to go. "Make sure my parents are okay." I don't say anything to him. He walks to me. "Call me later," he whispers softly, and I nod at him, and I can tell that he's uncomfortable with Julia here. He bends to kiss my cheek, I smile at him, ignoring the stinging of my eyes. "Julia." He turns to her and nods. "There are two burgers in the bag."

"Thank you." She doesn't even make eye contact with him. He walks to the door, and I smile at him, trying to stay strong, and only when he closes the door do I turn on my sister.

"You have got to stop," I demand, wiping the tear from my face. She turns and looks at me. "You can't hold a grudge forever."

"It wasn't going to be forever," she says softly. "It was just for today, and I was going to forgive him tomorrow."

"Well, you better be nice to him," I warn, walking to her. "He left here because you were here."

"I only came over because I was worried about you," she says to me. "You went to meet his parents without any backup. What happened?"

"They were so nice," I share, and then I swallow. "His name is Michael Horton," I say and she just looks at me, and her eyebrows come together. "He plays hockey for the Dallas Oilers." Her mouth hangs open.

"Shut the front door." She reaches into her purse and takes out her phone. "I'm going to google him." I walk over to the counter and take out the burgers, waiting for her to find him. "Oh my God," she says, looking at me. "He's not kidding."

"His father is Max Horton," I finally say softly.

"No, he's not, you're lying," she says, the tears coming down, and she wipes them away. "No." She shakes her head, and I nod. "Oh my God," she sighs, putting her hand to her mouth. "It's a sign."

"I don't know what it is," I say, sitting down. "All I know is that this baby is going to have more love than it knows what to do with," I confirm, taking a bite of my cheeseburger. "And for that I couldn't ask for anything more."

"I'll apologize to him." She sits down beside me. "You have to invite him to Mom's tomorrow."

"What?" I shriek out. "Why?"

"Because she needs to meet the father of her grandchild," she says. "And it gives me a chance to talk to him one-on-one."

"I don't know," I say, looking down at my food. "What if Mom is mean to him?"

"When has Mom been mean to anyone?" Julia asks, and I shrug.

"When has someone left one of her daughters pregnant?" I counter.

"Ohh, good point," she agrees, opening the other

burger. "Only one way to find out." She takes a bite and looks at me. "Might as well kill two birds with one stone."

TWENTY-THREE

MICHAEL

I WALK BACK into the apartment, and the tension in my neck is almost pushing me down into the floor. I can hear talking in the kitchen, and when I walk in, my parents are sitting at the counter with Alex eating. "What are you doing back here so soon?" my mother asks, looking at me with worry.

"Her sister showed up," I tell them softly, going to the empty chair beside Alex and sitting down. My stomach rumbles, so she slides her plate over to me.

"You look like shit," Alex says, earning my parents to both hiss her name out. She looks over at them. "Are you trying to tell me that he doesn't look like shit?"

"He's going through a lot," my mother reminds her. "But you do look tired."

"So," I start, taking a piece of chicken and cutting it. "What did you guys think?" I look at my parents, who share a smile with each other, and then look at me.

"She's wonderful," my mother praises. "She's so pretty, charming, and so strong to do that all by herself."

"And smart," my father says, grabbing his own piece of chicken.

"Well, not that smart," my sister says with a smile on her face. "She had sex with you." She nudges me with her shoulder, and even I laugh at that joke.

"Where is Uncle Matthew?" I ask.

"Went to Cooper's house," Dad says, "to see the kids."

I finish the plate and then look at my parents. "I'm going to head to bed," I tell them, and they both smile at me. Alex gets off her stool and walks away to one of the spare bedrooms.

"You got a package," my father says when I walk toward my bedroom. The yellow envelope is on the front table, and I grab it on the way to my room.

Heading straight for the shower, I turn it on to cold and let the cold water just hit the back of my neck. I'm wrapping the towel around my waist when the phone rings and I look down to see it's Jillian. "Hey," I greet, the smile coming to my face right away.

"Hi," she says, her voice a bit weird. "I have something to ask you." I can tell that she is nervous. "And it's okay if you say no."

"Okay," I say, not sure I could ever say no to her. I sit on my bed, grabbing the yellow envelope.

"Every Sunday, we have lunch at my mother's place," she says. "And well, I was wondering if you would like to come with me and meet her." She huffs out the last word and then I look down at my phone and press the

FaceTime button. It does a special ring, and then it says connecting, the circle going around and around. It's a couple of seconds before her face fills the screen, and I can see she's lying down.

"So you want me to meet your mom?" I inquire with a shy smile, looking down at her, and my heart speeds up in my chest. Even today, when I kissed her, I thought the world would stop spinning. I thought time would stand still. It wasn't a kiss that I really wanted to give her, but with my lips on hers, everything felt like it was going to be okay.

"Might as well rip it off like a Band-Aid," she says as she blinks. "I called her, and she also invited your parents."

My eyes go big. "Do you think that is a good idea?" I ask her, wondering if she's lying in her new bed.

"What is the worst that can happen?" she quips, and I get up from the bed, and she sees my chest. "What are you wearing?"

"A towel." I smirk at her and walk out of my room. "Mom!" I shout her name and then hear her voice in one of the rooms. I knock on the closed door, and then Alex comes out of her room.

"What are you doing?" She looks at me with a gross look on her face. "Why are you naked?"

"I'm not naked," I argue. "The towel covers everything." She looks at my hand and sees Jillian on the phone.

"Gross! Were you playing with yourself in your room?" she accuses, pretending to vomit while Jillian just laughs.

The door opens, and my father stands there in his boxers. "Dad, seriously, can you not be gross?" Alex says, turning and slamming her door shut.

"I'm in the bedroom with the door closed. Am I supposed to wear a suit?" he says to the closed door, and I look down at Jillian, who just rolls her lips.

"You really think this is a good idea?" I ask, and she smiles and nods.

"Jillian's mother would like to invite the two of you over for lunch tomorrow," I say to my father, looking over at my mother who is in bed with the cover at her waist.

"We would love to," my mother agrees. "Count us in."

"Me, too," Alex calls from her room.

"You aren't invited!" I shout back at her, shaking my head, and she opens the door up again. Coming next to me, she pushes her face into the phone screen.

"Jillian, can I come?" she asks her softly, and I roll my eyes.

"Don't fall for that soft-voice shit," I warn Jillian. "She's like Medusa. You look into her eyes and turn to stone."

"Talking about turning to stone," Alex teases. "Someone is excited to see his girlfriend." She points down at the towel. I gasp and cover myself as Jillian just laughs.

"I am not," I deny, shaking my head and looking over my shoulder at my father, who just shakes his head.

"Sick," he says, closing the door.

"Well, that was fun," I say, walking back to my room. "I love when they visit." I close the door behind me and see her eyes shining bright. "Are you in your new bed?"

"I am." She smiles and turns over. "At first, I thought it was hard like a rock, but then, you get sucked into it."

"I'm glad you like it," I say softly to her. "How was dinner?"

"Good," she says and then looks at me. "I wish you hadn't left."

I smile. "I figured you needed some sister time."

"No, you didn't," she rebuts and sits up in the bed, her shirt falling off her shoulder. "You left because Julia makes you uncomfortable."

I roll my eyes. "She doesn't make me uncomfortable," I hedge. "But I know she doesn't like me, and I don't want you to be stressed, so I took myself out of the equation."

"Well, next time, don't," she says. "I wanted you to stay."

"For the record," I say, looking at her. "I wanted nothing more than to stay. I wanted nothing more than to spend the night with you by my side." Her eyes go soft, and she yawns. "Go to bed and call me tomorrow when you get up," I advise. "What time should I be at your house?"

"I can meet you at my mom's," she says, and I glare at her. "Fine, if you can be here by eleven thirty, that would be great."

"I'll see you then," I confirm, and then I remember. "Hey, how many weeks are you exactly?"

"Seventeen," she answers. "Why?"

"I bought a couple of baby books, so I wanted to know." I hold up the book I bought. "The *What to Expect When You're Expecting,* and the other one is *The Expectant Father's Guide.*"

"You bought books," she says in shock.

"Well, yeah," I say. "I want to know everything." I open the book to seventeen weeks. "The baby is the size of a hand. Do you have stretch marks?"

"I'm going to bed," she deflects. "I will give you complete access to my stomach tomorrow after my mother's house, and you can inspect it."

I look at her. "Just your stomach?" I ask her softly, lying down in the bed. "I really like you, Jillian." The words come out without me even knowing what I'm saying.

"I really like you, too, Michael," she says softly. "See you tomorrow." She hangs up the phone, and I get up, slipping on boxers and shorts.

I walk out of the room at the same time as Alex walks out of her room. "I need water," she says, and we walk into the kitchen. She looks over at me. "If me coming tomorrow is going to be too much, I'll stay back."

I shake my head. "I need all the help I can get," I share honestly. "Her sister isn't exactly welcoming, and I don't expect her mother to be that happy to see me."

"Why?" she asks, grabbing a juice bottle.

"I left her alone for the first seventeen weeks of her pregnancy," I admit, sitting on the stool and taking a deep breath.

"It's not like you did it on purpose," she reminds me. "It's not like you knew and didn't give a shit. Granted, you're an idiot," she offers. "But the minute you found out, it's not like you walked away."

"I thought I heard you two," my mother says, coming into the kitchen in her robe. "What were you two talking about?"

"Michael thinks that Jillian's mother and sister hate him," Alex blurts, taking a sip of her juice.

"I didn't say hate," I say, looking at my mother, who looks like she's ready to rumble.

"Well, what did they say?" she asks, walking to the fridge and grabbing some water.

"They didn't say anything," I reply, getting up. "I just, can we not go crazy tomorrow?"

Alex just looks at me and laughs. "Yeah, let's for once act like normal."

"We are normal," my mother says in a shocked voice.

"I want you all on your best behavior tomorrow," I plead to both of them as they look at each other. I point at both of them. "This means a lot to me." They both nod at me, and I walk out of the room, seeing my father there listening.

"It's going to be okay, son," he reassures me, slapping my shoulder.

"I married your mother without anyone there," he shares. "When they found us, your grandmother wept the whole time, and I thought Matthew was going to throw me off the balcony." He laughs. "It can't get worse than that," he says, walking into the kitchen.

"I really fucking hope not," I say to his retreating back, going into my bedroom and reading the pregnancy books. "I really fucking hope not."

TWENTY-FOUR

JILLIAN

"WHAT TIME WILL you be here?" my mother asks, and I can tell she is a bit nervous about having Michael and his family over. I mean, it's a big deal, and I know she wants to make sure everything is perfect.

"He just texted me that he's going to be here in ten minutes." I slip on the gray short-sleeved t-shirt dress that hugs my body. It goes to my knees, and I slip on my white running shoes. I don't even look in the mirror because I know I'm going to hate the outfit, and I don't have any time to change. Nor do I have any clothes to change into. "I'll text you from the car," I say, and she hangs up at the same time as there is a knock on the door.

I grab the jean jacket that I put on my bed and walk out of my room to the front door. He stands there in dark blue jeans, and a white button-down collar sticks out from under his navy blue sweater. His eyes sparkle when he smiles at me. "Hi," he greets softly, bending to kiss me. I wait for his lips to hit mine, but instead, he kisses the corner of my mouth.

"Hi." The word comes out in almost a whisper.

"You look amazing," he says, looking me up and down.

"You look pretty good yourself," I reply, grabbing my purse and locking up. He slips his hand into mine, and I don't pull away from him. When we walk out the front door, I see Max is standing in the middle of the pathway with his phone in his hand.

Alex is in the back seat of the SUV with Allison next to her. They look over at me as we wave to each other.

"Hey," Max says when he looks up from his phone toward us. He is wearing the same thing as Michael is wearing. "How safe is this neighborhood?" he asks, and I shrug.

"Dad," Michael scolds as he walks with me to the SUV and opens the passenger door, and I just shake my head.

"I'll sit in the back, so your father has room," I offer, walking to the back door and opening it. "Do you want me to sit in the middle?" I ask Alex, who just slides over. When I get in the SUV, the first thing that hits my nose is the smell of flowers. "Hi," I say, looking around as I take a couple of inhales.

"If you think you smell a flower store," Alex says, looking at me. "It's because the trunk is filled with every single flower known to mankind," she says, looking over at Allison.

"It's not every flower," Allison rebuts as Michael and

Max get into the car.

"Did you do your Sherlock Holmes investigation, Dad?" Alex says from beside me.

"It's just not safe that you can just walk in," Max says, looking over his shoulder at us in the back seat. "There have been seven break-ins this year?" he questions, and I just stare at him.

"How do you know that?" I ask as Michael looks at me and shakes his head.

"It's a crime-mapping service," he explains, holding up his phone, and my mouth hangs open.

"Can I get the address so we aren't late?" Michael tries to change the conversation, and I give him the address.

"If you think this is bad," Alex says from beside me, "he got a list of sex offenders in the area when I went away to college." She shakes her head as she looks at her father. "The person who took care of the dorm room actually did a dance when I decided to switch to an apartment the second semester."

"I don't know why," Max says, turning to look ahead.

"You called her weekly for updates," Alex hisses. "And wanted to know confidential information on other dorm members."

I roll my lips as I think about how over the top he is, and then I look over at Michael, wondering if he's going to be the same as his father. We pull up to the house, and I lean forward to open the back door when Michael talks. "Best behavior," he says in a warning, and I laugh.

I get out, and Alex gets out after me, shaking her head. She is in black jeans with a black and cream button-down long-sleeved silk shirt. Her feet are in sky-high heels. "I can't wait to touch your bump," she says to me as she smiles and looks down at it.

"You can touch it," I say to her, and she looks at Michael, who just smirks.

"I touched it last night," he gloats, puffing out his chest as I shake my head. Alex puts her hands on my belly and leans down.

"Hey, little one, it's your favorite aunt," she coos, and I look around to see if Julia is anywhere near to hear her. "I'm going to give you all the candy."

"That's enough," Michael says when the trunk slides open, and I get my answer about what kind of father he is going to be, pretty much just like Max.

"You look so pretty," Allison says when she comes around as she gives me a hug. She's wearing her own black jeans and a soft pink long-sleeved shirt with a sash around her throat tied in a knot. She walks over to the trunk and grabs the biggest flower arrangement I've ever seen.

"Oh, my," I say, and Alex just shakes her head.

"There is more," she says, walking to the trunk as she grabs another flower arrangement in one arm, holding it sideways, and all I can do is stare at how big it is. In her other hand, she carries a big brown bag.

"What in the world?" I ask, and she just shrugs.

"This is them doing things normally," she says as she waits for her father, who carries three brown boxes.

"Michael," I say his name when he closes the trunk, and he's holding one brown bag in his hand. He looks over at me.

"I know," he says, coming next to me. "But you have to pick your battles. This is one I choose to lose."

"Do I want to know what is in the bags?" I ask, and he shakes his head.

"Dessert," he shares, looking down at the bag he has. "We couldn't get one cake like a normal family," he says, looking over at his mother. "So we took one of everything."

I close my eyes. "I'm afraid to ask about the flowers," I say, looking at the three bouquets in front of me. "You ready?" I ask, and again, he shakes his head. I slip my hand into his to give a united front. "It's going to be fine." Walking with him to the front door of the house is nerve-racking for me, so I can't even imagine what Michael is going through. "Here we go," I say, opening the front door and walking in. The smell of roast hits my nose right away. I walk into the living room right off the front door, and my mother comes around the corner.

"Oh my goodness," she says when she sees them with all the gifts in their hands. She is dressed in jeans and a sweater. She looks at me first, and I can see she has tears in her eyes. "Hi," she greets, coming to me and kissing my cheek. "And you must be Michael," she adds, giving him a soft smile as he nods his head.

He hands her the brown bag in his hand. "It's a pleasure to meet you," he says nervously to her. "Thank you for inviting us."

"Mom, this is Allison and Max," I introduce, pointing at them. "And Michael's sister, Alex." Who just smiles at her.

I'm about to say something else when I hear footsteps behind my mother, and my sister comes in. She smiles as soon as she sees us, and then her eyes go big. She scans the room, and then her eyes go to Max's, and I can see tears welling in her eyes.

"Oh my goodness," Allison says when she sees Julia wipe away a tear. Her eyes are looking down and then looking back up at Max.

"I'm sorry," she says. "It's silly. Please ignore me." She turns her head.

"Welcome to our home, I'm Sharon." She walks over to Allison and holds out her hand.

"Thank you so much for having us," Allison replies, holding out her hand to shake my mother's. "You have a lovely home."

Both of them are blinking away tears. "Can I help with any of these bags or flowers?" my mother asks as she walks over to Alex.

"Let me help," Julia offers as she walks over to Max, and she just stares at him.

"This moment," she says, and I look over at Michael, who puts his hand around my shoulder and pulls me close as I wipe away my own tear.

"What am I missing?" Max asks and looks over at me.

"Their dad used to watch every single hockey game when he was alive," my mother says, and she looks at Julia. "You were his favorite, and they used to watch you two together."

"Oh my God," Allison says, walking over to Max.

"Put down the boxes," she tells him, and he looks around for someplace to put down the boxes. He doesn't move. Instead, he bends and puts them on the floor next to the couch.

He looks over at me and smiles, then turns back to Julia, who has her head down as she silently cries. "It's nice to meet you," Max tells her, and she just looks up at him.

"Can I have a hug?" she says, and Max takes her in his arms. She wraps her arms around his waist. "I'm sorry," she finally says when she steps back. "It's just…" She shakes her head. "He would have gotten a kick out of meeting you," she shares, and I look up at Michael, who just smiles at me. "He would have probably had some choice words about the situation, too," she continues, and my mother gasps.

"Julia." She hisses her name, and we all laugh.

"But he would have loved to meet you," she finally says.

"The pleasure would have been all mine," Max responds graciously.

"Why don't I take some of this stuff in the kitchen? So the moms can talk," Julia says, looking at Allison and my mother.

"I'll take these." Max picks up the boxes, and Michael looks at me, not sure what to do.

"You go and help your dad and Julia," I suggest and then lean in. "Let her get to know you."

He nods, not sure he should leave me alone. "It's a girl thing," I say, and he just looks at his father for some advice. Max silently nods his head at him, and they turn to follow Julia into the kitchen.

"Gosh, this is hard," Alex ponders. "Do I want to stay and see the moms cry?" She points at our mothers. "Or do I want to go into the kitchen and listen to Julia gush over my dad, making me want to gag," she says. "I'm going to go for gagging." She walks out of the room.

"I'm so sorry," Allison says. "She speaks her mind. I want to say she gets it from her father." She wrings her hands. "But she doesn't."

"Please sit." My mother points at the couch, and my mother sits on the couch facing her. My mother leans over and grabs a couple of tissues.

"I would like to start by saying that we couldn't be happier and prouder of Jillian." Allison looks over at me, and I walk to the single couch and sit with my hands in my lap. "And I know what our son did."

"He did nothing wrong," I say, my voice quivering. "Nothing wrong." Allison tilts her head to the side as she smiles at me for protecting him.

"You've raised a strong woman," Allison praises, and my mother looks over at me.

"I have to be honest," my mother says, wiping the tears from her eyes. "I did not behave in a way that I'm proud of," she admits, looking at Allison, wringing her hands in her lap. "It was a shock, and the only thing I worried about would be how hard it would be for her." She looks over at me and smiles at me with tears running down her face. "But hopefully, she can forgive me."

"Mom." I get up and go to her. "There is nothing to

forgive." I put my hand around her shoulder.

"We want to be as involved as she will let us be," Allison says, grabbing her own tissue. "I know we can be over the top." She laughs. "But the one thing we do is we love, and we love hard." She looks at me. "We want to be there for you and Michael and the baby. Whatever you need, whenever you need it." I wipe my own tears away. "You say the word, and we are there." She takes a deep breath. "We've been talking, and we want to be there for everything, and the thought of not being around is almost too much to bear." I get up and walk over to her side of the couch.

"I want you to know…" I have to stop for a second to compose myself. "When I found out I was pregnant, the only thing that ran through my mind was making sure my baby would have love." I put my hand on my stomach. "I will never ever make this baby feel like it took something away from me or it stopped me from doing anything."

"That's for both of us," Michael says as he walks into the room. The three of us look over at him. "I'm sorry for interrupting," he apologizes. "But I wanted to just tell you I'm sorry I wasn't there from the beginning." He swallows, and I get up to walk to him. "But nothing and no one would have kept me away from them."

Alex and Julia walk into the room and look around at us. Julia turns back to Alex. "Tequila?"

"Tequila," Alex confirms, and they walk back out of the room. I shake my head, and Michael puts his hand up to wipe away the tear.

Max comes out of the kitchen. "They are doing shots of tequila in there," he says, pointing over his shoulder. "And the timer went off."

My mother claps her hands together. "I love you all already," she says. "Let's eat."

Allison gets up. "Let's eat."

They walk out of the room, leaving Michael and me alone. "That wasn't so bad," he says, tucking my hair behind my ear.

"You missed the hard part." I point at the couch where our mothers were. "Promise me something."

"Anything," he says, and looking into his eyes, I know he means it. He waits for me to say something, and all I can think about is kissing him. "Kiss me."

He groans and closes his eyes. "Why do you decide it would be a good idea for us to make out in your mother's living room?" he asks, and I laugh. "How about we put that make-out on hold until I drop you off at home?"

"Promise." I put my hand up, and he slips his pinky in mine.

"Oh, you can bet on it," he assures me and leans down to kiss my lips softly.

"They are making out on the couch," I hear Julia say from behind me. "Looks hot and heavy. Should I break it up?"

"She's already pregnant. He can't do more damage than that," I hear Alex say with a giggle, and I can't help the laugh that comes out of me.

"Great," Michael sighs, looking over my shoulder at Julia. "Let's get this over with," he says, and Julia just laughs.

"Something tells me that everything is going to be okay," she says to him, pushing his shoulder with hers.

TWENTY-FIVE

MICHAEL

"THANKS FOR BREAKFAST, Mom," I say to her, putting my plate away in the dishwasher. "I hope I don't vomit on the ice." I look over at my father, who laughs as he picks up his coffee cup and brings it to his mouth, finishing it off.

"You'll be fine," she says, cleaning up the kitchen. By the time I rolled out of bed, she was already done making breakfast. My father puts his plate away and then walks to the door where he grabs his jacket.

My mother is slipping on her shoes when my father yells, "Let's go, Alex," down the hallway toward the closed bedroom door. We can hear her grunting, and I can't help but laugh.

"Will you send us pictures?" My mother looks at me and hugs my waist. "I want daily pictures."

"I'll try," I agree, kissing her head. Yesterday at lunch, it was such a surreal experience. I thought I was going to be a nervous wreck, but once we got all the talking out of the way, it was as if we did lunch every single week.

"Is she even awake?" My father looks over at my mother as the door opens, and my sister comes out of the room. She's wearing yoga pants and a sweater and her black glasses.

"I'm up," she mumbles. "Why are there so many fucking windows in this house?" she asks, rolling her suitcase behind her.

"Hey, Alex," I chirp, putting my hands on my hips. "Want some tequila?" I ask her, and I can tell she's glaring at me.

"I don't know why you are on my case." She pushes my shoulder. "I was doing it for you," she says, and I throw my head back and laugh. "I was trying to make you look good."

"You drank a bottle of tequila for me?" I point at myself.

"Yes," she hisses. "And it wasn't a whole bottle. It was half." She folds her arms over her chest. "Julia finished the other half."

"I told you to stop drinking," my mother scolds her, and she puts her head back, looking at the ceiling, and groans.

"Are we not late?" She avoids the questions, and my father opens the door as the four of us walk out.

"You call me if you need me," my father reminds me when he presses the button.

"God, you make it sound like he's dying," Alex says, and my mother slaps her arm. "He's having a child. He'll survive." She shakes her head as the elevator gets there. She steps in, and we take the elevator to the garage where Matthew is waiting for them.

I hug my mother goodbye, and then Alex comes to me. "Don't fuck it up," she warns, giving me a side hug and then rushing to the truck.

"Is she going to throw up?" Matthew looks back at the car and then at us, and we both shrug. "We'll see you guys in a couple of weeks," he says, and I look at them.

"Give or take," my father says, slapping my shoulder as he gets into the car with Matthew. I wave at them and get into my own SUV.

I put my seat belt on as I pull out of my parking space and call Dylan. He answers after two rings. "Asshole," I say as soon as he answers the phone.

He groans. "It's not my fault," he says, and I can hear him breathing heavy, and I look and see that he's probably working out right now.

"How is it not your fault?" I ask him as I make my way toward the arena. We have practice today and a game tomorrow.

"She called me," he explains. "And then she was asking why her parents flew to Dallas."

"And you said?" I ask him.

"I hung up the phone on her," he says, proud of himself.

"And then?" I ask, laughing to myself.

"Then she called me back," he replies. "I told her I didn't know and to call you." I don't say anything. "She knew I was lying."

"So you couldn't lie to her?" I ask him, and he groans.

"The last time she found out I lied to her," he says, "she put baby oil in my sunscreen." He hisses out, "I was a fucking lobster for two weeks."

"God, that was bad," I recall. Shaking my head, I remember how bad it was. "You had blisters everywhere."

"Don't remind me," he says. "I heard the lunch was good, though."

"It went really good," I say. "Alex got shit-faced."

Now it's time for him to laugh. "I was wondering why she was sending me pictures of the walls, but they were blurry. I think I even got one of her eyeball." His voice goes low. "So what are you going to do about Jillian?"

"I don't know what you mean," I say to him.

"Are you going to marry her?" he asks.

I laugh. "You have to stop hanging around with Uncle Matthew," I say as I get to the arena and park my SUV at the same time as Cooper gets there. He gets out of his own SUV as he stares at me. "I'm going to let you go. Cooper is here, and from the looks of it, he's not happy with me."

"I heard," he says. "He called me to ask me if I knew."

"And you said no, right?" I say to him, and he laughs. "I'm not telling you anything again." I hang up on him and get out of the SUV.

"Hey," I greet, looking over at him and seeing that we are both wearing the same tracksuit with the team logo on it.

"Don't fucking hey me," he says. "I can't believe you."

I roll my eyes. "I didn't know she was the girls' teacher," I defend, putting my hands up. "I mean, it's not like we discussed what we did for a living."

"She is the sweetest, kindest person I know," he says, and all I can do is smile, proud that my child is going to have her as a mom. Everything about her is amazing, from her smile to her laugh and even the way she glares.

"You slept with her. Did you even know her name?" he asks, and I turn to walk into the arena.

"Of course, I knew her name," I say. "She just didn't know I played hockey or what my last name was."

"Did you dip and go?" he asks, and I look around to make sure that no one can hear us.

"No, I wanted to see her again, but I was waiting for her to call, and she never did, and then my phone got stolen," I say, and his eyes go big. "Yeah, so that happened."

"Pregnant," he says the words again. "Like she's having your baby." He slaps my shoulder. "Your life will never be the same again."

"Thanks," I say, walking into the room and seeing everyone getting dressed for the on-ice practice.

"Ice in ten minutes." The coach sticks his head into the room. "If anyone is late, we start with suicides." He takes his watch out and starts a ten-minute timer.

"Ugh," I groan, getting dressed as fast as I can. I'm one of the last to get on the ice, and when his timer goes off, we look around, and everyone is busy counting.

"Good timing," he says. "Manning, start the stretching."

We get in a circle at center ice as we start the warm-up. We do drills, and he makes us skate for three hours. I skate off the ice, and I have sweat pouring down my face; I huff out as I hand my gloves to the equipment manager.

Walking into the dressing room, I peel off my shirt and untie my skates. Sitting down on the bench, I'm drinking water when my phone buzzes, and I look down and see that it's Jillian.

Grabbing the phone, I walk out of the room and away from the reporters waiting to interview a couple of us. "Hey," I answer, putting the phone to my ear and stepping into an empty office, and closing the door.

"Hi," she says, and my whole face fills with a smile. "Am I catching you at a bad time?" she asks, and I can hear her walking.

"I just got off the ice," I say, huffing. "Going to get some lunch. How are you?"

"Good, a touch tired," she admits. "But hey, I feel better than Julia does this morning." She laughs.

"Alex wasn't faring any better," I say, sitting on the desk with my face to the door in case it swings open.

"I got a picture," she says, and I laugh.

"Apparently, I'm part of the group text that they started yesterday," she says, laughing. "I had to mute the conversation at ten o'clock when to them it was the witching hour." I can't help but laugh. "Anyway, I just got a call from my doctor that she had to bump up my appointment from Friday to today at four," she explains, and my heart speeds up. "It's fine if you can't come."

"I'll be there," I confirm right away. "Can you text me

the address?"

"Are you going to be done at work?" she asks. "How does it even work?" I'm about to answer her when there is a knock on the door. I get up, opening the door, and see Cooper standing there. He mouths, "Press," to me, and I nod my head.

"I'll explain everything to you tonight," I say. "I have to go and meet the press."

"Okay," she says. "I'll see you at four."

"I'll be there." I hang up and walk out of the room, the phone buzzing in my hand, and I look down and see the address to the doctor's office.

I walk back into the room and look over at Cooper, who just looks at me as he answers questions. I put a shirt on when one of the reporters comes over, and they ask the standard questions. It's about thirty minutes later when they finally walk out of the room.

"You good?" Cooper asks with a worried face.

"Yeah," I assure him, looking around and seeing the room is empty but the two of us. "Jillian has a doctor's appointment at four."

"You're going, right?" He folds his hands over his chest, glaring at me.

"Of course," I say, pulling the shirt off me and undressing to go into the shower. The whole time, I pretend I'm not nervous, but if truth be told, I think I'm going to vomit.

TWENTY-SIX

JILLIAN

"DON'T FORGET TO bring back the yellow paper tomorrow," I tell the kids when they get up and start packing their things. I look up at the clock and see I have five minutes before the bell officially rings. I always have them clean up early so they aren't rushing to get out of here. They walk over to their hooks as they shove the paper into their bags. "It's for pizza day, so if your mom and dad don't sign it, you get no pizza."

I look over at the door and see the kids from the sixth grade coming to help the younger ones get on the bus. "Hi." I wave to them as they look for the kids they need to escort to the bus. "Okay, picker-uppers," I say to the kids who get picked up by their parents. "Get in line so I can walk you guys out."

I walk over to the door as ten kids line up in front of me. "Okay, we have to tippy-toe," I tell them quietly. Walking backward out of the class to make sure that they all follow me as I put my finger to my lips, showing them to be quiet.

When we get to the door, I look out and see the parents waiting in the schoolyard. Stepping outside, I let the kids run to their parents. Mia runs over to Erika, who is walking into the schoolyard with her son on her hip. He smiles when he sees Mia in front of him. Erika bends to kiss Mia's head and then looks up at me and smiles. She walks to me as I wave goodbye to the kids. "Hi," she says with a smile and a soft voice. She and Cooper have always been so polite and kind to me.

"Hi." I smile and hold back the hair that is flying with the wind, looking down at the baby. "He got so big."

"He did." She puts her cheek to his head. "I heard the news," she says, looking around. "I also heard you met my father-in-law."

I laugh. "I did," I say to her. "He is…" I try to come up with the right word.

"He is something," she fills in. "I won't keep you, and I know how ears perk up, so I just wanted to tell you that if you need anything."

I smile at her. "Thank you so much."

"It can get lonely when they travel," she says right before Emma comes out, and I just look at her, and I really need to sit down and ask him all the questions.

"Have a great night," I say, turning to walk back into the school. Older kids are still lingering as they take their time leaving. Walking into my class, I hear the ping from the phone right away, I sit down at my desk and pick up the phone to see thirty-seven missed text messages.

"What in the hell?" I say, opening them and seeing it's just Alex and Julia.

Julia: When are you coming back down?

Alex: I just stepped into my house, and let me tell you flying hungover. Would not recommend.

Julia: YOU FLEW PRIVATE.

Alex: It's still an airplane.

Julia: Did you lie down?

Alex doesn't answer. Instead, she sends a picture of her on the couch in the plane curled up in a ball with a cover on her head.

Julia: You had a couch.

I shake my head, reading through the back-and-forth, and finally add to the conversation.

Me: Can someone explain why I'm on this thread?

I look down to see the three dots come up, and Julia is the first to answer.

Julia: We didn't want you to miss out on the fun.

I shake my head and grab the Tupperware container of fruit on my desk, looking at the clock and seeing that I have thirty minutes to get to my appointment. Cleaning off my desk, I grab my fruit as I walk out of the school toward my car.

Once I park and get out of the car, I look around to see if I see Michael anywhere. Making my way into the doctor's office, I smile at the receptionist. "It won't be long," she says to me. "You can have a seat."

I walk over to an empty seat and take out my phone, seeing I have more missed messages.

Alex: Why don't you guys come to New York for the

weekend?

Julia: Ohhh, I want to go to New York.

Alex: I'm staying in the loft in Soho. You guys should definitely come.

I don't even bother answering them, my head spinning as I look at the clock on my phone and see that he's a couple of minutes late. The door opens as the nurse steps out and calls my name. "Jillian," she says, and I take a deep breath getting up. I ignore the burning in the pit of my stomach as I walk back with her. "How are you doing?" she asks when I walk in, and she takes me to the scale right outside of the doctor's office.

"Let's get you weighed," she says, and I step onto the scale. She comes over and looks down, writing the number in the file. "You've gained three pounds," she says, smiling at me, and I look down at my stomach.

"That is good," she assures me, and then we walk over to one of the closed doors. "Doctor will be right in," she says to me, and then I see the receptionist look over at us.

"Jillian," she says my name. "Someone is asking for you." I feel relief.

"Yes," I reply, looking at her. "That's the dad."

She just nods as she opens the door for him, and he steps inside. He nods his head at her as he looks around. His face is filled with worry until his eyes land on mine. "Hey," he says, walking to me, and I take him in. He is wearing blue track pants with the matching jacket. The team logo is on the leg of his pants and the crest of his jacket. Another Dallas baseball hat on his head. "I'm so sorry I'm late," he apologizes once he gets close enough to me. "I had a phone call." He stops in front of me and then leans down. My whole body tingles as I see his lips come toward mine but he moves his head to the side, kissing the corner of my lips. "You look pretty." He smiles at me as I try to control the erratic way my heart is beating.

"If you can get undressed." The nurse finally cuts in as she looks from me to Michael. "She'll be right in."

I nod as I walk into the doctor's office and see the desk in the corner with a computer on it. The chair/examining table is in the middle of the room. The ultrasound machine right next to the table. "I'm afraid to move," Michael says from the door. "Or touch anything."

I laugh as I pick up the hospital gown. "I have to change." His eyes go big.

"I'll turn around," he offers, turning to look at the door as I slip out of my white loose dress. My matching white bra and panties set leaves little to the imagination since it's lace. I slip the gown on. "I'm really nervous," he says, and I look at his back as he puts his head back. "Like so nervous I almost vomited in the car."

"Why?" I say, walking to the table and sitting down, looking down to make sure that everything is covered. "You can turn around."

He turns back to face me and steps to the side in the corner, making sure he doesn't touch anything. "Relax," I say. "Also you need to stay over here." I point at the back of my head. "You stay there and well." I shake my head, and he laughs, walking toward the back of me.

He looks at the pictures on the wall. "What is going

to happen?" he asks, taking off his hat and scratching his head.

"Well, last time she came in and checked my stomach to see if my uterus was measuring fine," I share, and his face turns white.

"Does it hurt?" He puts his hand to his stomach. "Will you or the baby feel pain?" I'm about to answer him when the door opens, and the doctor steps in.

"Hello, hello." She smiles at me and then looks over and sees Michael, her eyes going big.

"This is the dad," I say, pointing at him with my thumb. Her eyes go big. "We ran into each other."

She smiles, not sure what to say. It was a different story three months ago when she sat me down to tell me I was pregnant. I did not handle that well, at all. I broke down and told her all about the one-night stand. I bet she didn't think that would come out of my mouth, she then sent me for some blood work and an STI test. Both came back negative. She walks to the rolling stool at the desk and opens my chart. "How are you feeling?" she asks as she reads the notes from the last time.

"Good, I have more energy some days, and other days, I can sleep all day."

"That's normal," she says. "You are in your second trimester, so your energy will start to pick up."

She closes the file and looks at me. "Let's get you measured," she says, and I lean back in the chair as she presses the button for my back to go lower. She comes to me and lifts up the gown, my stomach on full display. She takes a white tape measure out.

"What is she doing?" Michael leans and tries to whisper in my ear, but the doctor can hear him since he's close to her head.

"I'm measuring her belly to make sure that the uterus is at the right size." She places one hand on the bottom of my stomach and moves up, pressing down.

"Whoa," Michael says to her. "That's got to hurt." He looks at me and then at the doctor, who just smiles at him.

"The baby is very well protected in there," she assures him, looking down and walking over to the files to write down the number.

"Is it okay?" Michael asks her, putting his hands on his hips, and I hold out my hand to him.

"She usually does all the tests, and then she tells me at the end." I look at him, and he puts his hand in mine. "Now it's the fun part," I say.

The doctor wheels over to me, grabbing the ultrasound machine and bringing it close to her. She grabs the white bottle on the side and squeezes the blue liquid on my stomach. "Are you ready?" She looks over at Michael, who is watching her like a fucking hawk. His eyes follow her every movement. She presses the button on the machine, dimming the lights in the office as she takes the wand and moves the gel around my stomach.

The sound of thumping fills the room. "That," the doctor says, "is your baby's heartbeat."

I look at Michael as he stands there with his mouth hanging wide. "It sounds like horses." He takes his phone out. "Can I take a video of the sound?" He points his phone to the machine as he takes a video.

"You sure can," the doctor confirms and then looks at me and smiles. "And here we are," she says as Michael looks at me, turning the machine around. "That is your baby," she says with joy in her voice.

Michael leans over a bit to look at the screen. "Oh my God," he whispers as the baby flips around. "Do you feel that?"

"I feel little flutters," I answer him as I look at the screen. His arm goes around my head as he leans more in.

"Look"—he points at the screen—"two hands and two feet." The tears run down my face as he looks at the screen in awe.

The doctor presses things on the machine, and we see dots as she takes measurements. "I'm just making sure everything is growing properly." She tells us. "Do you want pictures?"

"I want one," Michael says to her and grabs his phone. She prints out a row of pictures, putting the wand back in its place. She grabs a towel and wipes my stomach, handing Michael the pictures.

"Congratulations, Dad," she says to him, and all he can do is beam with pride.

TWENTY-SEVEN

MICHAEL

"CONGRATULATIONS, DAD," THE doctor says to me as she hands me the long black-and-white pictures of my baby. I don't know why, but the minute she says dad, my chest puffs out, and all I can do is smile.

"Thank you." I look back down at the pictures. "Our baby," I say, my finger rubbing the picture. The lights turn back on, and I look over at the doctor who opens Jillian's file back up.

Jillian sits back up and holds out her hand for the pictures. I hand them to her. "Okay, so," the doctor says, and my head whips to look at her. "From the measurements, I'm going to say that you are going to probably have a big baby."

"What?" Julia says in almost a whisper. "But how?"

"I was almost eleven pounds," I reveal, and the doctor tries to hide the smile on her face when Jillian gasps out.

"What?" She glares at me, and I just shrug, looking

back at the doctor.

She takes a look at me and then at Jillian, turning to look back at the file in front of her. "Heartbeat is healthy," she says. "How are the hormones?"

"Fine, fine," she says quickly. My eyes fly to Jillian, her eyes are big and she just shakes her head.

"Okay," the doctor says, closing the file. "If there is nothing else." She looks at Jillian. "I'll see you in a month." She gets up and smiles at us.

"Thank you," I say as she walks out. I wait for the door to be closed before I look back over at Jillian.

"Are we going to talk about the hormones?" I ask, and she avoids my eyes.

"I have to get dressed," she deflects. "You can wait for me outside." She points at the door.

I roll my lips, trying not to laugh. "Okay, we'll discuss it later," I say, walking to the door and pulling it open. "If you don't want to tell me, I can always google what it means."

"While you're at it," she says, getting up, coming to the door, and she looks so fucking cute. "Google what not to do to piss off the woman who is carrying your child." She slams the door in my face.

I smile at the door, taking the phone out of my pocket and sending my parents the sound of the heartbeat.

Me: The baby's heart beating.

I press send and then send them a new picture of the sonogram. The door opens, my eyes find Jillian's, her eyes go from me to the phone. "Did you google?"

"No," I deny, shaking my head, "I just sent my

parents the sound of the heartbeat." I press play on the audio. "It's the most beautiful sound in the world," I say, wanting to bend and kiss her, but not sure if I can or even if she wants me to.

She walks past me to the front desk as she turns to me. "Do you have your schedule for next month?" she asks, and I nod my head and pull it up.

It takes three tries to finally schedule the appointment. "And we said no, right, to the 3D ultrasound?" the receptionist asks Jillian, and I look up from my phone to see her.

"Sadly," she says. "My insurance doesn't cover it." She shrugs. "I'll see the baby in 3D when he or she comes out."

"Schedule the appointment," I say, angry that she had to do all of this before without me. The pit in my stomach is burning. "I can afford it."

"It's a lot of money," she says, looking at me and then at the secretary, and I know she has no idea what I make, nor does she care. "Are you sure?"

"I'm sure." I smile at the receptionist, who makes sure she does it the same day as the next appointment. When I walk out of the doctor's office, I turn to talk to her, but my phone rings with a FaceTime from my father. "It's my dad," I say, and she smiles.

"Well, answer it," she urges, and I press the button, his face finally comes on the screen, and I can tell he's been crying.

"Hi," I say, getting my own tears in my eyes. "Did you hear?"

"Did I hear," he confirms, laughing while he wipes the tears from the corner of his eyes.

"He sobbed like a baby," my sister,, Alex says from somewhere in the room. I put my arm around Jillian and pull her into the screen with me so she can see.

"Jillian." He says her name, and his voice cracks.

"Oh, good God," Alex says from behind him. "What else did the doctor say?"

"Where is Mom?" I ask her, and Alex just shakes her head.

"In the bathroom sobbing," Alex says. "She threw a spoon at Dad and blamed him for coming home early." She snickers, and my father grabs the phone from her.

"She's right here," he says, walking in the house. I look over at Jillian, who has her own tears running down her face. I lean in and kiss the side of her head. "Angel," my father says, and I can see that he's in their bedroom. "Jillian and Michael are on the phone."

He gets on the bed with her, and I can tell that she was crying. "Hi, guys." She tries to smile, but she sobs out. "I heard the audio."

"Mom," I say, and Jillian punches me in the side to shut me up.

"It's beautiful," she says. My father kisses her lips as she looks up at him. "We wish we could have been there."

"Oh, good God," Alex says, coming into the room pushing my mother over. "What else did the doctor say?"

"That it's going to be a big baby," Jillian says.

"Michael was close to eleven pounds," my mother

says proudly as Alex cringes and pretends to throw up.

"Bet you regret sleeping with his fat head right about now." Alex pushes her face into the phone.

"Alex," my parents hiss out at the same time as Jillian's stomach growls.

"Okay, I'll call you guys back after we eat," I say, hanging up the phone. "You hungry?"

"I'm carrying a human. I'm always hungry," she says. "This is me getting hangry."

"What do you want to eat?" I ask her, and I want to touch her. I want to hold her hand. I want to hug her because I just want to fucking be able to do all of that, and it kills me that I can't just do it.

"Greasy food." She smiles at me. "Like running-down-your-arm greasy."

"There is this burger place," I start to tell her.

"I like where this is going," she tells me, her eyes lighting up.

"I can get the food and meet you at your house so you can relax a bit," I suggest, and she smiles so big and wide.

"You did check Google." She laughs. "Smart man."

"What do you take on your burger?" I ask her as I walk her to her car.

"Everything," she says. "Oh, and get fries." She opens her car door. "And onion rings." I laugh at her.

"I'll order one of everything," I say, and she nods her head.

"I'm assuming you aren't going to let me pay." I glare at her question.

"We have things to talk about, Jillian," I share, and I'm not joking. "Lots of things."

She rolls her eyes at me. "Bring me food, and we can talk." She starts the car, and I watch her drive off.

I get into the SUV, calling my father right away. "Hey, how do I get Jillian added to my insurance?" I ask him, totally unaware of how any of this works. "Or how do I get her and the baby their own insurance."

"I'll call my guy tomorrow and get them their own," he says without skipping a beat. "I should have asked her for her information when I was there."

"She didn't want to get an ultrasound because her insurance wouldn't cover it," I say, the burning coming back in my stomach. "Dad, I felt like a deadbeat," I finally admit. "Like I couldn't take care of my family."

"One," he clarifies. "A deadbeat father is someone who knows about their kid and chooses not to take care of them. Two, from the minute you found out, you have taken care of your family." Even though he says the words, nothing reassures me. "Three," he huffs out. "I really think you and Jillian need to sit down and discuss this."

"No shit," I say. "Okay, I'll send you all her information tonight when I get it."

"Okay," he says. "She really has no idea how much money you make?" he questions, shocked.

"Even if she did, it's up to me to make sure they have everything that they need."

"She's one of the good ones," he finally says, and I nod my head. "Call me if you need anything." He hangs up. I pull up to the little diner that my uncle Evan showed me once when we came to visit. He brought my aunt Zara here on a date, and they have the best burgers you will ever have.

Walking in, I take a seat at the counter and wait for the waitress to come over. I order two of everything on the menu. "Someone is hungry," she says, and twenty minutes later, I'm walking out with three bags full of food. By the time I get to Jillian's, the oil has seeped through the bags, my SUV smells like a drenched french fry.

She opens the door when my hand is mid-knock. Her hair is pinned on top of her head. "I was wondering if you were okay?" She lets me in, and I can smell the soap on her. She stands there in shorts and a sweater, her face free of makeup as she glows, looking at the food. "You were not kidding about greasy," she says, grabbing one of the bags, and it's like my tongue is stuck. "It smells so good," she praises, walking over to the counter and getting on a stool. "Oh, did you want plates?"

I laugh at her, shaking my head. "God, no."

I put the two bags in my hand on the counter, and she just looks over at me. "What did you order?" she asks.

"I got two of everything." I sit next to her and take off my baseball hat, putting it on the counter.

"You know I already have a collection of your hats." She sticks her head in one of the bags and grabs a fry.

I pull my track jacket off when she holds out a fry for me. Instead of taking it in my hand, I bend and take it with my mouth. My cock springs to action as I look up and see the same look she gave me that night when we first met.

She pulls out one of the burgers and hands it to me, then grabs one for herself. I open the two bags beside me and pull out the food for her. "Are those fried pickles?" she asks, clapping her hands.

I pass her the container as she takes one. "Thank you," she says to me with a huge smile. "For today."

"You are more than welcome," I say, looking at her as she takes a bite of her burger. "Now that you are eating, we need to discuss things."

TWENTY-EIGHT

JILLIAN

"YOU ARE MORE than welcome," he says as I take a bite of the greasy burger, and it does not disappoint. "Now that you are eating, we need to discuss things." I stop mid-chew and look over at him.

"I think we should discuss a couple of things," I suggest as I swallow the bite that I have in my mouth. My stomach automatically gets sick, and for the first time, I know it's not the baby this time.

"Good," he says, taking a bite of his own burger. "I called my father and asked him to add you to my insurance." I'm about to argue with him. "The baby will go under me as soon as he or she is born." I can't really say anything to him about that, so I'll leave him with that one. "How much have you spent on the baby since you found out you were pregnant?" he asks, looking over at me.

I shrug my shoulder. "I'm not sure." It's an honest

answer.

"I'm going to write you a check for forty thousand dollars," he says, and all I can do is look at him, my mouth hanging open a bit.

"One," I say, putting up my finger. "I haven't come close to spending forty thousand dollars." I take another bite of the burger. "Two, are you out of your mind?"

He laughs, and I have the need to lean over and rub my nose along his jawline while I kiss him. "Completely out of my mind." Putting down his burger, he gets up to get himself a glass of water. "Today when she asked you about the ultrasound."

I raise my hand to stop him from talking. "It's not that big of a deal." His eyes go dark, and I can see him fighting off tears.

"It was a big deal to me." His voice is cracking. "My job is to make sure that you and the baby never want for anything." He comes back over to the stool beside me. "And I was not doing my job."

"Michael." My hand goes to his arm. "I never felt you weren't taking care of the baby. Not once." My thumb rubs his big arm. I want to get off my chair and hug him. I want to get lost in his arms.

"Then let me pay you back," he whispers. "I can never repay you for taking care of the baby alone." He looks back at his burger and picks it up. "There is no monetary price I can put on it."

My heart breaks that he had this thought at the doctor's office. "How about I check my papers, and then we can decide on an amount?" I try to meet him in the middle.

"I have a question."

"Okay." He takes a bite of his burger.

"It might sound stupid." I take a bite of my own burger as he waits for me to ask him the question. "But how does your job work?" He chuckles. "Like do you go to work every day?"

He shakes his head. "So when we don't play, that day we have practice and then off-ice training. When we play, we usually have to be at the rink about four hours before. Some of us even go in the morning and skate and then nap before the game at night. There is always off-ice training the day of the game."

"So today, you were at the rink all day long?" I ask, and he nods, taking another bite of his burger.

"Tomorrow is a game day," he informs me. "So I will go and get a skate in the morning and then come home at noon. I'll take a nap for a couple of hours and then head in for the game." I'm so intrigued by all of this, and I've never ever been interested in anything that has to do with hockey. "I got Julia tickets for tomorrow's game." He looks over. "You want to come with her?"

"You got Julia tickets?" I ask, shocked.

"Well, she was talking with my dad yesterday, and she sounds like she really misses it." He shrugs. "So I got her tickets. They are lodge tickets."

"I don't know what that means." I take a fried pickle. "But it sounds expensive."

He shakes his head. "It's the perks of playing with the team."

"Okay, but what happens when you leave?" I ask.

"The games away."

"It depends," he says, taking his phone out and showing me his calendar. "We play tomorrow, and then the next day, we leave for six days."

"Six days?" I try not to think about how it's going to be not seeing him.

"Some road trips are two days," he points out. "We just got back from two weeks on the road."

"Oh my gosh," I say, not even imagining what it would be like for him to be gone for two weeks. "That's so long."

"It gets old very fast." He shrugs. "But it's a job right now." I nod. "I'm going to buy a house," he finally says, and my stomach sinks once again. "That's why I was late." He takes a sip of water. "My aunt called me, and we were going over a couple of things."

I nod, not able to say anything. Four days ago, it was just me and the bean, and now, it's the three of us. "How is this all going to…" My finger goes into a circle.

"I have no idea," he answers, blowing out a breath. "I don't think there is a playbook for this kind of thing." He laughs nervously. "And even if there was one, I think we need to make our own rule book. My main focus is you and the baby." My heart does a pitter-patter when he includes me and not just the baby. "It's you and the baby and helping in whatever I can do to help."

I nod at him. "That sounds like a good plan." I avoid his eyes. "I mean, people have babies all the time when they aren't with each other anymore." I get up to get away from him, the sting of tears itching to come out.

Going to the fridge, I take a bottle of juice out and drink it, leaning on the counter looking at him. "I think that as long as we put the baby first, everything is going to fall into place." I wait for him to say something, anything but all he does is watch me. I want to know what is really going on in his head. I want to know how he expects us to raise a baby. I want to know how it's going to be if he meets someone or if I meet someone. I put my hand to my stomach as my stomach does the wave.

"Are you going to be sick?" he asks, pushing away from the stool.

"No," I reply. "Just a little bit of a flutter."

"Today," he says, scratching his head. "It was insane." The smile fills his face, and all I want to do is sit next to him. But I have to remind myself that he's here for the baby.

"What part?" My curiosity is piqued. Everything is piqued when it comes to him. My body wakes up in ways I can't even put into words.

"Hearing the baby's heartbeat." His eyes light up from the smile that is on his face. "Then seeing him flip and flop in your stomach."

"Or her." I tilt my head to the side. "It could be a girl."

"Do you think it's a girl?" he asks. "Like do you feel it's a girl?"

"Honestly, I think it's a boy." I shrug. "I have no idea why."

"Honestly…" He leans back a bit. "I don't give a shit as long as the baby is healthy."

"Same." I smile at him. "As long as he or she comes

out healthy and a normal size, I think it's all I can ask for." He laughs. "Who the hell gives birth to an eleven-pound child?"

"My mother." He chuckles. "I think Zara and Zoe were eight pounds and six pounds."

"That's fourteen pounds of babies." My tone is shock.

He gets up and starts cleaning up the counter, and I ignore the need to tell him to stay longer. I ignore everything, putting up a solid front. "Okay, one last question," he says once the counter is clean.

"And go." I look over at him as I'm washing my hands.

"What did the doctor mean by how are the hormones?" he asks, and I grab a dish towel to dry my hands. I scratch my head. My nipples are already ready to be played with.

"Why can't you ask me another question?" I groan, and he claps his hands.

"I knew it was a good one," he jokes. "What is it?"

"I don't know why you even care." I try not to look at him, but again, something about him just pulls me in.

He puts his hands on his hips and raises his eyebrows. "I'm not leaving here until you tell me."

Don't tell him, my head screams. If you don't tell him, maybe he'll stay. I close my eyes as I gather up the courage to tell him. "It's just that when you're pregnant," I start, avoiding looking at him. I look out toward the living room. "Your body gets extra hormones."

"Okay," he says, not happy with the answer I just gave him.

"And well, these extra hormones can, you know." I

move my head back and forth, hoping he picks up on what I'm trying to say.

"You know." He mimics my head moving back and forth.

"Oh, good God," I snap at him. "It's made me horny," I finally say and close my eyes, putting my hands on my face. His laughter fills the room, and I swear I want to die. "Stop laughing," I mumble, moving my hands from my face. "It's really not funny."

"You're horny?" he asks.

"I'm not horny right now, like this minute." I fold my arms over my chest to hide the way my nipples have become hard. The last thing I want him to know is that I want to climb him like a tree. "But I have been occasionally in the last couple of weeks."

"So you've…" He smirks, looking down at my lady town. "You've been playing?"

"Okay, time for you to go," I deflect, walking to the door and opening it. "Thanks for dinner."

He walks to the door, the smile on his face even bigger than before. "If you want, I can help you out before I leave." *Yes*, my body yells in my head. Just lie in the middle of the bed and let him help you. He put you in this situation, so it's only fair he helps you out.

"Suddenly, I'm the opposite of horny," I lie through my teeth. I look down at lady town. "Yup, totally like shriveled up." I close my eyes. "I'm going to shut up. You can go." When I open my eyes, he's still there in front of me, but this time really close to me.

"Well…" His hand comes up to my chin. "I'm the

opposite of shriveled up." My eyes go against me, and I look down to see his cock ready to come out and play. "Lock up after me." He bends his head, and my eyes close, waiting for his lips to hit mine. Instead, I feel his lips on my forehead. "See you tomorrow," he says when my eyes flutter open. I watch him walk away from me, and he turns to face me, walking backward. "If you need me in the middle of the night." He smirks. "Call me."

TWENTY-NINE

MICHAEL

"HORTON!" THE COACH yells my name, and I jump over the board, sliding on the ice, going on the attack. Manning brings the puck up, slowing down his speed so we can all get into the zone at the same time.

Manning slaps the puck at the goalie, but he sticks his legs. The puck bounces off it and goes into the corner. I hustle around the guy in front of me and head toward the net. Cooper is the first at the puck as he passes it back to Manning at the blue line. He turns his body, faking to pass it to the other defenseman, but instead, he passes it back to Cooper in the corner. Out of the corner of his eye, Cooper sees me slip right in front of the goalie. Cooper doesn't even keep the puck on his stick for a second before sliding it to me. My stick comes out just a touch to tip it right over the goalie's shoulder.

I see the puck hit the back of the net and the red light siren goes off at the same time as the fans jump to their feet. I skate to the boards, and Cooper comes over and punches my arm. "That was all Grandpa," he says of the play he taught us when we used to scrimmage with him.

Manning comes over. "Nice little play, you two," he says to me, and we all skate to the bench, going down the line to give everyone a high five.

"We've got five more minutes," the coach says when I get back on the bench. I look up at the Jumbotron in the middle, showing we are up by two. With two minutes to go, they pull the goalie, and Manning gets the puck and clears it to their end, scoring an empty-net goal and giving us a three-goal lead.

The horn goes, and we all make our way over to the goalie. After I knock my helmet with the goalie, I skate to the middle of the ice as we wait to thank the fans for coming like we do all home games. My eyes go up to the box where I know she is sitting. She stands there with Julia beside her, and they are both clapping.

A smile fills my face when I see the smile on hers. Julia leans over and says something to her, making her throw her head back and laugh. I skate back to the bench, getting off the ice. After placing my stick with all the other sticks, I make my way back toward my spot. Grabbing one of the Gatorades from the middle of the room.

Coach comes in before the press does. "Cooper, Michael." He points at us as we sit side by side. "Not sure where that play comes from but good fucking play."

I smirk and look over at Cooper, who holds his fist up to me. I fist-bump him, laughing. "It's a family play,"

Cooper boasts, smiling as the coach just nods at us and walks out of the room before the press descends on us.

"To be born into hockey royalty," Wilson says, getting up and taking off his shirt to walk toward the showers.

"He has sex every single night," I say, getting up. "You would think he would be less frustrated."

Cooper gets up next to me. "Maybe they don't let him finish."

"Or maybe he's just an asshole," I reply, shaking my head as my phone beeps.

Jillian: Do you want us to wait for you?

I look over at Cooper. "I'll be right back," I say, grabbing my phone and walking out of the room. Dialing her number, she answers right away. "Hi." I lean against the concrete wall.

"Hey," she huffs, and I can hear all the people around her as she tries to make it out of the arena.

"I don't know how long I'll be, and I know you have school in the morning." I turn, wishing I could see her if only for a second. "What time do you leave for work in the morning?"

"I have to leave tomorrow at eight," she says.

"Would it be okay if I brought breakfast to you?" I say softly. "I leave tomorrow at ten."

"I'm up at six thirty," she says.

"I'll see you then," I confirm, wanting to talk to her longer but knowing I have to get back into the room. "Okay, I have to go meet the press."

"Out of all the excuses I've ever had from a man, that has never been one of them." She laughs.

"Good to know I stick out." The pit of my stomach burns.

"Oh, you stick out all right." She laughs. "See you tomorrow." I disconnect the call and walk back into the room.

"You okay?" Cooper asks me when I sit back down. "You look like someone kicked your dog and stole your cat."

I look down at my skates. "Yeah, just…" I shake my head when the press comes into the room, pushing Jillian to the back of my mind.

When I get back home, I pack my bag and slide into bed, turning to look out the window at the black sky. The one lone star in the sky blinks as my mind spins around and around, and I try not to think about what is really bothering me. My eyes drift to sleep, and when the alarm rings at five thirty, I fly out of bed, slipping on black dress pants and a white button-down shirt. It's a travel day, and we have to travel casually.

I'm out of my apartment by six o'clock, loading the SUV with my travel bag. I make my way over to Jillian's, stopping by the same place I got her food the last time I showed up at her house. By the time I'm parking the SUV, it's six thirty-three.

Getting out of the SUV, I take a look around and notice how quiet it is. I try not to make too much noise when I knock on the door. The door opens softly, and I see that the apartment is still dark. "Hi," she grumbles as she wipes the sleep away from her face. "Sorry, I just got up."

My heart speeds up. "I can go," I say, ignoring the burning that starts again at the pit of my stomach. "I can leave the food, and you can go back to bed."

"No." She reaches out her hand to grab my arm. "Don't go." Her voice is soft as she pulls me into the apartment. "Let me just go to the bathroom." She walks toward the bathroom. "Make yourself at home."

I put the bags on the counter, taking out the containers as I listen to water running in the bathroom. Something in my chest feels heavy, and I don't even know how to explain it if someone asked me. Grabbing two plates and utensils, I put them on the counter and sit on the stool waiting for her, nervously tapping the counter.

My head turns to look at her when I hear the door open. She comes out with her hair piled on top of her head. Her black-and-white shorts are loose on her, and she has a pink T-shirt that says Let Me Sleep. "I should have called," I say when she gets on the stool beside me.

"I had the alarm set." She turns to look at me, the sleep still in her eyes. "But it just took me a while to fall asleep last night."

"Was everything okay?" I ask as worry sets in.

"Yeah, it was fine. It was the high of the win." She smiles at me. "What an adrenaline rush it must be."

"It's always good to win," I agree, grabbing her plate and putting food on it. "A lot better than losing."

"How do you turn it off?" she asks. "Like do you get home and are wired?"

"Yeah," I answer her honestly. "It takes a couple of hours to relax by the time I get home. I usually eat something." When I hand her the plate, her fingers graze mine, and I ignore the pull to her. "Then I turn on the television and just flip through channels until I'm tired."

"What time did you go to bed?" she asks, grabbing a piece of bacon and chewing on it.

"Last time I saw the clock, it was after three." Grabbing a piece of toast, I take a bite.

"Aren't you tired?" I nod at her.

"But I can sleep on the plane." I scoop some eggs on my plate. "It's a five-hour flight to Vancouver."

"How long are you there for?" She grabs her fork and takes a bite of the eggs.

"We get there today, and the game is tomorrow. Then we leave Vancouver right after the game and head to LA." I try to remember the schedule. "We play LA the day after, then San Jose the day after that, and then we get back." She just looks at me with her mouth open. "Then I'm home for ten days."

"My hat's off to you guys." She smiles. "I don't know how you do it."

The rest of the breakfast flies by faster than I want it to, and I know I have to get going, or she's going to be late. I get up and take our plates to the kitchen, rinsing them off and putting them in the dishwasher. "Thanks for having breakfast with me."

She gets up. "Thank you for wanting to have breakfast with me." She waits for me near the door.

"I'll call you tonight," I say, trying to gather up the courage to kiss her. My hand goes to the handle of the door.

"Text me when you land." She looks up at me as I stand here in the doorway of her apartment. "Just so I don't worry."

I smirk at her. "You worry about me." My hand comes up, going to her face as my thumb rubs her soft cheek. "I like that." My voice goes into a whisper as my face also leans down, and I want to kiss her so bad, but I'm not sure she wants me to. My lips go to her cheek. "I'll text you later." I look at her, and all she can do is nod. I smile and walk out of her apartment with my shoulders feeling like they're holding up a thousand pounds. I wait for her to call me back, hoping she calls me back, but nothing.

When I get into the SUV, I start it and drive away from here before I do something stupid. Stopping at the red light, I connect my phone and call Dylan. "How are you up?" he asks, laughing.

"Travel day," I respond, making my way toward the airport.

"Saw that little play last night." He laughs, making me laugh.

"You watching my game?" I tease him.

"Did you not read the group text that Granddad sent?" he asks, and I look down, seeing I've missed a hundred and one messages. "Who taught him how to do a group message?" I chuckle. "I had to put it on 'do not disturb' because it was going off every five seconds."

"He was just proud," I say, and then my voice trails off. "I just left Jillian's."

"And?" He knows I have a lot more to say.

"And I really fucking like her," I admit, the lump in

my chest getting heavy again. "Like really fucking like her." I shake my head. "I left, and all I wanted to do was to kiss her, but I didn't." I'm upset with myself for not just taking the kiss I wanted. "What do you think I should do?"

"Here is a crazy thought." He stops, and I wait for it. "Why don't you tell her?" I roll my eyes, not saying a word. "Dude, she's having your kid."

"Yeah, but what if she doesn't want me like that?" I ask. The fear that she doesn't is almost too much to bear.

"What if she does?" He turns it around on me. "What if she does want you like that, and she's waiting for you to make a move, but you're too busy jacking off? Instead of being like 'I like you, you like me.'"

"Wow, powerful. Did you read that in this month's *Cosmo*?" I chuckle as I get to the airport.

"Laugh, but you'll be thanking me later," he huffs out. "Also, who the hell is your sister dating?"

"What?" I ask, shocked. "I didn't know she was dating anyone."

"She posted a picture of her with a guy on her Insta," he fills me in.

"It could be a friend." I grab my phone and look over to see that people are loading the plane already. "Okay, I got to go."

"Tell her!" he yells right before I hang up the phone.

"Yeah, tell her," I mumble to myself, getting out of the SUV and grabbing my stuff. "Just tell her."

THIRTY

JILLIAN

MICHAEL: JUST LANDED. You can stop thinking about me.

I laugh at the text and answer him back.

Me: New phone, who dis?

I laugh, waiting for his reply as the kids come back into class from music. I look up and see that the bell is going to ring in a couple of minutes. I get up and make them grab their bags and start the routine of when they leave. Twenty minutes later, I'm packing up my own bag when the phone pings.

Michael: Want to have dinner with me?

I sit in my chair and answer him back right away.

Me: I would love nothing more.

I press send before I can think about it or harp on it or tell myself it's a bad idea. When he left this morning, I wanted nothing more than to get on my tippy-toes and kiss him. The flutters in my stomach had nothing to do with the baby moving and everything to do with the man standing in front of me. I wanted to yell at him to come back. But I let him go. I felt his touch on my cheek while I got dressed. The whole day, I could see him in my head, wondering if he fell asleep on the plane or not.

Getting home, I walk in, and I can't put my finger on it, but just feel like it's missing something. Walking to the bedroom, I kick off my shoes, move to the bed to grab my pjs, and make my way to the shower.

Slipping off my pants and shirt, I look at myself in the mirror. My breasts have gotten bigger for sure, my nipples darkening. My stomach is much bigger than when he was with me, and I'm assuming so is my butt. *Maybe he doesn't find me attractive*, I think to myself, the thought making my stomach burn. Maybe it was just a one-night thing for him, and I should let it go. The maybes drive me crazy, and I finally give in to the tears that come. There is just so much that is unknown, and to me, it drives me crazy. I'm the one with the plans all the time. I'm the one who knows what I'll be doing in five years. I'm the one who had everything mapped out. Except for the baby. I rub my stomach. "We've got this," I say to him or her as I rub cream on my stomach to prevent stretch marks.

Brushing my hair out, I braid it to the side of my head. I can hear my phone ringing from my bedroom. I run to it and see that Michael is trying to FaceTime me. I press connect without even thinking twice about it. The little circle going around and around telling me it's connecting.

His face fills the screen, his smile falling when he takes one look at me. "What's wrong?" he asks, his tone tight and his eyes fill with worry.

"Nothing," I say, confused as I look at his blue eyes. His forehead creases as he just stares at me.

"You look like you've been crying." His voice goes soft as his eyes roam my face as if he'll be able to tell something. "Are you hurt?" He gets up from wherever he was. "Is it the baby?"

"No, no," I deny, feeling silly. "The baby is fine." I put my hand on my stomach and show him that it's still perfect. "See, still okay?" I fake smile, and he just stares at me, waiting for it. "It's nothing." I shake my head. "Where are you?"

"In my hotel room." He sits up, and I can tell he's shirtless. I wonder how long he's been in bed. I wonder if he's naked or with his boxers on. The thought of him being naked sends shock waves through me. "Why were you crying?"

"Why are you shirtless?" I counter, and he shakes his head, chuckling.

"You answer my question." He tries to one-up me. "And then I'll answer yours." He looks at me.

"Fine, you go first." I sit on the couch and look at him. *He's so hot* is the only thing I can think of. Watching him on the ice last night was all that and a bag of chips. Every single time he was on the ice, I was invested. I didn't know any of the rules, and I didn't care. All I cared about was no one touching him. It got a bit rough at some points, and then when he scored, my heart just exploded in my chest. I jumped out of my seat and screamed as loud as I could, no doubt making the baby bounce up and down.

"I just got to my hotel room, and I took off my shirt. I was going to get into my sweats, but I wanted to call you first." He looks suddenly shy. "Now, why are you crying?"

"It's…" I look at him and then look out the window, trying to get the courage to say what is on my mind. "It's just my body is changing, and I don't know." I shrug, ignoring the sting of new tears that threaten to come. "I didn't feel." I stop myself before I say sexy. "Attractive."

"Jillian." He says my name, and I look up at him. "You are hands down the most beautiful woman in the world." His words hit me in the chest. "You are the sexiest woman I've ever seen."

"You're just saying that." I shake my head, not sure I want to hear what he has to say. "Because I'm carrying your child."

"No," he snaps at me. "I'm not just saying that. Do you know what I did today?" I just look at him. "I left your place, and all I could think about was kissing you. All I wanted to do was kiss you." He smiles shyly. "I mean, I wanted to do more than kiss you. I wanted to lay you on the bed and have my way with you. It's sick and twisted, and I don't even know if your head is in the same place mine is." He just keeps talking without giving me a chance to say anything. It's almost like a dam that has been broken, and he can't stop what is coming out.

I listen to his words, and I'm shocked. "What?"

"Yeah," he says. "I don't even know if you want me like that."

"Well…" I take a big inhale. "I do," I admit. "I want you to kiss me." I leave out the part that I was so aroused thinking of him last night that I had to take my vibrator out. "I've waited for you to kiss me since the last time." I might as well just give it to him all since I've already said this much. "I just figured you didn't find me attractive."

"What. The. Fuck?" he hisses out. "I was trying not to be, you know…" He just looks at me. "Annoying and in your face."

I'm about to say something when there is a knock on the door. "That's for you," he says with a smile. "We are going to table this conversation for when you open the door."

I walk over to the door and open it. "Jillian?" The man says my name, handing me a bouquet of white roses and a paper bag. "Have a nice day," he says, and I close the door.

"What is this?" I can't help the smile that fills my face. "You sent me flowers," I say excitedly. "I've never gotten flowers before." I prop the phone up on the counter. "Ever." I put my face into the phone. The sound of his laughter fills the room as I open the brown bag, seeing the containers stacked all the way to the top. "What is this?" I say, taking one out.

"It's chicken and steak with sides." His eyes light up.

"Oh my goodness." I open the first container, seeing the chicken and then the steak, and there are two different potatoes, baked and mashed. "What did you do all this for?"

"Well, I can't be there to take care of you," he says softly, turning on his side, and I wonder if he got to sleep in the plane. "So I wanted to make sure you were okay."

I shake my head. "That was very thoughtful of you," I say, swallowing the lump in my throat. "And the most thoughtful thing anyone has ever done."

For the rest of the conversation, we play twenty questions, and I spend the whole time with the biggest smile on my face.

When I wake up the next morning, the first thing I see is a text from him. Sent to me at midnight my time. Which was ten p.m. his time.

Michael: Good morning, beautiful. I hope you have a great day. Call me on your lunch break.

I get out of bed, get ready, and head to work. When I walk into my class, there is a paper bag on the middle of my desk with a pink ribbon tying the handles together and my name in black marker across it. I pull the ribbon and look inside. A white envelope lies on top of two containers. One of fruit and another of yogurt and granola.

Counting down the days until I can eat breakfast with you again.

Michael

I shake my head and snap a picture of it and send it to Julia, who calls me right away. "This guy…" she says. "He's good."

Laughing, I sit in the chair, and my fingers go over the words on the white card. "It was on my desk." I try not to smile too much, but I can't help it.

"And he sent you flowers and dinner?" She huffs out, "Damn. I need me some of that." I called her right after I got off the phone with him last night. My whole body was giddy, but I kept our conversation to myself. That was just ours and would only be ours.

I can't help the laughter that escapes me. "Well, I'm sure he did it because I'm carrying his child."

"I can tell you right now that he's not doing this just because you are having his baby," she says. "I think he genuinely likes you."

I shrug, scared to admit I like him more than I think I do. I'm scared to admit to anyone just how much I like him. The bell rings, and I let her go, and the whole morning I count down the minutes until I talk to him.

THIRTY-ONE

MICHAEL

I LOOK OUT the small square window as soon as the wheels of the plane touch down. Putting my head back on the seat headrest, I close my eyes, and all I can see is Jillian and her huge smile. I swear her laughter is stuck in my head. Although I hated the travel of the past five days, it was the best thing to happen to us. It was as if the phone was the safety net, and we finally gave in to what we felt and thought.

The first night I was away, when I called her and she was crying, my heart literally stopped in my chest. I had this sense of dread fall over me, and the only thing that was going through my mind was how I would be able to get back home. Being so far away killed me until she told me why she was crying. The dread went away, and I knew then and there that I would never hold back from telling her how I felt. No matter how scared I was, it didn't matter. What mattered more was Jillian and how she felt. I would set my alarm every morning to make sure I spoke to her before she went to school. When it was her lunch, I would usually be headed toward the rink, and even though I tried, we missed each other a couple of times. But for dinner, I was there with her all the time. I had meals delivered to her every night, and we would talk while she ate. It was a good thing I was two hours behind, so even on game night, I still got to talk to her. Every day I thought of things to send her, and the smile she gave me when she would call me was priceless.

"Well, gentlemen," Wilson says, getting up from across the aisle. "I won't miss your faces for the next four days." He smirks, and I just shake my head as he walks off the plane.

"Anybody going to tell him that he's a douche?" Ralph mumbles, getting up from the seat in front of me as he grabs his bag. The road trip was not one any of us want to talk about. It was loss after loss, and it didn't help that Wilson also got suspended for five games for an illegal hit. He took his frustrations out at the wrong time.

"He couldn't care less," Manning says, grabbing his own bag. "Wilson cares about one person."

"Two people," Cooper says, putting up two fingers, everyone looking at him waiting for who the second person is. "Him and his dick." We all laugh. It's no surprise that he's the biggest player, and he gives zero fucks about it either.

I grab my own bag as I walk off the plane behind Manning and right in front of Cooper. The heat and wind hit my face right away because the sun is high in the sky.

"See you guys in four days," Manning says loudly, looking around. "Stay out of trouble." He looks at Cooper and me.

"I'm married with children," Cooper points out. "He's the one off sowing his oats." Cooper is the only one on the team that knows about Jillian. Actually, my family all know about her, but I haven't announced it to the team yet.

"I'm not sowing any oats." I shake my head, turning to look at Cooper. "Don't call me until Monday," I say.

He throws his head back and laughs. "I'm going to send out a group text to all the family, telling everyone how depressed you are and how sad you look," he jokes, and I glare, not sure he wouldn't do it for fun. "And how you want to hear everyone's voice."

I stop walking and hold up my finger, flipping him the bird. "Fuck you."

He throws his head back, laughing out loud. "I will call your father," I counter. "And tell them I saw Erika crying and that you were talking to another woman." It's the best I can come up with.

"Nice try. Everyone knows that she owns me," he says, unlocking his car doors. "So joke's on you."

"Whatever," I mumble. Getting into my own vehicle, I start the truck. I think about going home first and dumping off my shit, but my head has other plans. I stop at the flower shop and grab all the roses she has in the shop. The bouquet in my hand is massive and heavy. I then stop off at the bakery I know she likes and grab a box of her favorites, and when I pull up in front of her building, I park in the same spot it seems I always find. Holding the flowers and the box in one hand, I walk up the pathway and pull open the front glass door, looking around and still hating there is no security.

I jog up the steps, and my heart beats just a touch faster when I get closer and closer to her door. I knock once, and my palms get all sweaty. I have to laugh at myself for being so nervous to see her. "Coming." I can hear her voice, and the smile comes again without a second thought. The sound of her footsteps are coming closer and closer to the door.

The click of the lock flips, and the door swings open. Her eyes go wide when she sees me standing here. When I spoke to her last night before the game, I told her we would be arriving later in the afternoon, so she wasn't expecting me until tonight. "Oh my gosh." Her voice pitches, and her face goes into a full-blown smile, making her eyes light up bright. Neither of us takes the first step as we just look at each other. It's a weird thing, having all this courage through a phone to say what we feel and want and then being in front of the other person, not sure what to say or how to act. "You're home," she finally says after a couple of seconds. Her hand still on the doorknob, she looks so fucking beautiful with her hair piled on top of her head. I can tell that she just got out of the shower because the bottom hairs on her neck are still a little wet. Her face is free of any and all makeup, not that she wears much or that she needs it. She's wearing a short-sleeved dress, and her little bump seems bigger.

"We just landed," I say and then step into her, suddenly wanting to drop all this shit on the floor and just grab her face. "I thought maybe I would bring you flowers myself." I walk into the house and put the flowers on the counter next to the box. Looking around quickly, I see that there are five vases scattered around the room of the flowers I sent her when I was away. "I also brought you some pastries." She closes the front door, not saying anything, and I'm suddenly worried that maybe I did the wrong thing. Maybe I should have just gone home and then come over afterward. "I should have called," I say softly, "instead of just showing up." I wonder how fast I can get out of here without looking like an idiot. I mean, more of an idiot. "I'm really sorry for just showing up here." The pit of my stomach burns.

She walks to me, and I literally hold my breath, not sure what the fuck is going to happen. My eyes roam her face to see if maybe I misread the whole situation. Maybe she just wants me by her side for the baby. Maybe she got to know me, and she's over me. The maybes come barreling to me, but then just as fast as the pit in my stomach got there, it slowly goes away when I see the smile on her face never leaves, and her eyes light up.

"I'm really, really happy to see you." Walking, she stands in front of me, my heart beating faster and faster for a whole different reason. She puts her hands on my hips, then her eyes go down as she shyly admits the next part. "Really happy." My hands come up to cup her cheeks in them, then I move her face to the left as my lips find hers. The minute my tongue slips into her mouth, we both sigh. Her tongue fights with mine, and I thought I remembered what it was like to kiss her. I thought I knew what to expect, but I was wrong. It is just so much better. The burning in my stomach goes away. The tightness in my chest eases up just a bit, and I can finally breathe.

Her hands move from my hips to my back, and when she pulls me to her, I feel her stomach. I let go of her face, and we just look at each other. The lust and need is in both of our eyes. I put my hand on her stomach. "Hi," I whisper to my child, my hand rubbing her stomach and looking back up at her. "Hi," I repeat and see that her nipples are perky.

My lips go back to find hers, and she moans when I do this. Her back arches into me, my hands move from her stomach to her breasts, and I can't help but roll her nipples between my fingers. She lets go of my lips so she can moan. Her head falls back, and her eyes close. "Jillian," I say her name, and she opens her eyes halfway. "We should talk about this," I say, not wanting to go any further until she knows I don't want to just do this one more time.

"Yes," she says breathlessly. "We should talk." Her hands go to my hips. She bites her lip. "But can it be after you give me an orgasm?"

I smirk at her. She would never have admitted this to me before I left. "I can do that." I put my hand around her waist and pick her up. "Where?" I look around for a second before her hands come to my face, and she kisses the shit out of me. Her legs wrap around my waist, and my cock just wants out. Our kisses become more frantic, so I let go of her lips to ask her one question. "Couch or bed?"

THIRTY-TWO

JILLIAN

"COUCH OR BED?" He lets go of my lips long enough to ask me, and my head is swimming. I knew he was coming back today. But I was too shy to ask him to come over and see me right away, so I just left it in the universe.

The whole morning, I kept looking over at the clock and then at my phone and then back at the clock, wondering where he was. Wondering when I would see him, I finally gave up and took a long shower. I was slipping on my dress when he knocked on the door. My whole body went on alert when I saw him, and I was wet before he even said hello. The last five days of talking to him through the phone and admitting how I felt and listening to how he felt just made everything between us so much more real. "Baby." He attacks my neck. "Cock or bed?" he asks, and he laughs at his own joke.

I laugh out. "Cock," I confirm, pointing at the bed.

"Definitely cock." I can't think when his lips are on me.

He walks toward the bed and places me down on the edge of the bed, my legs opening for him. "God," he says when he sees my nipples are trying to rip through the dress. He leans in, taking one in his mouth, wetting my top. My head flies back as he goes from one nipple to the next. I put one hand in the back of me to hold me up as I look down at him. His hands roam up my bare legs, pushing the dress higher. I lift my hips and take charge, pulling the dress up and tossing it to the side.

"You were naked," he says, his eyes going a deep blue. His hands come up to cup my tits, rolling my nipples between his fingers. My eyes close, and my whole body wakes up and wants him to touch me. "This whole time."

He leans in and takes one of my nipples in his mouth. My eyes open to watch him go from one nipple to the next. "Michael." I say his name more as a plea than anything else. "I need…"

"What?" He looks up at me while biting down on the nipple in his mouth, and my hips fly off the bed. I've never in my life been this needy, like ever. "What do you want?"

"I need you to touch me," I plead breathlessly in a whisper as he kisses down my chest, stopping at my stomach. I sit up. "I know I look different," I say, swallowing the lump that is going to come up and ignoring the burning that is flowing up my neck.

He shakes his head as he kisses my stomach. "You look even better than you did that first time." He leans up to kiss my lips. "And you blew me away that first time.

This," he says, bending his head again. "Is the sexiest thing I've seen in my life."

I want to tease him, but he kisses my hip. "Lie back, baby," he tells me, and I lie back, looking at him. "I've dreamt about this moment," he says right before he licks my slit. "For a month." I want to watch him, but my eyes close as I just feel him. "You're so wet for me." I want to tell him all the things, but the only thing I can do is open my legs wider. His tongue licks up again, this time flicking my clit, then sucking it in.

"Michael." I lean up on one elbow to watch him between my legs. He slips a finger into me at the same time as his tongue enters me. "Yes," I say, my hand going to my nipple and then twisting it, making my toes curl.

"You are squeezing my fingers," he says to me, and I can't even focus as he finger-fucks me.

"Faster," I urge, lifting my hips to get him to go deeper into me. My arm falls down, and I'm on my back "More." I move my head side to side. "I need."

I can hear him chuckle as he licks up. "Michael." I say his name again. "I need your cock." I close my eyes as soon as I hear the words come out of my mouth, but I'm too far gone. "I need more." He stops licking, and I look down and see him stand, his eyes just watching me as he pulls his shirt out of his pants. "I really wanted to undress you," I say, but my hand slides between my legs. "But this whole week," I finally admit to him. "It's been crazy." My fingers slip inside me.

"Have you touched yourself?" he asks, unbuckling his belt, and all I can do is nod.

"Every night," I whisper out. "Sometimes twice." God, I wish I could shut up right about now. "I just." I stop talking when I hear his zipper go down. My body moves on its own as I sit up. My hand slips out of me as I frantically help him pull his pants down, and I suck his cock into my mouth the minute I slip his boxers down enough.

"Fucking Christ," he groans as I take him as deep down into my throat as I can with the taste of his precum on my tongue. I close my eyes as I suck his cock, another thing I've been dying to do. "I don't know," he says as my hand jerks him off at the same time as my mouth. "Fuck, you need to stop." I shake my head, not willing to let his cock go. I moan, moving my mouth up and down. "Jillian," he says my name, and when I look up, I can see that his head is back. His eyes close as his hips move. "I'm going to." I close my eyes as his hand goes to my head and he grunts out and empties himself into my mouth. I don't stop until the last drop, and when I do, I'm proud of myself.

"That was…" I say, and his eyes open as he takes me in.

"That was." He unbuttons his white shirt, and I have the chance to see his chest.

"I want to lick every single part of you," I declare, and my hand flies to my mouth as he laughs.

"Good," he says, shrugging off his shirt. "I plan to spend the whole day either buried in you." He kicks off his shoes. "Or with your pussy in my face." My eyes close, and I shiver at the thought of all that. "The only time I'm not going to be in you or tasting you," he says, and I open my eyes to see his pants fall to the floor. "Is when you eat."

My hand comes up to hold his cock, stroking him. "Much bigger than my vibrator," I say, and I really wish I would stop talking.

"Jillian," he says my name through clenched teeth. "I'm going to try to go slow."

"Don't," I say, letting his cock go and scooting back on the bed. "Please don't go slow or soft."

He crawls onto the bed. "Not this time." I put my feet on the bed, and my pussy opens for him. "I need it hard." I watch him kneel in front of me, his cock in his hand as he slides it up and down my slit, and my ass bounces up. "Michael," I hiss his name. "If you don't put that cock inside me." I glare at him as he smirks. "I'm going to throw you on this bed and take it myself. Actually." I sit up. "You sit down." I point at the bed.

"You want to ride," he urges, sitting down with his back to the headboard he bought me. "Far be it from me to say no."

I throw my leg over him to straddle, grabbing his cock in my hand. His hands go to my hips as I guide my pussy to his cock. I slide down his cock, so slow I feel every single vein. He fills me fuller than I've ever been filled. "Jillian." He hisses out my name when I sink all the way down, my ass hitting his thick legs. His hands go from my waist to my ass as he squeezes it in his palms. "Fuck, you are so tight."

"God," I say, grabbing his shoulders and rise up to the

tip and then sliding back down. "This is so much better," I moan, and his hands go from my ass back to my hips. "Than I remembered." I pant out as he takes a nipple into his mouth. "I feel so fucking full," I say as his hands go back to my ass, and he pushes me up off his cock, and then I fall down again. "It's so good." My head falls back as my body craves more of him.

My body takes over, and I start to move faster and faster on him, trying to get him deeper every single time I slam down on him. "Michael." I say his name in a pant, looking in his eyes. My mouth goes to find his. His tongue slips into my mouth as I rise up and down on him. This time, I go slower and take my time. His hands move from my ass to my tits, where he plays with my nipples, and I swear I can come with the way he rolls them. I don't want to let go of his lips, but I'm so close to finally coming. "I'm there," I confirm, the feeling starting in my stomach every time I rise up and then fall down on him. "So close."

"After you come." He takes a nipple in his mouth, and I swear my pussy clamps down on his cock. "I'm going to flip you over and fuck you so hard." I close my eyes as my toes curl, and I come all over his cock. I swear I can't move. I can't even see as I come and come and come on his cock. "You done?" he asks when I open my eyes, and I swear he picks me up by my hips and turns me around on my hands and knees, pulling me to the edge of the bed where he stands behind me. "Fuck, you look good with your ass up in the air for me," he says, smacking down on one ass cheek at the same time that he sinks into me in one long thick thrust. "Fuck," he mutters at the same time my eyes roll back in my head.

I open my hips wider. "Again," I say to him, one hand holding my chest up while the other slips between my legs. "Harder," I demand as he slams into me over and over again.

The sound of his skin slapping against mine fills the room, along with our heavy breathing. "Your pussy is like a vise," he says, and I want to suck his cock. "Squeezing me so tight."

"I'm going to come!" I exclaim as my hand moves back and forth against my clit. "Right there," I say, and he grabs me so tight and slams into me so hard I'm surprised I don't fly off the bed. It's also the exact thing I need to come again. "I'm coming." fisting the sheet in my hand.

"Me, too," he says as I come on his cock, and he plants himself in me. I can feel him pulsing inside me at the same time I squeeze his cock. I push back on him, and he groans out as I look over my shoulder at him, his eyes closed, his hands still gripping my hips. I know I'm going to have his mark on me, and it makes my pussy squeeze him again. His eyes open as he stares at me.

His chest has a sheen of sweat from fucking me. "You're fucking hot," I say to him, moving slowly forward and then pushing myself back on him. "I want you."

"You have me." His hands drop from my hips as I get up on my knees while he is still inside me. His chest to my back. "You have me," he repeats to me when I look over my shoulder at him. "You fucking own all of me." His lips find mine as his tongue comes out, and it takes a minute longer before he turns me onto my back and fucks me with everything that he has, and it's fucking glorious.

THIRTY-THREE

MICHAEL

"HARDER," SHE SAYS from beside me as I slide into her. I woke up five minutes ago, and her ass was pushing into me. My cock was already up and waiting to get back into her. My hand came up and cupped her tit as I played with her nipple. She moaned out right away, pushing her ass back into me. When I rubbed my cock up and down her slit, she was wet and ready, so I slid in softly. "Michael." She moans out my name. "Harder." She pushes back at me, and she squeezes my cock. I roll her nipples and pull just a touch making her back arch, and I know she's close. I've gotten to know all of her body in the last, close to twenty-four hours. After I had her twice in the bed, we took a shower where I had her again. It was a tight fit, but she bent over, and all I could do was slide into her. "Right there," she says, and I bury my face into her neck as she comes on me, and I pound into her harder and harder. The sound of slapping fills the room, but it's drowned out in her loud moans. When she goes limp beside me, I close my eyes and follow the hero over the cliff.

She moans contently and snuggles back into the bed. "That was better than last time," she mumbles out, and I laugh as I slide out of her and get off the bed.

"You've said that every single time." I walk back to the bathroom and wash myself off. I walk back into the room, and she hasn't even covered herself back up. Her naked body lies there teasing me.

She turns to look over at me. "I can feel your eyes on me." She laughs, turning back over and still not bothering to cover herself. "Don't you need protein or something?"

"What, why?" I chuckle and look around for my boxers, putting them on.

"You worked out for a good eight hours." She turns over to face me, putting her hand on her little bump. "That needs some sort of protein."

"You were there the whole time." I point at her, and she laughs.

"I was there, but I didn't do all the work." She stretches. "If anything, I might be dehydrated from all the orgasms I had."

I throw my head back and laugh. "I don't know why you are complaining, you asked for them."

"Oh, trust me." She smiles mischievously. "The last thing I'm going to do is complain."

I sit on the bed, leaning over and kissing her stomach. "Morning, baby," I say, and then she jumps up. My stomach rises to my throat as I think I hurt her, the fear running through me as I look at her.

Her eyes go wide. "Oh my God," she says, sitting up. "Oh my God." She puts her hand on her stomach.

"What is happening?" I ask, putting my hands on my head, looking around for the phone in case I have to call nine one one.

"I think the baby just kicked," she says with tears in her eyes. "Come here." She takes her hand off her stomach and motions to me to come to her. I get on the bed, going to her side, she grabs my hand and puts it back on her stomach.

"Is this normal?" I ask her, the need to have my father here with me to ask him questions just fills me. "Should I call my father?"

She puts her free hand on my face, cupping my cheek. "It's normal," she says softly. "Usually, it's just flutters, but today, when you said good morning, I felt a kick and it was so strong. It was the best fucking feeling."

My eyes fill with tears as I lean down. "Hey there, little one," I coo softly, and her stomach moves under my hand, and my reflex has me whipping my hand away from her stomach. "Oh my God," I say. "Do you think I poked him with…" My eyes go big. "I knew I should have gone soft." I shake my head as she laughs at me.

"It's perfectly fine to have hard sex," she assures me, putting her hand on her stomach and looking down, waiting for the baby to kick her again.

I get off the bed and go to my phone, grabbing it from the pocket of my pants. "What's the doctor's number?"

"We are not calling the doctor." She shakes her head,

moving her hand over her stomach to see if she feels the baby anywhere else. "The baby is very well protected."

"How do you know?" I ask her, putting my hands on my hips. "Who told you that?"

"Google," she says, getting up. "I googled it this week when I was using my vibrator." My mouth just hangs open. "The baby is very high up there, and you do have a big penis, but it's not that big." I roll my eyes at her, and before this, I would have probably debated on how big my penis is. "You are very well endowed," she says, trying to roll her lips to keep herself from laughing.

"Okay, that's enough." I hold up one hand and grab my phone, pulling up my father on text message.

"I can't even text my father." I look at her. "What the hell am I supposed to ask him? Did you bang Mom when she was pregnant?" I close my eyes when Jillian laughs. "I don't want to know that. I mean, I could ask Cooper." I tilt my head to the side. "But I don't want to know that either."

"Michael." Jillian says my name. "Trust me, sex during pregnancy is normal." I look at her and then down at her stomach. Her eyes go to her stomach as she puts two hands on her belly. "Tell your father, you are okay." I wait for her to say something or to feel something, and she doesn't. "I guess the baby likes your voice better." She steps to me and puts her hand on my chest. My eyes go down to look at her hand on me. "I'm okay." Her voice comes out softly. "The baby is okay."

"Are you sure?" I ask her. She smiles and gets on her tippy-toes and kisses my lips.

"I'm going to go to the bathroom, and then you can google," she teases, turning and walking to the bathroom.

I sit on the bed, opening my browser and asking the question. The bathroom door opens, and Jillian comes out wearing a robe. "Are you hungry?" she asks, and I look up.

"I am," I admit to her. "Do you want to get dressed, and we can grab something and head to my place?"

"Only if you promise me that you aren't going to freak out, and if I want to use your body and your big dick, you'll let me." I shake my head as she wraps her arms around my neck. "Promise me." And it's at that moment where I know I would promise her anything.

I push her hair over her shoulder. "I promise." I kiss her lips. "Now let's get dressed."

She slips on tights and a white tank top, her small belly sticking out. "You look sexy." I smack her ass when she comes next to me after I finish buttoning up my white dress shirt.

"You don't look so bad yourself." She laughs, grabbing a sweater and putting on her sneakers. "I'm ready."

We walk out of the apartment, and I grab her hand, slipping my fingers with hers. "I like this," she says softly when we walk toward my SUV. I open the door for her as she stands in front of me. "Can I kiss you?"

"Why would you even ask me that?" I look down at her, and she just shrugs, avoiding my eyes.

I put my hand under her chin and raise it. "You can kiss me any fucking time you want to." She leans in and kisses me, getting into the SUV and not saying anything more.

I get into the SUV, starting it, and something isn't sitting right with me. "Why would you ask me that?" I look over at her.

"I don't know." She mimics me, putting her back to the door. "I don't know the rules. I don't know if you want anyone to know we, you know." She uses her fingers, pointing at me and then to herself. "Are together." I watch her struggle with what to say, and I grab my phone and pull it out of my pocket and call her. She laughs, shaking her head. "What are you doing?"

"Well, you obviously have something to say, and you always tell me when you're on the phone." The ringing stops, and I can hear her voice in the phone as it goes to voice mail. "You going to tell me, or am I going to have to go into your house and call you?"

She shakes her head. "I don't even know how to explain it," she starts. "If people see us together, what are they going to think?" I look at her, confused. "Do you think if I wasn't having your baby, we would be together?" she finally says and takes a big exhale right before her eyes meet mine.

"Like if I wasn't having your baby, would you want to be with me?"

I hold up my hand. "Yeah, I got the gist of the question the first time you said it," I say. "Is that what you think?" I ask her, and she just shrugs.

"I have no idea what to think," she answers me.

"What would you say if I told you that I came to see you the week after?" I say, and she just looks at me, confusion filling her face. "The Sunday after I came here, and you weren't home." I admit it finally to her, "I waited for about an hour, and then my sister and my cousin convinced me that it was a bad idea."

"What?" she whispers.

"Yeah, they said it looked like I was a stalker and that your neighbors would most likely call the cops on me since I was sitting in my car that whole time." I shake my head. "I knew they were idiots. I even wanted to leave a note, but then Dylan said that it would scare you off."

She leans over the middle console and crushes her lips on mine. "For future reference," she says, her hand going to my cheek as she rubs it with her thumb. "Don't listen to your cousin."

I laugh. "Noted," I agree and push the hair away from her face. "Now, did that answer your question?" She nods her head. "Good." I kiss her again. "Now let's get some food." She sits back in her seat and fastens her seat belt. "Because there is more that needs to be said."

THIRTY-FOUR

JILLIAN

HE KISSES MY lips. "Now let's get some food." I sit back in my seat and fasten my seat belt. "Because there is more that needs to be said." I look over at him, not sure what more needs to be said. "Grab my phone," he says. "And check the Uber app and see if there is anything there you want to eat." Grabbing his phone I look at him for the code. "It's one two three four." I laugh.

I scroll the list, my mind still reeling from what he just said. He showed up at my house, waiting for me. I can't even believe I heard the words. "You showed up at my house." I repeat the words to him again, shock still in me.

He nods his head. "I got up that Sunday, and I was irritated that you didn't call me." He winks at me. "Since I rocked your world."

"Obviously." I roll my eyes, and he laughs.

He shrugs. "I just wanted to ask you why you didn't

call."

I look down at my belly, putting my hand on it. "Julia said I would look desperate if I called you the same day." He groans out. The feeling of disappointment comes back to me, just like that day when she said I shouldn't call him. I just wanted to talk to him and hear his voice. "I should have called," I admit to him softly.

He reaches over and brings my face to his for a kiss. "How about from now on, we don't listen to your sister or my sister?" He chuckles.

"Or your cousin," I add in, and he just nods, going back to his seat. I look over at him and change the subject. "What do you feel like eating?"

"You," he says, grabbing my hand from my lap and bringing it to his lips, my stomach feeling flutters again. Every single time he touches me, it's like the first time. It gets my heart going, and my body becomes alive.

I look back at him and then the list. "Pussy is not on the list." I smirk at him as he looks at me, smiling. "Sadly, neither is cock." I wink at him.

"Are you sure?" he jokes with me and pretends to scroll the list.

"Nope, nothing." I shrug. "I even checked under the dessert, and it's not there." He laughs out loud, looking over at me.

"So, what does that leave us with?" he asks as we make our way over to his place.

"This would go a lot faster if you just tell me what you want to eat," I say, and we toss an idea out, and by the time we park in his parking spot, the food is already on its way to us.

He gets out of the SUV, and I follow him meeting him in the back where the trunk is. He grabs his luggage, shutting the trunk and then looking at me. "Give me a kiss."

"I mean, when you ask like that," I say, walking to him and leaning my head back. His kiss is soft and quick, his hand grabbing mine as we make our way up to his place.

He unlocks the door, and just like the last time, I'm blown away. "I swear my whole apartment fits in your living room," I say, looking around. "I don't think I could ever get used to living here."

"Good," he says, pulling my hand toward the bedroom, and if I thought I couldn't get over the living room, I stop in my tracks at the bedroom.

"Holy moly," I gasp, looking around. The whole back wall looks like the headboard, the bed facing a fireplace with a television on top. I shake my head. "Where is your bathroom?" I ask him, folding my hand over my chest, and he just smirks and points at the door on the right-hand side. I walk forward, looking over my shoulder at him before walking over and opening the door and stopping in my tracks. "Shut the fuck up," I say, shaking my head and walking into the bathroom. "This is the size of three of my apartments." I go to stand in the middle of the marble bathroom right under a crystal chandelier. The shower is all glass and the size of my whole bathroom. I throw my head back when I think of how he had to get into my tub/shower and duck to get in.

"This is a bit bigger than normal," he says, and I turn to look at him. He leans against the doorjamb.

"How crammed did you feel in my shower?" I ask him, and he shakes his head smiling, not bothering to answer. "Be honest." The doorbell interrupts him. "Saved by the bell," I say, walking out of the bathroom.

He stops at the door on the way to the kitchen, grabbing the bag of food. I can not for the life of me get comfy in this house. I walk behind him as he makes his way to the kitchen, sitting at the big white counter. "Sit," he says, pointing at the chair.

He hands me my burger and fries, and I watch him open his, taking a bite and then getting up to go to the big double-door stainless-steel fridge. He grabs two bottles of water and comes back. "Thank you," I say, grabbing a bottle, taking a bite of my burger. "This is good."

"It is," he says, leaning over and kissing my neck. "Not as good as you are going to be on that couch after this."

"We are not getting on that couch." I look over to the white leather couch. "With grease on our hands."

He laughs. "Well, I won't be here long." He takes another bite of his burger and looks over at me. "I'm going house hunting tomorrow." My eyes go big. "My aunt set up five houses for me to see."

"Wow," I say. "That is a lot of houses."

He nods his head, taking a fry. "I want to discuss our relationship." I look over at him, my stomach starting to burn.

"And what relationship is that?" I ask him, trying to

get my heart to beat normally.

He looks over at me. "Well, I want to be with you," he says, and I can't help but smile shyly. "And from what you told me, you want to be with me."

I tilt my head to the side. "Did I say that?" I look around, pretending to think. "I don't know if I said those exact words." I laugh.

"I'm going to tell my parents we're together," he says.

"Isn't it going to be weird?" I ask him, wondering how they are going to take it.

"I don't think it's going to be weirder than this girl I met is having my baby," he says, and I can't help but laugh. "What about the baby?" His tone turns serious, and all I can do is look at him. "I don't want to keep that we are having a baby secret."

"Okay," I reply, not sure of what he's asking me.

"So I'd like to announce it on my Instagram," he says, and my eyes go big. "I spoke with Candace, who takes care of my social media. She's my uncle Evan's sister, and she's married to Ralph, who plays with me."

"I'm going to need you to make me a family tree," I joke, grabbing the water again and taking a sip while he laughs.

"I was thinking we can take some pictures and put out a statement on my page," he says, and I let it sit in my head. "Or we don't have to do it." He takes it back nervously. "I just don't want it to be a secret. I don't want you to be a secret or the baby."

I smile at him. "Well, when you put it like that." Leaning into him, I kiss his neck. "Let's do it."

"I'll speak with Candace," he says, getting up.

"I'm going to tell Julia and my mother," I say, and he nods his head.

"Also." He holds up a finger. "We have dinner with each other every night when I'm home, and we can."

I chuckle. "Okay, I'll have dinner with you."

"Second." He holds up another finger. "And we sleep together."

"I like that very much," I admit to him. "I think that should be number one."

He laughs. "Good, where do you want to sleep tonight?" He pushes off from the counter and cleans up where he was eating. "We can stay here, or we can go back to your place."

"Since we are compromising," I say, tapping my hand on the counter. "How about we alternate?"

"I'm going to be honest," he says, leaning against the counter facing me, folding his arms over his chest. "I don't give a shit where we sleep as long as you are beside me."

"I think my panties just melted off." I laugh at him, and he comes over to me, picking me up as if I weigh nothing. "Where are we going?"

"I'm going to see how melted those panties are." He carries me to his bedroom, where he gives me a thorough inspection.

I leave him in the shower, going to the bedroom wearing one of his T-shirts, when my phone rings from the kitchen. I walk out and look and see that it's Julia trying to FaceTime me. I click connect, waiting for her face to fill the screen. "Well, well, well," she says when she sees me. "If it isn't my long-lost sister." I throw my head back and laugh.

"It's been less than twenty-four hours." I look over at the clock on the wall and see that it's been over twenty-four hours.

"Last time I spoke to you," she says, sitting up on her couch. "Was when you said I'm going to take a shower and call you back." I roll my eyes. "That was over thirty-six hours ago."

"Michael showed up," I admit, walking back toward the bedroom. The shower is still running from when I left him in there.

"Okay?" She waits for it as I climb into the middle of his bed.

I roll my eyes at her, ignoring the way my body is reacting to this news. Ignoring the beating of my heart. Ignoring the heat that is flowing up my neck. "I'm not in love with him."

Julia just stares at me seriously and then throws her head back and laughs out loud. "If you weren't in love with him, you wouldn't be having his baby." I open my mouth to say something, and she holds up her hand. "I know, I know that you love the baby, but a little piece of you had to love him to even think about doing it alone."

"I mean, I obviously liked him, or I wouldn't have slept with him," I admit to her, and I hear the shower turn off. "But I'm not in love with him."

"Okay." She rolls her eyes. "Keep telling yourself that."

"I have to go," I say, annoyed as I sit in the middle of his bed.

"Say hi to the baby daddy for me," she says, and I quickly disconnect before she mentions I love him, and he hears it.

Looking up when I see him walking out of the bathroom with a white towel around his waist, I can still see little droplets of water on his chest, and I swallow. "I love you naked," he says, coming to the side of the bed and dropping his towel, showing me his cock. "But you're even sexier in my clothes." He gets into bed beside me, and I look into his blue eyes, and my heart stops in my chest at the same time I realize that I am, in fact, in love with him.

THIRTY-FIVE

MICHAEL

"HEY, DAD." I look at the phone when his face fills the screen. I can tell from the back wall that he is in the home gym.

"Hey, son," he says, and his face fills with a huge smile. "Where are you?"

I attach the phone to the plastic device that holds it up. "I'm in the car. I just left practice," I say, pulling out of the parking lot. "And I'm headed over to get Jillian so we can go look at houses."

"That sounds good," he says, and I look at him as I wait for him to finish because I know that he has more to say. "Your aunt sent me a couple of the houses that she picked for you."

"Yeah," I say, smirking, shaking my head looking at him, not that I'm surprised by any of this. In fact, I'm more surprised that he didn't get on a plane and fly out to visit them with us. "And?" I wait for it.

His face forms the same smirk I just gave him. "There is one I really like, but I'm going to hold off on my opinion until you two see the house," he says, making me laugh.

"That's a first," I tease, making him laugh.

"Did she agree to move in with you yet?" he asks, and I look at him.

"Dad, it's not that easy," I explain, my stomach burning. "We've only been dating for a week." I point out to him, and he actually rolls his eyes at me.

"I knew that I wanted your mother to live with me, and we weren't even dating," he says, and I shake my head. "We got married, and we weren't even living together."

"Yes, we were." I hear my mother's voice as she comes to stand by my father. He looks at her with so much love, his eyes have always been for her, and he would die without her.

"Your family didn't even know we were dating." My father puts his arms around her and brings her in to kiss her lips.

"This is very true," my mother confirms, looking at me. "Here is some crazy advice." Both my father and I groan out. "How about you just ask her?"

"That's not good advice," my father counters. "You just need to convince her that she needs to move in with you."

"Wow, this is all great advice," I tell them. "But I have to go."

"Call us when you make a decision about the house," my father says, and I disconnect the phone when I get back to my place. I take the elevator up to the apartment, and the minute I step foot into it, I can hear the television playing. "Hey," I say, walking into the kitchen and seeing her sitting on the bench. I wrap my arms around her, and she tips her head back, her eyes lighting up. "Missed you."

In the last week, we have alternated staying at her place and at mine, and when I have games, she opts to stay with me at my place so I don't have to travel so far. I never had such a connection with someone before. It feels like I've known her forever, like we've been together since we were younger. I can't explain it even if I tried to. "Hi." She kisses under my jaw. "Are you hungry?"

"I ate at the rink." I rub my nose to hers. "Did you fall back asleep when I left?"

She smiles. "I did, but the bed was cold without you." I hold her face in my hands, kissing her lips.

"We have to leave in ten minutes," I remind her, and her eyebrows shoot together. "We have three houses to visit today." I look around. "I hate this place," I say. "It's cold, and the only thing good about it is you sitting here."

"Well, when you put it like that." She gets up, and she is wearing my shirt, her stomach sticking out just a touch. "I'll come with you." She walks past me, and all I want to do is take her in my arms, so I do. My hands go straight to her ass. "If you continue doing that, we are not going to leave in ten minutes."

She pushes my chest away from her and then walks back to the bedroom. I follow her as she gets dressed next to the small bag she brought over yesterday. Just looking at the bag with her clothes in it gets my blood going, but I push it down, knowing that if she likes a house today, we are going to have to have a whole different conversation, and it's a conversation that I'm not going to lose.

"So what's in door number one?" Jillian looks over at me as we sit in the SUV and head to my least favorite house of the bunch.

"House number one is six bedrooms, ten bathrooms," I say, looking over at her, and she just looks at me with her mouth hanging open. "A media room."

"You lied to me," she huffs out, and I'm taken aback by what she just said. "We aren't going to look at houses," she says. "We are going to look at mansions." I laugh nervously, grabbing her hand and bringing it to my lips. When we pull up to the house, I look at her reaction, just in case she actually likes it and doesn't want to tell me. I can tell from her face she isn't impressed, and I breathe a sigh of relief. The whole time I watch her face to see if she likes it when she stands in the middle of the monstrosity of a house. "What does one do with all this space?" she asks, going around in a circle. "How long does it take someone to clean?"

I laugh at her. "If someone buys this house." I look around. "I can guarantee that they have money to hire a cleaning lady."

"How much is this house?" she asks, and I smile and look away. "Michael."

"Five point two," I say, watching her face.

"Million dollars?" she gasps, and the fact she still

doesn't know how much I make is refreshing. The fact she doesn't know what my family is worth is even bigger.

"Okay, let's go check out house number two." I hold out my hand, and she grabs it.

"What are the other two worth?" she asks, and I shake my head, opening the SUV door for her. I don't tell her because the third one is the house I want. But I'll only get it if she likes it because if I have my way, she's going to be living there with me. "What did you do today, Jillian?" She mimics a conversation that she is going to have. "I went to see million-dollar homes wearing eight-dollar Gap flip-flops."

When we pull up to the second house, she has the same look as the last one. It's the same as the first house. But when I pull up to the house I want, I look over at her and see that her eyes glisten. "This house only has five bathrooms," I say, and she shakes her head, getting out.

"You know you're slumming when your house only has five bathrooms," she jokes as we walk up the circular walkway. The white two-story house has a great layout plan, and if I have my way, lots of rooms to fill up. "I like that little balcony." She points up at the balcony on the second floor. "This house also doesn't look huge," she says, and when she walks in and gasps. It might look small from the outside, but the minute you walk in, you are greeted with the big family room that goes all the way to the back The whole back wall is windows, showing you the backyard. "I take it back." She looks around, seeing that the stairs are on the left to go upstairs, and you can look down from upstairs. On the right-hand side is the dining room, and she walks over to it to peek inside it. I don't say anything the whole time. I watch her eyes as we move from room to room.

The house is open concept, another thing I love about it. "So what do you think?" I ask her when we stand in the middle of the kitchen. That one has a massive island, exactly like I had growing up, which pulled me to this house even more.

"I think it's stunning," she says, her eyes lighting up. "And I like it better than the other two."

"Do you see yourself living here?" I finally take the leap and ask her, and she just looks at me. "Do you see yourself living here?" I ask her again.

"With you?" She points at me. "One day on, one day off." I look at her dressed in black pants and a white button-down long top that shows off her belly just a bit. Her hair is piled on top of her head, and she is the most beautiful woman I've ever laid eyes on. The fact that I get to hold her hand at night and share a life with her is more than I can thank anyone for.

"No." I shake my head and my heart speeds so fast I'm afraid of everything that is happening right now. "I mean, you move your stuff in here with mine, and we share the house."

"I'm a teacher." She points at herself. "I can't afford this house."

"But I can," I counter. She puts her hands on her hips, and I hold up one hand to stop her. "I know you don't care what I make."

"I don't know what you make," she answers honestly.

"I mean, you play a professional sport. How much can you possibly make?"

"I make enough to afford this house for us." I try to shy away from what I make a year.

"You want to live together?" she asks, looking around. "Like together together?"

I walk to her. "I want to move into this house," I say when I get in front of her, and she looks up at me. "I want to come home to you every single night," I explain. "I want to get up in the morning and have your stuff on the counter with my stuff. I want us to get dressed in the same room and have all of our stuff mingled together." My hands cup her face. "I want to bring the baby home here and grow together as a family." She blinks away tears. "I want us to build a home together." My thumb grabs the tear that escapes her eye. "I want it all, Jillian, and there is no one in the world I want to do it with besides you." I kiss her lips, feeling her hands going to my hips. "What do you say, Jillian?" I question when I let go of her.

"I say that if someone would have told me six months ago that I would meet this hot-as-balls guy…" I chuckle at the way she calls me hot. "By accident." She laughs. "Have the best sex of my life." I smile as I look into her eyes. "And then get pregnant and have a baby with him, I would have told them they were crazy." I take a deep breath. "But I guess the universe had other plans for me." I let her speak, not interrupting her because I just laid it all out for her, and it can be a lot to take in. "I don't suppose you'll let me contribute for the house." I glare at her, and she laughs. "And I don't suppose you'll let me pay for anything." She shakes her head. "Are you sure this is really what you want?"

"There are two things I've ever been sure about in my life," I say. "One, that I would play hockey." I laugh. "I mean, at times I was fed up with it, but I couldn't deny how much I loved to play it, and the second is that there is no one in this world I want beside me but you."

"Oh, that's smooth." She smiles. "And you said you had no game."

I laugh, thinking back on the first date we had or the accidental date we had. "Only for you."

"This is insane," she says, and I just look at her. "I mean, not as insane as sleeping with a guy on the first date and then having his baby, but this has to be number two." I want to tell her that we can be totally insane and get married, but one thing at a time.

"So what do you say, Jillian?" My voice goes soft as I get lost in her eyes. "Want to build a home with me?"

She looks down, and for one split second, I'm afraid she's going to say no. But when her eyes look back up into mine, I find peace. "Fine."

THIRTY-SIX

JILLIAN

I LOOK DOWN at my belly, feeling the kick our child is giving me. I look up into his eyes. The only thing I can say is "Fine." The smile fills his face as he grabs me around my waist and pulls me to him. "Your child is happy with this decision."

His eyes go wide as he puts me down and gets on his knees in front of my stomach, something that he does every morning and night. He puts his hand on the side of my stomach. "We got a house." The baby kicks him as if he understands. "And I can't wait to bring you home and show you all the things."

I look down at him. "Don't forget to mention we only have five bathrooms," I joke with him, and he laughs. I grab his face in my hands. "I wouldn't care if we had five bathrooms or one bathroom." I want him to know. "I wouldn't care if we had to live in my one-bedroom condo."

"I know," he says softly. "It's one of the things I love most about you," he shares, and the only thing I can hear is I love you. I'm about to say something to him when his phone rings. He pulls it out of his pocket as if he just didn't mention the love word. "It's my dad," he says, getting up and pressing the connect button.

He puts his arm around me, pulling me to him as Max's face fills the screen. "Hey, you two," he says, and I wrap my hands around Michael's waist.

"Hey," Michael greets. "We have some news for you guys," he says, looking at me, then back at his father.

"You guys are getting married!" Max shrieks out with a megawatt smile.

"No," Michael denies. "Not yet." My head whips to Michael. "One thing at a time."

"I'm sorry, what?" I say, and they both ignore me.

"We are moving in together," Michael says, and Max claps his hands.

"Allison!" he yells. "They found a house." He comes back to us. "Which one?"

"The white one," he says, and his father just smiles.

"I had a feeling that would be the one you picked," he says, and Allison comes into the picture.

"Did you guys pick a house?" she asks, standing in front of Max. Michael tells her all about the house and starts to show her the backyard.

"There is no pool?" Max asks.

"No," Michael says.

"You need a pool," he says, and Michael nods his head. "I'm going to call the one who did Cooper's pool."

"How much is a pool?" I ask, and he just shakes his head.

"It'll be our gift," Allison says, and I just look at the both of them.

"A pool," I say, not sure I heard them.

"And a tree house," Max counters. "We also have news."

"If you tell me Mom is pregnant," Alex says from behind them somewhere, "I'm going to stab myself in the eyeball and hopefully bleed out." I hear a laugh I recognize in the back, but I just listen to Allison laugh.

"What's the news?" Michael asks.

"We bought a house," he says, and I look over at Michael, who also looks confused.

"You're selling the house?" he asks his father, and he just shakes his head.

"No, this is your home," he says and then smiles at Allison. "We bought a house in Dallas," he says, and my mouth opens. "Zoe sent us one of the listings that you got."

"Which house?" Michael asks and I put my hands on my head.

"The one with the pool and the slide," he announces happily.

"The one with ten bathrooms," I say, shocked. "That house is massive."

"It's a little bit smaller than the one we have," Alex says, then I see Alex's face come into the screen. "Did you guys pick the one with the big kitchen?" Michael nods, and I'm shocked when I see Julia's there. I grab the phone from Michael.

"What the hell are you doing there?" I ask her, shocked. "You said you were spending the weekend with your friend."

"I am spending it with my friend." She laughs. "Alex invited me for the weekend."

"Don't worry," Max says. "We are bringing her back tomorrow."

"Bringing her back?" I say. "How, carpool?"

"No." Alex laughs. "God, no, we have the plane booked."

"Yeah, of course you guys do," I say, shaking my head. "This is a little bit too much," I mumble, and Michael grabs the phone from me.

"Okay, I'm going to let you go, see you guys tomorrow," he says, putting the phone down and then looking at me.

"Ever since I found you again," I say. "It went from snail pace to a hundred."

"We need to call your mother and tell her about the house," he suggests, and I just look at him. "She needs to know that I'm going to take care of you." I can see the struggle that he is going through, and I walk over to him.

"Why would you even say that?" I ask. "She knows you're going to take care of me." I look around. "I don't think she knew it would be in a million-dollar house, but she knew," I reassure him.

He puts his hands on his hips, looking at me. "Is that a bad thing?"

"How spoiled is our baby going to be?" I ask him a

question that I don't even want to know. I don't even bother to wait for him to answer it. He just smiles at me, the smile that makes me weak in the knees. The smile that makes my heart speed up and makes whatever is going on around me not even matter. The smile that I wake up to and go to bed with. "I love you," I finally admit to him. He's about to say something to me, and I hold up my hand. "And not because of your family or who you are. But because all you want to do is make me happy. All that you have done this whole time is put the baby and me before anyone and anything."

"With every single fiber of my being," he says, pushing my chin up with his finger to look at him. "I love you." He kisses my lips. "I think the earth shifted the night I met you for the first time, and then when I found you again, it's as if my life had a purpose. It's so strange how you can love someone so much yet be afraid at the same time." I put my hand up to his face. "Thank you, Jillian, for giving me the world."

I shake my head. "See," I say, getting on my tippy-toes. "That's smooth."

He throws his head back and laughs. "I'm really going to have to bring the big guns out when I propose."

"Can we calm down and do one thing at a time?" I say to him, but if he asked me, there is only one answer I would give him, and that would be a yes.

"Yes, one thing at a time." He agrees with me. "First, we call my aunt and make an offer on the house." I nod, and he picks up his finger. "Then maybe I can persuade you to have sex with me in the middle of our new kitchen."

I shake my head. "I'm not having sex with you in the middle of a house that we don't actually live in."

"What if they accept the offer?" he asks, and I glare at him.

"Fine." He puts up his hands. "Have it your way. We'll just have sex in the SUV." He turns, picking up his phone. I walk back to look at the backyard, and I have to admit having a pool will be kick-ass.

The phone in my pocket beeps, and I take it out. Seeing it's a text from Julia.

Julia: This house is insane.

Julia: They literally just bought a house on the phone.

I laugh, turning to look at Michael.

Julia: Congrats on making it Instagram official.

Me: What do you mean?

Julia: Go check out your man's Instagram.

I quickly open Instagram, and there it is at the top of my newsfeed. A picture of the ultrasound with Baby Horton written under it.

Michael Horton: Baby Horton coming off-season. Jillian and I couldn't be happier to welcome our little one. He or she is already loved more than we can say. Thank you to my girl for giving me the world.

I wipe the tear away from my cheek as I finish reading it, and he gets off the phone. "It's ours," he says, and I just shake my head and hold up my phone.

"You announced our baby." My voice comes out a bit shaky, and the smile fills my face. "And you called me your girl?"

"Well, you are my girl," he says, putting the phone in his back pocket.

I walk to him. "How official is this our house?" I ask, and he just smirks.

"Official enough," he says. "The owners don't even live here, and all this furniture is staged." I look around the house.

"So no one would care if we had sex on the table?" I point over to the table. "Or the couch."

"Or the beds." He comes to me, picking me up. "Or the showers," he says, walking back up the stairs. "We can stay here all night and do every single surface."

"Challenge accepted," I respond, and we do spend all night here. Well, almost all night, we do fall asleep in my bed many hours later.

THIRTY-SEVEN

MICHAEL

"WHAT TIME IS everyone going to be here?" Jillian sticks her head out of the walk-in closet, and all I can do is smile at her. She's fucking beautiful. "Don't you look at me like that, Michael Horton." She is also very feisty these days, and I don't know if I blame her. She is due in six weeks. "Do you not see what state I'm in?" She points at her belly. "There is no more room for this child to grow into, but according to Alex, you had a big fat head, so I'm going to be giving birth to a turkey."

I get off the bed and walk over to where she is standing in her bra and panties. "You look beautiful." She glares at me. "And both Julia and Alex said you don't even look pregnant from the back." Her look goes from a glare to a death stare.

"Speaking of them…" She looks around when she hears voices. "Are they here?" She grabs a robe and heads out of our bedroom. It took a month for us to close on the house, and by the time we closed, the pool was already installed and working. In that month, we would sit down and go through pictures on Pinterest. Little did she know that I would send everything to my mother. When we got the keys to the house, and we came over, she was shocked but not surprised that I made it happen.

"Julia?" she calls her name over the railing.

"Yeah," Julia says from somewhere in the house. "I'm in the west wing," she jokes, and my laughter is taken away when Jillian looks over at me. "I brought you lemon cake with blueberries."

"She better," Jillian huffs, turning to me. "Are you not going to kiss me?" She looks at me almost as if she is going to cry. "You didn't even kiss me good morning."

"Baby," I say, taking her in my arms. "I said good morning when I kissed you awake." I kiss her lips. "You also said if I took my cock out of you, that you would break it off." I push into her so she can feel said cock.

"You know I love you," she says softly, kissing my neck, and her hands start roaming.

"If you finish that sentence," Alex warns, coming out of one of the bedrooms she deemed hers, "I'm going to jump over this railing." She walks past us. "Seriously, you two. Like, can you not leave her alone?" she huffs, walking down the steps. "I caught you two going at it in the kitchen."

"It's our house!" I yell at her.

"Well, people eat on that counter," she retorts, walking downstairs.

"Why are you here?" I shout, then stop when I feel

kisses on my neck.

"You're sexy when you huff and puff," she says, turning and waddling down the stairs. I shake my head and look up at the ceiling.

"Why did we say it's okay for our sisters to come and go?" I put my hands on my hips and look down at my girl.

"Michael," she says when she gets to the last step. "Alex lives in New York, and Julia is here all the time because you don't want me alone when you aren't here."

I walk down the stairs and into the kitchen. "Eww," Julia says. "Go put a shirt on. Why are you coming into the kitchen naked?" Alex and Julia sit at the counter eating cereal out of the box with their hands.

"I'm wearing shorts," I point out. "And my woman likes my chest," I say, looking at Jillian, who just nods. I'm about to say something else when the front door opens. "It's like Grand Central Station." I grab a coffee cup and feel lips on my back and look over to see Jillian smiling at me.

"Why aren't you dressed?" I hear my mother's voice and put my head back.

"It's nine o'clock," I say, pouring the coffee for myself.

"Michael," my father says from behind my mother. "Your sister-in-law is sitting right there, and you are shirtless."

"Not sister-in-law," Julia denies. "He didn't put a ring on it. I don't even know what to call myself, so it's baby momma's sister." She shrugs. "And I'm uncomfortable with him not being dressed."

"I feel the same," Alex says, looking over at my parents. "I mean, how would you feel if I walked around without a shirt?"

"Dad," I say, looking at him, and he just glares at Alex.

"I'm not going to." Alex holds up her hands. "Now, are we ready for the glam?" She claps her hands, and I look over at Jillian, who just stares at her. "It's your baby shower. You didn't think we wouldn't have a glam squad coming."

"I love glam squad," Julia says, getting off her stool.

"Since when do you love glam squad?" Jillian laughs, shaking her head. "I have to eat, or I'll be hangry," she says, and my mother comes over to grab her.

"We have everything set up at our house." She looks at Jillian, who looks at me. "The party planners are already setting up, and the team is due to be there in twenty minutes. We have all the food set up in the kitchen."

"I thought we said low-key baby shower?" Jillian reminds her, and Julia can't help but laugh. Jillian looks over at her and glares. "We sat down and said low-key, just family."

"Yup," my mother says. "We are just a touch over fifty…" She trails off when Jillian's eyes get bigger.

"Do you want to just get in the truck in your robe?" Alex says, trying to change Jillian's mind. "Since your outfit is already there."

"It's so pretty," Julia says, and Jillian looks over at me.

"Go have fun," I say, smiling, the knot forming in my stomach. "It's for the baby."

"I can't wait for when the baby is here, and none of you use that excuse." She grabs a piece of cake. "The baby is up," she says, and my mother puts her hands on her stomach and then gets tears in her eyes.

"Oh, here we go," Alex says. "I'm going to get my bag." She leaves the kitchen, followed by Julia. Jillian just stands there eating her cake while my mother and father both try to feel the baby.

"It's like *National Geographic*," Jillian says, eating another piece of cake. "What are you going to be doing while I get glammed up?"

"My dad and I are going to put the crib together." I point at my dad, even though we are not going to be putting the crib together.

"Okay," Julia says, coming down the stairs. "I brought you a dress, so you don't have to leave your house in your robe like Tony Soprano."

"Thank you." She grabs the dress, changes, and in five minutes, she's kissing my lips and heading out the door.

"You ready?" My father looks over at me, and I nod. "I just have to get dressed. Where are we meeting this guy?"

"Matthew's place," he says, and I look over at him. "You didn't think Matthew wouldn't have gotten a place here." He shakes his head. "His grandchildren are here."

"Oh my God, how many people are actually coming to the baby shower?"

"Fifty," he says. "Women plus the men."

"She's going to lose it." I shake my head.

"Well, your mother hired Erika as the party planner," he says, and I put my hand to my mouth. "Yeah, she's not going to be happy." We walk out of the house and head toward my uncle Matthew's new house, and four hours later, I'm walking into the baby shower.

"Oh my God," I mumble to myself when I walk up the driveway, and there is a balloon display next to the door in yellow and green. I push open the door, and I can hear people chattering already.

In the middle of the foyer with the high ceilings, a balloon pyramid is coming down with a teddy bear dangling. There is a path of roses that leads you to the backyard, and if I thought inside was something, nothing could prepare me for outside.

"Holy shit," Cooper blurts, coming to me. "Did you see outside?" He shakes his head. "Your mom went all out."

"I thought mine was extreme," Erika says. "This tops that."

"Dear God," I say. "How is Jillian?" I ask, looking around.

"Beaming," Erika assures me, and they both walk away.

"There he is." I hear my grandfather and look over at him as he walks toward me from the stairs. He grabs me by my neck like he's done from when I was younger.

"Hey, Grandpa," I greet, hugging him. "Did you guys just get in?"

"We did with Dylan," he says. "It's the only reason

Alex picked us up." He laughs. "She almost took off without him."

"What did he do?" I ask, shaking my head. It's not a party if Alex and Dylan are not arguing.

"Something about her dressing appropriately for a baby shower." I shake my head, and we walk out of the house together.

To the side is a wall of balloons spelling OH BABY in big letters and standing in front of them getting pictures taken is my girl. She's wearing a mint green dress that is off the shoulder and ruffled across her chest and goes tight all the way to her knees and ruffles. Her hair is long and curled, and she smiles at the photographer.

"There he is." I look over and see Dylan there. He walks to me wearing dress pants and a white button-down shirt rolled at the sleeves. "The dad." He slaps my arm, "You ready?" he asks, and I tap my pocket.

"Oh, good, you're here," my mother says, coming up to us. "Dylan, you look skinny." She shakes her head, and he laughs. "Alex told me to tell you that. You look fine." She then turns to me. "You need to go and take some pictures with Jillian." She points toward my girl, and I look around. I walk to her, and when she sees me, her whole face lights up.

"Hey," I say, leaning down and kissing her lips. "You look…"

"It's all glam." She laughs. "Did you look at all of this?" She looks around the backyard. "I had a feeling that your mother's low-key and my low-key were two totally different keys." She shakes her head.

I laugh and look at her while the guy takes pictures. "Everyone that we love is here," I say, looking around at the tables scattered all over the lawn. My aunts and uncle are all around, and so is Jillian's mom, who stands with Julia as they talk to my uncle Matthew.

"Look here," the photographer says.

"You having fun?" I ask, and she smiles big, nodding.

"The baby has been very active." She puts her hands on her stomach. "I'm afraid that this baby is going to love parties."

"That isn't a bad thing," I say, the collar at my neck getting tighter even though there are two buttons open. "I love you," I say, and she looks up at me, smiling.

"I love you, too," she says, and the photographer just keeps snapping pictures.

"When I was younger…" I start, and the whole speech that I planned before is out the window. "God, I'm messing this up," I say, and she just tilts her head. "I went over this with my father today." I put my hand in my pocket and take out the red box. "Jillian." I get down on one knee. The gasp and shock from everyone who didn't know, which is almost everyone, fills the backyard. Her hands go to her mouth. "There is no one else I want beside me for the rest of my life," I vow. "There is no one else in this whole world who can complete me the way you do. When I come home every single night, my heart settles down just from looking at you." I look down and then look up. "Grow old with me, Jillian." I smirk at her. "Will you marry me?"

"Oh my God," she says, looking around. "You don't

have to do this."

"I know, I don't have to. I want to. There is nothing more I want in my life than to have you as my wife."

"Is she going to say no?" I hear Alex who looks over at Julia, who just smiles.

"Nah, she's too in love with him to say no," Julia says, shaking her head.

"So what do you say?" I look at her, and she bends down, putting her hands on my face.

"You can't take it back," she warns, kissing my lips.

"Never," I assure her, slipping the ring on her finger.

"I guess this means I'm his sister-in-law." Everyone chuckles at Julia's remark as I stand and take Jillian in my arms.

"Who knew a blind date with Zander would lead to the love of my life," she says, looking down at the ring on her finger. "Later, we can discuss how much this ring cost."

THIRTY-EIGHT

JILLIAN

"HOW DID THEY take it?" Julia asks from her side of the table while picking at the fruit bowl I just set out. It's a nice day, so we are lounging by the pool area.

I shrug. "I think good. What was I supposed to do? Maternity leave was six weeks, and I would have to be back right at the start of school." My voice trails off. "I just don't know how I would be able to leave the baby that soon."

"Hey," Julia says. "You have the opportunity to stay home, you stay home."

"I want to be a stay-at-home mom," Alex says from the couch area right off the table. When the pool was installed, I thought it was nice, only to come home two days later to find another construction crew. This time, they were making a shaded area for the baby. When that was done, Michael had someone come in and do a whole kitchen area because heaven forbid there isn't a sink and fridge out there.

The back door opens, and I look up to see Michael in shorts and a top with a white baseball hat. "There's my girl." Walking to me, he bends to kiss my lips and then rubs my stomach.

"Whoa," Dylan says from behind him, dressed in the same attire since they went to play golf this morning. "That is a lot of skin." I sit back in the chair and rub my stomach. I'm seven days overdue and miserable. I swear I don't know how much longer I can do it. He puts his hands on his hips. "Can that like explode at one point?" He does the sound of a bomb going off, making me chuckle and look down.

"You're such an idiot." Alex sits up and comes to sit next to me.

"It's an honest question, Alex," he says, and she shakes her head, grabbing his hat off his head and then walks over to the pool. "Alex," he calls her name, and she looks over, right before she steps into the pool. "The washing machine shrank your bottoms again." We laugh at him while she flips him the bird.

"How are you feeling?" Michael sits in the chair next to me and grabs a strawberry.

"Babygeddon is in your hands," Julia says, getting up. "I'm going to take a nap." She gets up and walks into the house. Ever since my due date has come and gone...actually, when I turned thirty-six weeks, it's been all hands on deck. Michael refuses for me to be alone at all. If I'm up, someone has to be up with me. If he's not with me, he has someone come and sit with me. Come to think of it, it's the only thing we argue about.

Dylan gets up from his chair to come eat some fruit with us at the table. "Where is your necklace?" He tries not to laugh.

"That was a good idea," Michael defends, shaking his head while I glare at him. The day he brought it home was the day we had our first full-blown, slamming-the-door-at-him sort of fight. I didn't talk to him for a full twenty-four hours, and it was hell for both of us.

"Bringing me a Life Alert necklace was the stupidest thing you've ever done," I hiss at him.

"It was in case you fell, and I didn't hear you." Michael tries to plead his case again, but I stand in front of him.

"Michael, if I fell, the house would shake," I grit between clenched teeth and start to storm away when I feel a gush come out.

"Oh my God," I say mid-step. Michael springs out of his chair. Alex stops moving and looks over, and Dylan flies out of his chair.

"What is that?" Dylan points at the puddle of water around my feet and running down my legs. He puts his hands to his mouth and gags. "I'm going to throw up." Michael just stands there, his face turning white like a ghost. "Oh my God, why is it still coming out?"

"Would you knock it off?" Alex hits his arm with his own hat, coming to me, a towel wrapped around her body.

"It's gushing out of her," Dylan says. I'm still standing in shock, looking down to make sure I didn't imagine it. Michael hasn't moved either, and his color is getting whiter. "Is it pee?"

"Her water just broke," she says without panic in her voice. She puts her hand in mine. "Let's go get you dressed." She looks over at Michael. "You come with me." Alex then looks at Dylan. "You start the phone chain." He just looks at her. "Call my mother, and she'll start it." She turns back to me and smiles to comfort me. "How are you doing?" she asks as she walks with me into the house. The whole time, water keeps leaking out.

"My water broke," I say, shocked, and I feel like I'm in a daze while we walk to my bedroom.

"Julia!" Michael yells from the hallway, and when she doesn't answer after the first time, he yells her name again. She comes out of the room, and I can imagine her annoyed expression. "It's time."

I stand in the middle of our bedroom, looking over at Michael, who is standing with his hands on his hips. The sound of Julia running to us fills the hallway. "Oh my God, why isn't she dressed?"

"I'm getting her dressed," Alex says, walking to the closet and grabbing me a big dress. "Michael, you need to load the car."

The sound of running up the stairs causes us to all look over. "Your mother is on her way," Dylan says, huffing out.

"I need to shower," I finally say, and all eyes are looking at me. "We had sex this morning." I look at Michael while the other three just groan.

"What the hell is wrong with you?" Dylan mumbles beside him. "You can't keep it in your pants. Look at her.

Does she look like she wants to have sex with you?"

"Enough," Alex says when the front door opens, and the sound of more feet fills the house.

"What's going on?" Allison says, pushing through Dylan and Michael to get to me. "Why isn't she dressed and in the car?"

"She needs to shower because Michael had sex with her this morning." Dylan fills them in, and I close my eyes from embarrassment but also the pain that shoots through my vagina. I put my hand on my stomach, and it's hard as a rock.

"That is probably what started the labor," Max says, as if this is an everyday thing. Out of all of us, I would never imagine Max and Alex to be the calm, cool ones. "We did the same thing with Michael."

Dylan puts his hands to his mouth again. "This time, I'm really going to be sick." He gags.

"There are things you share," Alex says with clenched teeth. "And there are things you never ever say in your whole life." She points at him. "That is one of them."

I pant through the pain, and when I open my eyes, I look at Allison. "That was a contraction." She nods her head and looks over at Michael.

"Start the clock," she tells him, and he takes out his phone.

"Should we call an ambulance?" Dylan asks with his phone in his hand as he contemplates calling 911. "I think we need like a police escort or something." He looks over at Max, who just nods and takes out his phone.

"I'm going to call Matthew." The whole family is

on baby watch with us, and his uncle Matthew was not kidding when he said they would take their vacation in Dallas. The whole clan is here, and that is a lot of people.

"No!" we all yell at him, and he looks at us.

"We need to just get her in the car and then we can go," Allison says, and I nod. "Let's just throw this dress over her and get her in the car."

"Can I please shower?" I look at her. "I smell like coconut, and I'm lathered in oil. They might think I'm a stripper."

"Doubtful," Dylan says, and we all glare at him. "Who would be stripping past their due date?" He tries to take it back. "They stop at least a couple of months before."

"Of course you would know this." Alex glares at him, shaking her head. "Why don't you get one of your stripper girlfriends on the phone and ask her."

"I don't have a girlfriend." He smiles at her proudly.

"You two," Max says to them. "Do this later."

I walk to the bathroom, turning on the shower. "I really don't think that is a good idea," Michael says, standing at the doorway. "Like I don't have any ideas, but I'm sure doing that is not good."

"It's going to take me two seconds," I say, and I close my eyes because another contraction comes. I focus on my breathing like they taught me during Lamaze class. "That was not too bad," I say, untying my top and bottoms. "Go make sure that everything is in the car."

"Dylan and my father are doing that," he says. "I'm not leaving your side."

I step into the shower and rush to get out. When I

wrap myself in the towel and rub down my legs, I notice blood. I don't want to say anything, but Michael notices also. His tone is tight and tense. "I'm giving you five seconds and then I'm carrying you out of here naked." I don't argue with him because even I'm starting to worry. Slipping my panties and the dress on, I walk out but then stop midway when another contraction starts. "She's doing it again," Dylan says from the hallway. He runs his hands through his hair. "We really should get a police escort." He looks at Max. "We can name-drop."

"She's not the president of the United States," Alex says, and I look up and see her dressed also. "Let's just get her in the car."

We get outside, and they get me into the car. I look over at Julia, who is wiping tears away. "Call Mom," I say.

"I've already sent someone to pick her up," Max tells me. "She is going to meet us at the hospital." I look up at him, and tears run down my face. "Now, let's get me a grandbaby, shall we?"

"Yes," I agree and get into the back seat with Michael next to me. While Allison and Max drive us to the hospital, I have two more contractions. Max pulls up to the front of the hospital.

My mother is there waiting for me with a wheelchair. Nervousness is running through her when she sees me. "Hi, baby," she says softly when I sit in the wheelchair. "Are you okay?"

"I'm ready to have a baby," I say, and she holds my hand as Michael pushes me into the hospital. "Where is your mom?" I look at Michael, who looks behind him.

"She." He hesitates. "She didn't want to overstep, so she is going to wait with my dad," he says, and I smile and look over at Allison, who is trying not to cry as she stands next to Max. His arm is over her shoulder.

"Allison," I call out her name. "Get over here with us." She looks up at Max with the biggest smile and lets him go.

"Are you sure?" she asks, standing next to Michael. "I don't want to be in the way."

"I wouldn't have it any other way," I assure her and then stop when I get another contraction. This time, I have to groan out my pain.

When we get into the delivery room, the nurse hands me a gown, and when I have to stop and bend over, she stops talking. "We are going to page the doctor and see how far along she is." She looks over at me. "When did the contractions start?"

"I've had back pain for the last two days," I admit and look over at Michael, who just glares. "But it wasn't like a stabbing pain."

"We'll get the doctor in," she says and walks out of the room.

"Michael Horton," Allison says, putting her hands on her hips. "You change that face right now."

"She was in pain," he counters, and I get on the bed with my mother, putting on my hospital gown.

"You chose a lively one." She smiles at me as she holds my face. "He loves you fiercely."

"He better," I say, looking down at my ring he gave

me seven weeks ago. "Look at what he did to me?" I point at my stomach that is so low I'm surprised I was able to walk. "And look at his fat head."

My mother laughs. "He doesn't have a fat head." She gets me into bed and looks down to see that my legs are tinted with blood.

"She's bleeding," she says out loud, shocked, and I look over at Michael who at this point looks like he's shaking with nerves.

"I think it's my mucus plug," I explain and then look over at Allison who looks like she is going to set off like her son. She walks over to my bed and presses the red button, not stopping until someone comes on the intercom.

"She's bleeding," Allison says and the nurse is unaffected by this, telling us she will get our nurse. "We should have had a private nurse and doctor come in just for you." I look over at my mother who nods.

"It'll be fine," I try to say, but another pain comes, and I have to yell. I moan through the pain. "That one felt like someone took a knife and stabbed me right in the vagina," I share between clenched teeth. "And then someone lit my crotch on fire."

The doctor comes in with the nurse. "Good morning," she says, looking at me and walking over to put her gloves on. "How are we doing?"

"My vagina feels like someone lit it on fire," I say, trying to sit up. "After a circus of clowns paraded through it with knives." Making her laugh.

"Well, let's see what is going on." She lifts my gown

up, showing everyone what I have to offer, but at this point, she could sell tickets and have an audience, and I wouldn't care less.

"I'm feeling a lot of pressure," I say, and she checks me.

"You are seven centimeters and fully effaced," she says, even though I have no idea what that even means. "Your blood pressure is low, and I'm going to monitor the bleeding." She gets up, taking off her gloves. "I'll be back in an hour."

"Or before," Allison says. "If we need you to check her, right?" I don't think this is the doctor's first rodeo, and all she does is smile and walk out of the room.

I can't even talk to her because another pain comes, and this one is worse than the last one. I have enough time to breathe before another one comes. "I need drugs," I say between contractions. "Michael." I look over at him. "You need to get me the nurse."

He presses the button, and the nurse comes in while Allison and my mother take turns wetting a rag and putting it on my head. "Michael," I say with tears in my eyes when another one comes. "I don't know if I can do this."

He leans down and pushes back my hair. "You can do this better than anyone else," he reassures me, and I shake my head.

I go through the longest three hours of my life. Every time a nurse comes in, she is thanking us for the special treats. The waiting room is filled with all of our family, and Matthew and Max keep ordering the nurses food, hoping they aren't asked to leave. So far, it's working. "I have so much pressure," I say, grunting when the doctor saunters in.

"Let's see what is going on," she says, and when I open my legs, I hear a gasp. "Okay, the baby is ready," she says, and the nurse springs into action, calling another nurse in.

"What is going on?" I look around and then at my mother and Allison, who stand side by side crying.

"The baby's head is crowning," the doctor says as the stirrups come up, and the nurse places my legs in it.

"Okay." The doctor comes back fully ready, sitting on the stool in the middle of my legs. "We are going to try pushing."

Michael stands on my side while my mother and Allison stand on the other side of me. Michael slips his hands in mine. "I love you," he says as another contraction comes.

"Okay, you are going to push," the nurse says, and she starts counting from one to ten the whole time I'm bearing down and pushing.

"That was a good one," the doctor says, and we repeat this for over thirty minutes. At this point, I have no energy left, and all I want is for this to be over. I lie back after pushing. I'm so tired I don't even have the energy left to wipe the sweat that is pouring down my face. My eyes feel so heavy, and my head feels as if it weighs a thousand pounds.

"The baby is too big," I say, panting. "It won't come out."

"Oh, that is where you are wrong," the doctor says. "I know you're tired, but I need one more big push." She looks over at our moms. "Grandmas, come see your grandbaby."

They both walk around to stand behind the doctor and both of them gasp. "The head is out, honey," my mother says, sobbing. Allison just shakes her head as she cries. Allison grabs her phone, coming up to stand behind Michael, ready to catch the shot of the baby.

"One more," Michael says from beside me, where he has been cheering me on this whole time and telling me I can do it. "You are so strong."

"We aren't having any more babies," I declare, and he just nods at me.

I feel the pressure again, and this time, I grunt out and push with my last remaining strength. "We have a baby." The doctor smiles while she grabs something, and my mother and Allison just scream. "It's a big baby," the doctor says. She tells me to push one more time, then she places the baby on my chest. The sound of wailing fills the room, and I'm overcome with love. It's a love that not one baby book tells you about. It's a love you would die to protect. The tears stream down my face as I look down at the perfect human I helped create.

"We have a boy," the doctor says, and I look over at Michael, who just kisses my head as his own tears stream down his face. "He's so beautiful," he says, kissing our baby who lies on my chest. "Dad, if you would like to cut the cord." Allison steps up and takes a picture of her son cutting his baby's cord. It's a picture that will be framed as soon as I can print it.

"Hi, baby," I say to my son as he opens his eyes and just looks at me. "He looks like Michael," I say, sobbing out. "How do I carry him for nine months, and he comes out with not a piece of me?" The whole room laughs, and when the nurse comes to take the baby, I look over at Michael. "You follow her, and you don't leave her side for nothing."

Allison steps out of the room, and I hear roaring go through the hospital a second later when she tells everyone we have a boy.

I'm a freaking mess. All I can do is cry every time I look down at him. The door opens, and Julia comes in with Alex beside her, both of them with tearstained faces. Max follows them, his face ashen as he looks around and spots Allison, who walks over to him. She buries her face in his chest.

"Everyone," Michael says, sitting beside me on the bed as I hold our son. "We would like to introduce you to Jamieson Max Horton." He looks at his father who is silently sobbing, and I look at my mother, who is being held by Julia. "Named after both our fathers."

EPILOGUE ONE

MICHAEL

Three Months Later . . .

I WALK INTO the house and close the door softly behind me, not knowing if Jamieson will be down for his nap. I listen in the entranceway to know which way to go. When I don't hear any voices downstairs, I head up to Jamieson's nursery and stick my head into the room.

His crib is pushed against the wall with the gift that Dylan had made for him. It's hockey sticks from each of the men in the family glued together with his name in tin across the middle of it. He gave it to him on his christening day as his godfather. I tiptoe into the room and see the bed empty and smile, knowing that he's probably taking a nap in our bed.

I walk down the hallway to the bedroom and see the curtains still closed. Jillian lies on her side in the middle of the bed with her eyes closed, and right next to her is our son on his side facing her. They own my fucking heart. "Morning," I say softly when I get close to the bed, and her eyes flicker open.

"Hi," she says, looking down at Jamieson as he just sleeps. "Did you just get in?" she whispers, and I nod. "It's like if he doesn't smell his next meal, he can't sleep." She wants to be mad, but then she leans in and kisses his head. "What time is it?"

"Just after ten," I say, leaning down and kissing her lips. When my alarm rang this morning, she wasn't the only one who groaned. Practice is back in full force in a couple of weeks, so I am doing my preseason training, and it sucks ass. "I'm going to go shower, and then I can take him and you can sleep." Jamieson was ten pounds four ounces when he was born, and since then, he's almost doubled in size. From the time he came out, he's been a master at eating, and nothing has slowed him down. He doesn't care much for the bottle, but he will take it if it's from someone other than Jillian. If he sees her or even smells her, he's not having it. He wants it straight from the source.

"Why don't you shower and come join us in bed," she says, turning back and closing her eyes. I look down at her and wonder how I could love her more. She's been the best fucking thing that has ever happened to me. And to think our meeting was all a mistake. Shaking my head, I walk over to the bathroom and shower in record time, knowing I'm going to go back to her.

I walk out with the towel around my waist and walk to her side of the bed, slipping in behind her. I grab her in my arms and bring her closer to me. "Why are you in bed naked?" she mumbles when she feels my cock on her ass. She moves her ass from side to side. One thing that has not slowed down is the fact that I want her all the fucking time. Waiting six weeks after Jamieson was born was honestly the hardest thing I've ever gone through. No matter how many blow jobs or hand jobs she gave me, nothing was better than sinking into her. When I bend to kiss her neck, she slowly turns over to face me, hitching her leg over my hip. "Nothing says good morning…" she says, rubbing herself against me and then stopping when we hear the front door open and close.

"We are changing the locks," I say, and she rolls her lips. "Third time is going to be a charm." I've changed them twice already when Alex showed up at two a.m. once out of the blue and then another time when Julia and Alex both showed up in the middle of the night, and we found them in the living room passed out on the couch.

"Hello?" I hear my sister and then feel the blankets move. I look over to see Jamieson's eyes open as he looks around. His blue eyes match mine as does his face.

"Oh, there you guys are," Alex says and then stops when she looks and sees the towel by the side of the bed. "Are you naked in the bed with your child?" she gasps, and Jillian just buries her head in my chest. She used to get embarrassed, but now she just rolls with it. "What is wrong with you?" she hisses and comes to the other side of the bed. "He's awake."

"For the record," I say, getting up on my elbow. "He just got up."

"For the record." She leans over and grabs him, bringing him up to look at her. She smiles at him. "Your parents are gross." She rubs her nose with his, and he smiles at her. "But they do make good babies."

"What are you doing here?" I ask her.

"Mom and Dad were going to take a walk, so we came to get the baby to give you guys some time to sleep," she says, then looks over. "Or have sex, apparently." She smiles at Jamieson. "Do you want to go for a walk with me instead of watching your parents bang? I think you do?" she asks him, and he coos at her as if he understands. "When did he eat?"

"About an hour ago, maybe less," Jillian says. "There is milk in the fridge." She kisses him up and walks out of the door. We listen to her walk to the kitchen and then grab the diaper bag at the door on her way out.

"Is it bad that I still want to have sex?" Jillian says. "Even knowing that they know what we are going to be doing?"

"Is it bad…" I say, turning her on her back and slipping into her, causing both of us to moan. "That I couldn't care less that they know?" I pull out of her and slam back inside her, her legs wrapping around my waist. "I missed you." Bending my head, I bite her lip.

"Liar," she goads me. "If you missed me…" She lifts her hips. "You would fuck me harder." I toss the covers off us and flip her to her knees. Grabbing her by her hips, I fuck her as hard as I can. We both moan out as we come together. "I think we should take a shower," she says, collapsing on her stomach. "I may or may not want to ride you." I pull out of her and slap her ass, making her moan.

An hour later, I'm in the kitchen when she comes down. She wears her black yoga pants with a white sweater crop top, and her wet hair is piled on top of her head. I smirk when she looks at me. "Would you stop?"

"I can't help it," I say when she comes close to me, and I box her in with my arms. "You're so fucking sexy." She lifts her face up, wrapping her arms around my neck.

"You aren't so bad yourself." She smiles, and I cover her mouth with mine.

"Can you seriously, for the love of God, leave the woman be?" I hear Alex and look over to see her standing there alone. "Like we get it, you love her."

Jillian laughs, pushing away from me and going to our son, who sees her and then starts to wail. "Oh, what is all the fuss about?"

"He's been cranky patty for the last twenty minutes, and he finished the bottle ten minutes into the walk," Alex says, and I hear the front door open and my parents walk in. "They let me come in to make sure you guys were done before they walked in." She walks to the coffee machine and grabs a cup of coffee.

"I'm going to change him and then feed him," Jillian says, turning him so I can kiss his cheek. "Thank you." She smiles at my parents. "For the break."

"Was it a break with mister poking at you?" Alex asks, and I shake my head as Jillian just laughs, walking away from us toward the stairs.

My parents don't stay long, and when I walk up the

steps twenty minutes later, I can hear Jillian's voice. "And that's when I met your dad," she says as I lean against the doorway. "He was not my blind date." She tells him our story every single day, and all he does is look at her with bright eyes as if he is taking it all in. She looks up and sees me, her face filling with a smile. "It was only one little mistake."

"Nah," I say. Going to her, I crouch down in front of her and look at my son and then back up at her. "It was something so irresistible."

EPILOGUE TWO

JILLIAN

Nine Months Later . . .

"YOU MAY KISS your bride." I don't even have time to react before Michael leans forward and grabs my face in his hands as the cheers fill the room.

"Fucking finally mine," he says right before his lips crash down on mine. The laughter fills my ears as I pull away from him, and he turns us to face five hundred of our closest family and friends. He puts his hand in mine and raises it high, making everyone cheer louder.

I look over at Julia, who hands me my bouquet, and then behind her as Alex holds Jamieson. She smiles down at him and claps her hands, making him clap his hands. He's dressed in the same tux as his father. We walk down the aisle, and I look over to see Julia walking my mother down, and behind her, Dylan is trying to get Jamieson off Alex. He just shakes his head at Dylan and then laughs.

Dylan puts his arm around Alex, and knowing Jamieson, he pushes it off. He loves his father and me. Julia tries and tries, but Alex, she's his best friend.

I don't have one second to breathe because as soon as we are down the aisle, the photographer grabs us to take pictures for the next hour. "I'm starving," I complain, standing with my husband. "Husband," I say, "your wife is starving."

"Well, let's get you fed." He grabs my hand and we walk over to the tented area where our reception is taking place. I haven't seen anything yet. It's all been a surprise. The only thing I chose was my wedding dress. The rest I left up to Allison and Max since they said they were paying for it. To be honest, I didn't care if we got married at home in our living room as long as I became his wife.

The sound of music fills the air as we make our way over to the white tent. I don't know what I was expecting, but it was nothing like I imagined. "Oh my God." My mouth hangs open as I walk into the tented area, except there is nothing that says tent. Sheer fabric is all around, and the floor is white. White and green flowers hang from the middle of the ceiling down toward the empty dance floor that has Mr. & Mrs. Horton written in the middle of it.

A long white table against the back of the tent for the bridal party is taller than the regular tables on the floor. The back of the bridal table is filled with green and white flowers. Long tables flank the dance floor as people mingle and come up to us as we walk in.

"I'm so happy for you two," Franny says, coming to

us and hugging Michael and then me. She's just shocked everyone with her announcement that she is moving to Dallas to become a producer on the *Sports Talk* television show on the most popular sports channel. What is shocking is that she did it without anybody knowing. For the last five years, she's been working under an alias on a YouTube forum and finally caught the eye of the owner of the media company. From what I heard, Matthew was not happy, but she was doing it anyway. "Now, if you'll excuse me, I see some men at the bar I need to get to know," she says, walking away, and Michael groans beside me as he looks over at the bar and spots Wilson. Her dress is backless as she maneuvers her way to the bar.

"If he touches her," Michael says, shaking his head. "Cooper is going to spit him like a pig." He's about to take a step forward when Alex comes over with Jamieson.

"I've tried everything," she says as he reaches out for me. "I think he's tired."

Jamieson puts his head on my shoulder. "Mama," he says with a sigh of contentment. I rub his back softly as I walk across the dance floor toward a chair and sit with him. Michael comes over with a whole plate of food for me.

"Do you want me to take him?" he asks, and I look down at my son, lying in my arms against my chest.

"No," I say, rubbing his cheek. "I can't believe he's one." I rub his chubby cheek as he sucks on his pacifier.

"It's almost time to have another one." Michael smirks at me, leaning over. My heart speeds up the same way it did when I first met him. He was hot in jeans and a shirt, but he's even hotter in a tux with my gold band on his finger.

His lips find mine. "Well, you knocked me up without even trying and using condoms." He laughs. "Can you imagine if we really tried?"

He shrugs. "Not sure what will happen, but it's always fun trying." He puts his hand around my chair. "So are we going to try?" he asks. "You told me no more kids."

I look down at my son and finally let him in on a secret that I found out right before I walked down the aisle. "We don't have to try for long." I look up at him, and his eyes go big.

"Shut up," he says. "When did you…?"

"Right before I walked down the aisle. I was feeling weird yesterday, so I stopped and bought a test and took it right before I got dressed." With his arm around me, I put a hand on our son. "Our family is going to be plus-one next year."

"God, just when I think I couldn't love you more," he says, kissing my lips. "My heart grows more and more."

"That may be the second nicest thing you've ever said to me," I say, lifting my hand to his face. His blue eyes shine through the tears that are forming.

"What was the first thing?" he asks, and my face fills with a huge smile.

"Why don't you come and let me buy you a drink." I repeat the words he said to me not too long ago. The words that changed both of our lives.

"Thank you for saying yes," he says, kissing me, and

it doesn't last too long before we are being pulled to pose for more pictures.

Four Months Later

"MAY THE BEST team win," Dylan says when we walk into the locker room right before our game. We play Montreal tonight, so Dylan had a couple of hours to come by and spend time with Jamieson and to catch up with our twin girls. Apparently, when you really try, you score twice. Bianca and Bailey are expected in four months.

"Congrats, Captain," I say when I walk into the locker room before the game, looking over at Manning. He is playing his one thousandth career game tonight.

He nods his head and smiles. "Never thought I would see the day," he says, changing into his workout gear.

My phone pings, but I don't pick it up right away, and maybe that was a mistake, but I hear commotion happening right beside me. I look up to see Cooper rushing in, followed by Dylan, who tries to stop him. But Cooper is on a mission. He grabs Wilson by his shirt and pushes him against the wall. I rush to his side, wondering what the fuck is going on. "My sister," he hisses, and I look over at Dylan, who has his eyes big, telling me that if we don't stop him, Cooper is going to destroy him. "You fucking piece of shit."

"Enough," I say, pushing Cooper away from him, but he never releases Wilson's shirt, and it's ripped off him. The whole room is quiet, and everyone, and I mean everyone, is watching. Our team, the Montreal team. The coaches, the trainers, and the fucking media, and I turn my head looking up at the screen to see it.

Wilson is once again caught in another scandal, but this time, it's rated R. Sex tape leaked with none other than his teammate's sister.

ONLY ONE LOVE

MARCH 2022

Made in the USA
Middletown, DE
05 January 2022